MUSIC
CITY
MURDERS

W.D. FROLICK

Author: W.D. FROLICK

Paperback ISBN 978-0-9950554-5-2
eBook ISBN 978-0-9950554-4-5

First Edition Copyright © 2017 by W.D. Frolick. All rights reserved.
Revised Edition March 2023.

Book design by: bookdesign.ca

DEDICATION

I dedicate MUSIC CITY MURDERS to Thomas William (Bill) Osmond, my Frozen North Music (SOCAN) partner. Bill passed away on March 6, 2018, after a courageous battle against cancer.

I met Bill, a fellow songwriter, at a Nashville Songwriter International (NSAI) meeting in Stouffville, Ontario, in 2001. It didn`t take long for us to become good friends, and we established **Frozen North Music,** where we could publish songs written by ourselves and other songwriters.

When Bill and I formed our partnership, we envisioned **Frozen North Music** on Music Row in Nashville. The building would look like a giant igloo, like the **Frozen North Music** logo. Our dream never came true. In **Music City Murders, Frozen North Music** and **FN Records** are alive and well on 16th Avenue in the heart of Music Row.

ACKNOWLEDGEMENTS

I thank beta reader **Peggy McGrady** for reading my final draft. Your suggestions were constructive—especially for the opening scene.

Mike Khul, my songwriter/artist friend in Nashville, Tennessee, thank you for your assistance and structural suggestions.

Lieutenant Patrick Taylor of the **Metropolitan Nashville Police Department (MNPD)**, your patience in answering my many questions about police procedure and the MNPD was invaluable. **Thank you!**

To **Jim Bisakowski** at **bookdesign.ca**, thank you for your excellent job formatting and your superb cover design.

A writer's profession is a lonely one. You spend many hours staring at a computer screen, racking your brain, trying to write a great line or scene. I'd probably be a basket case if it weren't for Rose's encouragement and support. **Thank you, my dear. I love you! I love you! I love you!**

CHAPTER 1

Quiet darkness and frigid February air saturated the still evening. A homeless Vietnam veteran wandered along the riverbank searching for refundable bottles, hoping to earn coffee money and maybe even a hot meal. As he searched, he spotted something unusual. Pointing the beam from his fading flashlight onto the water, he was shocked to see the bloated body of a woman caught in debris near the shoreline. In the dim light, her lengthy hair waved lazily in ripples created by a gentle breeze. The man turned and ran as fast as his tired old legs would carry him as he stumbled up the icy incline toward Titans Way.

* * *

The score was 1-0 in favor of the Red Wings with just under ten minutes to play in the third period when Detective Mike McMahon felt a vibration in his jacket pocket. He retrieved his cell phone and read the screen—Rose Goodwin. *Shit! So much for my Saturday night off!*

"Hi, Rose, what's up?" He knew her answer would not be good news.

"Hey, Mike, where are you?"

Just as he was about to speak, the home crowd, trying to rally their team, started to chant, Let's go, Preds! Let's go, Preds! Let's go, Preds! To stifle the noise, he placed a hand over his ear and yelled, "What did you say?"

"Where are you?"

As the chant subsided, Mike said, "I'm at the Bridgestone with Suzanne watching the Preds game. Why?"

"We just caught a homicide at East Bank Greenway, across from Nissan Stadium. Meet me in thirty minutes. I'll fill you in when you get there."

Before he could reply, she hung up.

"Shit!" Frustrated, he shoved the phone back into his pocket.

Mike turned to Suzanne and said, "I just got called to a crime scene. Do you want to stay and take a cab home, or would you like me to drop you off on the way?"

"Can't it wait until after the game?" Suzanne pouted.

"Sorry, sweetie, it can't. There's no rest for the wicked in my line of work."

"I don't want to stay without you. If you can drop me at my apartment, that would be great. I'll be waiting for you when you get home." She flashed a beautiful smile and winked.

When she looked at him that way, his heart skipped a beat. "This could take a while, babe. Don't wait up. I'll get there as soon as I can."

At 10:13 p.m., Mike parked behind a CSU van and several police cruisers opposite Nissan Stadium. As he slid out of his car, a mobile news truck from Channel 2 TV pulled in behind him, and reporter June Murray and her camera operator jumped out and came running after him.

"Detective McMahon, can you take a minute to fill us in on what's happening here?" she yelled.

Continuing to walk, Mike shouted, "Sorry, June, I can't tell you what I don't know."

Shining his flashlight on the ground, Mike cautiously navigated the icy slope toward the Cumberland River. When he arrived at the crime scene, he ducked under the tape and flashed his badge at the officer standing guard. He signed in and headed to where the forensics team had gathered by the river. The battery-charged portable lighting made the night seem like the middle of the day.

Mike spotted Rose talking with ME, Tony Capino. In his late forties and slightly overweight, Tony stood about five and a half feet. He had a full head of jet-black hair and a round, clean-shaven wrinkle-free face. He always maintained a friendly disposition despite his gruesome job. Tony, a highly regarded forensic pathologist known for his excellent work, had been the ME for ten years.

Detective Sergeant Rose Goodwin was Mike's partner. She was an African American with a slim, athletic body. Rose had sparkling, intelligent, blackish-brown eyes, and a wild afro hairdo, making her look taller than five feet four inches. An attractive woman, she had a dazzling smile whenever she chose to display it, but that didn't happen too often these days— especially at crime scenes.

Two years ago, when Mike was a "rookie" detective, Rose, an experienced, well-respected homicide detective, became Mike's partner and mentor. As members of the Homicide Unit, which is part of the Criminal Investigation Division and the Investigative Service Bureau, Goodwin and McMahon became part of a unit that works on serial murders, high-profile murders, and missing person cases.

Seeing Mike, Rose walked toward him. Pulling him aside, she said, "Hey, McMahon, I'd better fill you in on the situation. Just before I spoke with you, I received a call from Lieutenant Foster, who had just spoken with the ME, Tony Capino. About a week ago, a murder took place in the parking lot of the apartment building of a young female songwriter. Mark Norris and Sharon Myers from the West Precinct initially caught the case. Since the killer used the same MO in this murder, Tony thinks we're dealing with a serial killer. That's why Foster said the case is now in our hands."

"I vaguely remember hearing something about it on TV, and our 'friend' Jeff Stone wrote an article about it."

"You're right, and it didn't get much publicity. However, this murder could change things if we have a serial killer on the loose."

They walked over to where the ME was standing.

"Hey, Tony, what do we have here?" Mike asked.

"We have the body of a young female found floating in the river," replied Tony.

While Capino talked with the detectives, a photographer snapped pictures of the body from all angles, and another tech operated a video camera.

Tony slipped into a pair of latex gloves and said, "It's time to take a closer look at the body."

As Capino knelt over the corpse, standing behind him, Mike and Rose could see the young victim. She had long, dirty-blonde hair and was in her early twenties. The victim wore faded blue jeans and was naked above the waist. She had multiple stab wounds near her navel and on her breasts. Badly bruised, the victim's face looked like it had absorbed several vicious punches. Mike felt cold, but the icy chill that ran down his spine resulted from the gruesome scene—not from the weather. McMahon had to glance away for fear of losing his dinner. He gulped a few times, trying to stop the bile from rising into his throat. After inhaling and exhaling a few deep breaths of cold air, his queasiness eased. Mike pulled out his cell phone and snapped several pictures of the victim.

"What's your take on this, Tony?"

"I estimate the victim was in the water for about a week. Judging from the body's condition, the killer was wild with rage. For some unknown reason, he drew a treble clef on her forehead. At least, that's what it looks like to me. I'd say he used a permanent marker that's water-resistant. The wire knotted around the victim's neck is a guitar string."

"Holy shit," Mike gasped. "Only in Music City would some nut job use a guitar string as a lethal murder weapon?"

"Yeah, crazy, huh," Rose said, trying to suppress a shudder.

"What's the significance of the treble clef symbol?" Mike asked.

"That's a good question. I attended a crime scene about a week ago. A young woman died in the parking lot of her apartment building. A guitar string severed her carotid artery and jugular vein, and she had a treble clef symbol on her forehead—drawn with a red marker. The victim's face took a pounding, and she had several stab wounds on her upper body. The only difference—unlike this victim, she was fully clothed."

"Based on what you're saying, Tony, the MO is pretty much identical," Rose said.

"Yeah, we could be dealing with a serial killer."

"Do you know who found the body?" Mike asked.

"An officer told me it was a homeless man. He spotted the victim caught in debris floating close to shore, and he ran up to the road and flagged a passing police car. The officers followed him down to the river, managed to secure the body, and called it in."

"Where's the homeless guy now?" Mike asked.

"I'm not sure. The guy must've taken off before anyone could get his statement."

"Was there any ID on the body?" Rose asked.

"I was just about to check."

As the ME searched through the victim's pockets, he only found a laminated Nashville Songwriter Guild International (NSGI) membership card in the name of Heather Brown. He placed the card into a paper evidence bag, labeled and signed it.

Mike jotted the name and her affiliation with NSGI down in his notebook.

"When I searched the body of Shannon Greenway a week ago, all I found was a laminated NSGI membership card, same as tonight."

"That's weird. Why wouldn't the killer take the membership card?" Rose asked.

"By taking everything else and leaving the membership card, I think he's sending us a message. What that message might be, I don't have a clue. I'd like to know what the treble clef symbol means," Mike said. He frowned, puzzled.

"Do you have any idea where the first victim was from?" Rose asked.

"I think the detectives at the crime scene, Norris and Myers, said they would do some digging and find out. I'm sure it's in their notes by now," Capino said.

"This victim could be from anywhere in the USA or Canada—probably just some innocent kid following her dream to become a famous songwriter or country artist. What a shame," Mike said.

Rose turned toward Mike, "Whoever did this is a demented psycho."

"You've got that right. We'd better find the son of a bitch before he kills again," Mike said. His puzzled look changed to disgust and then to anger.

"I'm hoping she fought before he wrapped the wire around her neck. Maybe we'll get lucky and find the killer's DNA under her fingernails. However, I wouldn't hold my breath on that possibility since she's been in the water for a week or more. That's it from my end. The next step is to do an autopsy and see if anything turns up," Capino said as he stood and waved at a man standing with a gurney several yards away. He pushed the gurney next to the body, and after a tech helped him place the victim into a body bag, they lifted the victim onto the gurney, and the man wheeled it away.

Before packing it in, Tony said, "I'll be performing an autopsy at ten tomorrow morning if you care to join me."

"We'll be there," Rose said.

"See you in the morning, Tony," Mike confirmed.

Rose turned to Mike, "There's nothing more we can do tonight. Let's go home and try to get some sleep. We can meet in the squad room around nine and head to the crime lab, and maybe we can start on the murder book when we get back. Let's get the hell out of here."

As they headed up the hill toward their cars, several reporters, including investigative reporter Jeff Stone from the *Nashville Star Daily*, followed them asking questions. Jeff Stone and Mike did not like one another. It started a year ago with a scathing article about Mike and Rose in a high-profile murder case. Stone's comments on their progress had been highly critical, and he had called Mike, a "rookie" detective with a lot to learn about solving murders. Mike had taken exception to the article, and he and Jeff Stone ended up in a face-to-face shouting match the next time they met. Fists would have been flying if it wasn't for Rose's intervention.

As they silently plowed their way through the pack of pestering newshounds, Rose finally said, "All I can tell you is that we have a young female who appears to be a homicide victim. I have no further comment now, and the MNPD will issue press releases periodically to keep you informed as the investigation progresses. Have a good night."

Jeff Stone asked, "Can you give us the victim's name?"

They ignored his question and kept on walking.

When Mike arrived at his car, June Murray and her camera operator ran up and asked for a brief interview. Mike reluctantly agreed to answer a few questions. He ended the interview by sending a message to the killer. "We don't know who you are, but we'll find out. We're coming to get you. You can count on it!"

It was 3:07 a.m. when Mike quietly let himself into Suzanne's apartment. He got undressed and slipped into bed, snuggling up next to her. He was cold, and the warmth radiating from her beautiful body felt good. Like a slide show, the young victim's bloated and badly violated corpse clicked through his head. It took Mike an hour to unwind before falling asleep.

CHAPTER 2

When Mike arrived at the usually cramped squad room Sunday morning, he found it almost deserted. Their Homicide Unit was temporarily in a leased building on Massman Drive. A new MNPD Administrative Headquarters and a new Family Justice Center were currently under construction on Murfreesboro Pike, the site of a former car dealership. The buildings wouldn't be ready for over a year, and Mike could hardly wait to move into a spacious new squad room.

Bleary-eyed, he sat behind his desk sipping coffee, hoping to clear the cobwebs from his head. He munched on a jelly doughnut while reading about the hockey game. The Wings squeaked out a 1-0 victory. The Predators outshot the Red Wings 42-18 but couldn't buy a goal. Goalie Petr Mrazek was hotter than a smoking pistol. Mike had mixed emotions. He was from Dearborn, Michigan, and grew up a Red Wings fan, but since moving to Nashville, he had become a Predators fan, with one exception—whenever they played the Wings, his heart was still in Detroit.

He glanced up as Rose came out of the ladies' room. She looked tired and half-asleep. Plunking down at her desk across from his, she said, "Good morning, Mike. You look the way I feel. To put it bluntly, you look like hell!"

"Thanks a lot, Goodwin. You sure know how to boost a guy's ego," Mike laughed.

Rose yawned and said, "That gruesome scene kept going through my head. I just fell asleep when the alarm went off."

"I know how you feel. I didn't get more than a few hours, and I hope this caffeine fix gets me through the day. The brutal scene of that poor girl's body also flashed through my head. I don't care how long you've been doing this job and how many murder victims you see; it sure doesn't get any easier."

"You've got that right. I'm not looking forward to the autopsy on this one at all," Rose said with a shudder.

Before leaving, Mike pulled a new three-ring binder from the bottom drawer and placed it on his desk.

"If we feel up to it, we can start the murder book after the autopsy," Mike said.

The binder would store all the information about the case. Typically, the murder book contains crime scene photographs and sketches, autopsy and forensic reports, and transcripts of investigator's notes and witness interviews.

"Let's remember to ask Norris and Myers for the info they gathered on the Shannon Greenway murder," Rose said.

"Good idea, partner. We can do that tomorrow."

* * *

Before the autopsy began, forensics tech Tim Marks prepared the body by scrapping and clipping the victim's fingernails and placing the contents into an evidence bag. Hopefully, any DNA might help to identify the killer.

It was nine-forty-five when Rose and Mike walked through the door. Tony Capino greeted them, extended a hand, and said, "Good morning, Detectives."

"Good morning, Tony," Rose said.

"Good morning," Mike said.

After greeting and shaking hands with Tim Marks, Tony gave each detective several disposable items. Each package contained a medical gown, surgical mask, latex gloves, and a head cover.

When they had suited up, Tony said, "It's time we got the show on the road."

The ME turned on a compact digital recorder from which a medical transcriptionist would type up his comments. Tim Marks picked up a digital camera, ready to snap pictures as the autopsy progressed.

The naked, mutilated, cold, bloated body of Heather Brown lay stiffly on a stainless-steel table. The state-of-the-art table contained a sink and a suction system.

Looking like two students by the side of a seasoned professional surgeon, Rose and Mike watched and listened intently as the ME began his external examination.

From the information he had previously written on a notepad, he stated the victim's height, weight, approximate age, and sex. He then measured the length and depth of each stab wound, four on the abdomen, two on the right breast, and two on the left breast. He noted that the stab wounds had been inflicted by a sharp knife with a serrated edge, like those found on hunting knives.

The ME pointed and said, "The victim died from strangulation caused by a wire identified as a steel guitar string. The killer's strength was such that the wire severed the carotid arteries and jugular vein, almost decapitating the victim. I believe the savage beating that fractured the victim's nose and jawbone and the stab wounds were inflicted after death by strangulation."

Next, he picked up a scalpel and made a large, "Y" shaped incision from each shoulder across the victim's chest and down to the pubic bone. He spread the skin, and then he used rib shears to split open the ribcage. The ME examined the lungs and heart and took blood and tissue samples. Next, Capino removed the lungs and heart and weighed them. He repeated the same process on the lower body, removing the spleen and intestines. An experienced pro, Capino, methodically performed the autopsy one step at a time.

Both detectives, feeling a little queasy occasionally, managed to survive the horrible stench by placing a few drops of scented oil inside their surgical masks.

As a "rookie" detective, Rose tried putting Vicks VapoRub under her nose at her first autopsy to help mask the stench. She soon discovered it opens your nasal passage to even more odor molecules.

Using Vicks, you were considered a wuss—with a capital "W." The good-natured ribbing she took ended that practice.

By the time the organs were back inside the cavity, and the body stitched up, it was almost two o'clock. Everyone felt utterly drained.

"I'll send you a copy of the autopsy transcript and pictures in a day or two. The full autopsy report could take a while," Capino said.

"No problem, Tony," Mike said. "Hope we don't have to do this again anytime soon."

"Hell, I thought you two enjoyed autopsies," Tony said with an amused grin.

"Not on your life," Rose said. She wrinkled up her nose and winced.

They all laughed, shook hands, and said goodbye.

On their way to the car, Rose said, "No matter how many autopsies I attend, I still can't get used to them. My stomach always feels like it wants to rebel and empty itself, and I have to look away and fight a feeling of nausea. I don't know how Tony can perform autopsies day in and day out."

"Yeah, I feel the same way. To do what Tony does for a living is not for everyone, and you have to be a different breed, but he certainly seems to enjoy his work."

"It's a dirty job, and I'm sure as hell glad it's not me who has to do it," Rose said as her stomach began to growl. "Hey, I can't believe I'm hungry."

"Me, too. You'd think we'd have lost our appetite after watching and smelling the pleasant odors of an autopsy. Let's pick up sub sandwiches and coffee on the way to the squad room."

Sitting at their desks, they devoured their food like two starving wolves. When their stomachs were full, they worked on the murder book until five o'clock, then called it a day.

"I'd better get moving," Rose said. "Paul offered to take Jill and me out for dinner tonight."

"Enjoy! I think I'll take Suzanne out for a bite as well."

Mike put the murder book into a drawer, grabbed his coat, and followed Rose.

CHAPTER 3

Monday morning, Goodwin and McMahon looked and felt much better. Both detectives had enjoyed a relaxing evening and slept well.

"What's our first move?" Mike asked.

"I think we should go and talk to someone at NSGI. I want to find out what they know about Heather Brown," Rose suggested.

"Sounds like a good place to start," Mike agreed.

As they were about to leave, Detective Sharon Myers came waltzing through the door, clutching a binder. She gave it to Rose and said, "I thought you two might need this book now that you've taken over our case."

"Thanks, Sharon," Rose said. "We appreciate it."

"Good luck. If you have any questions, don't hesitate to call me."

Before either of them could reply, without another word, Sharon Myers turned around and left.

"She didn't sound happy turning the case over to us," Mike said.

"That's Sharon. I've known her for several years, and she never sounds happy. If she smiled, I think it would crack her face," Rose said with a grin.

"Did you notice how she emphasized the word 'our' when she said now that you've taken over our case?"

"Don't worry about it. No detective likes giving up a case."

"Yeah, I guess you're right. I'm sure I'd feel the same way," Mike said.

On the drive to NSGI, Rose opened the binder and said, "I'll read you the highlights. Shannon Greenway was twenty-three years old.

She was a member and a director at NSGI. She lived in Nashville but originally came from Chicago two years ago. Her parents live in Chicago. Detective Sharon Myers notified Shannon Greenway's parents of their daughter's death. The day after her murder, searching the victim's apartment didn't reveal any clues about who the killer might be. Interviews with the building manager and neighbors of the victim did not result in any leads. No one saw or heard anything the night of the murder. Emma Neilson, a tenant in the apartment building, discovered the body the next morning on her way to work. Detectives Myers and Norris interviewed the president of NSGI and several songwriter friends of the victim. No one had any idea who might have wanted to kill Shannon Greenway. At this point in the investigation, there are no leads or suspects. From the sound of these notes, it doesn't look like we have much to go on."

Mike sighed. "At least we know a little about the first victim. Now, let's see what information we can gather on the second victim, Heather Brown."

The name plaque on her desk read Rita Thompson. She had sparkling blue eyes, blond hair in a pixie cut, and several freckles dotted her pretty face.

"Hello, Rita, I'm Detective Sergeant Goodwin, and this is my partner, Detective McMahon."

After they presented their badges, Rita asked, "Are you here about Shannon Greenway's murder? Two other detectives were in last week asking about her."

"We're not here about Shannon Greenway, Rita. We've taken over their case, and we have their notes." Rose said.

Rita looked confused.

Mike said, "We're looking for information on another NSGI member. Her name is Heather Brown. Would you happen to know her?"

"Yeah, I know Heather; we've written a few songs together, and she's an excellent songwriter."

"We need to find out where she lives," Mike asked.

"What is this concerning? Is Heather in trouble?"

"It's nothing we can discuss now," Rose said. "Do you have her address and phone number on file?"

"I'm sure I do. Let me check," Rita said as she nimbly typed on her keyboard.

"Yes, here it is." She clicked the mouse, and the printer sprang into action.

A few seconds later, before handing it to Rose, she reviewed the page and said, "Her cell phone is on here, but she also gave her boyfriend's home phone number and address. I think that's where she lived for a while before she moved into a house she rented with some girlfriends. Heather used to live in Franklin, but we no longer show that address. She hasn't updated her new address or home phone number yet. I guess she forgot, and I keep forgetting to remind her."

"Thanks, Rita," Rose said. "We appreciate your help."

They said goodbye, leaving Rita with a confused expression on her face.

As the detectives headed toward their newly assigned four-door black Dodge Avenger, Mike said, "Since we don't have her new address or phone number, I guess we'd better start with her boyfriend."

A half-hour later, Mike pulled into the double-paved driveway of a dated red-brick bungalow. Shabby and run down, it sat on a sloping wooded lot. The black roof shingles were weather-beaten and beginning to curl, and the window frames desperately needed painting.

Sitting in the car behind an older model blue Chevrolet Impala sedan, Mike dialed the number Rita Thompson had provided. After a few rings, a male voice answered.

"Hello."

"I'm Detective McMahon of the Metro Nashville PD. Is this the phone number for Heather Brown?"

"Yes and no," the man said. "She doesn't live here, but she's here a lot. She uses my number sometimes, and for some reason, she doesn't like giving out her cell phone number. Can I take a message?"

"And your name is?" Mike asked.

"I'm Charlie Cook—Heather's boyfriend. Or maybe I should say I was her boyfriend, but we're still friends."

"Are you the owner of the house?"

He laughed and said, "Don't I wish. I just rent the basement apartment."

"Where does Heather live?" Mike asked.

"She rents a house with three other girls near Vanderbilt University."

"We'd like to speak with you in person. Do you mind if we come by and ask you a few questions?"

"What's it about?" Cook asked.

"It's about Heather Brown," Mike replied.

"What about Heather?"

"We'll explain when we see you."

"Okay. Come to the back entrance. I'll meet you there."

"Thanks. We'll be there in a few minutes."

They went to the walkout basement entrance, and Rose knocked on the door. In less than thirty seconds, Charlie Cook greeted them. He ushered them into a small, damp-smelling, sparsely furnished apartment. They showed their badges and introduced themselves.

Cook, a huge man, stood well over six feet, six inches. A greasy dark-haired ponytail touched his shoulders, and Cook's prominent nose had a slight bend, looking broken and not fixed, but it didn't appear to be out of place on his large, stubbly, square-jawed face that sprouted a black goatee. He almost looked ruggedly handsome. He viewed the detectives suspiciously from deep-set dark-brown eyes. Mike judged Cook to be in his mid-twenties and weighing around two hundred and seventy-five pounds. He reminded Mike of a WWE wrestler similar in size to the famous Hulk Hogan.

Cook smiled and invited them to sit on a worn-out beige leather couch. He asked, "Would you like coffee, water, or beer?"

"No thanks. We're fine," Rose assured him.

"Do you mind if I have a beer?" Cook asked.

"Go right ahead," Mike said.

Charlie went into the kitchen and came back clutching a bottle of Bud.

As Cook flopped onto his recliner, Mike asked, "Do you mind if we record our conversation? It keeps me from getting finger cramps."

"I don't mind, Detective. Go right ahead."

Mike pulled out a compact digital recorder, placed it on the coffee table, and turned it on. He stated the date, time, location, and names of all persons present. Then he asked, "Mr. Cook, when did you last see Heather Brown?"

Charlie pondered for a few seconds.

"She left over a week ago. We had a little spat about somethin' stupid, and Heather decided to go home and visit her parents. She wanted to surprise them and break the good news about the staff writer's deal with Frozen North Music. Why do you ask?"

"Heather Brown's body was discovered in the Cumberland River last night," Rose said.

"Oh, no, what happened? Was she murdered?" Cook asked, appearing genuinely shocked.

"Yes. Let me show you," Mike said. He pulled out his cell phone and displayed a picture of the victim's battered face. "Take a look. Is this Heather Brown?"

As Cook stared at the picture, his face turned pale. Springing to his feet, he dropped the bottle, and beer spilled onto the carpet. Charlie made a mad dash to the bathroom, arriving at the toilet bowl without a second to spare. After emptying his stomach, he splashed cold water onto his face, rinsed out his mouth, and took a few deep breaths. White as a sheet, he returned to the living room. He gulped and whispered, "Yeah, that's Heather."

"Are you positive?" Rose asked.

"Yeah, I'm sure."

They gave him a few minutes to calm down.

"What was the spat about?" Mike asked.

Cook hesitated for a few seconds.

"She thought I was jealous about her gettin' the publishin' deal."

"Were you?" Mike asked.

"Were I what?"

"Jealous."

"No, I'm not jealous, just a little ticked off that Heather got the deal, and they passed on me. We're both songwriters, and I think my stuff is as good as hers."

"You said you were Heather's boyfriend. Did you break up?" Rose asked.

"Yeah, she said she needed space and time to think. We agreed to stay friends and continue to write songs together."

"After she left, did you try to call or text her?" Mike asked.

"I would've, but she told me not to. She said she'd call me when she was ready. Heather was pissed off and needed time to cool down." Charlie was trembling, and tears filled his eyes.

"Do you remember the day and date she left?" Rose asked.

Cook hesitated, looked away, then back at Rose, and said, "Yeah. It was over a week ago—it was Friday, January 27th."

"Are you positive that was the date?" Rose asked.

Cook took a moment before replying. "Yeah, I'm positive. It was the night of our spat. She took the week off from her job at the Songwriter's Bar & Grill. We hung out, wrote a few songs, and we were goin' to the Bluebird Friday evenin' to eat and catch some of our friends playin' in the round. After our spat, she decided to visit her parents over the weekend. She had to be back at work for the evenin' shift on Monday."

"What did you do after Heather left?" Mike asked.

"After she left, I decided to go to the Bluebird, hook up with my friends, and have a few beers."

"Do Heather's parents live in Nashville?" Rose asked.

"No. Heather's parents live in Horse Cave, Kentucky."

"What time did Heather leave for Kentucky?" Mike asked.

"I think it was around seven thirty that night."

"And what time did you go to the Bluebird?" Rose asked.

"I left right after Heather."

"What time did you get to the Bluebird, and when did you leave?" Mike asked.

"I got there around eight or eight fifteen and left around midnight. I was home and in bed by one. I hope you don't think I had anythin' to do with Heather's murder?"

Staring directly into Cook's eyes, Rose asked, "Did you?"

His face reddened, and anger flashed in his eyes. He raised his voice and said, "No, I didn't. I told you where I was that night, and I have witnesses who can vouch for me."

Mike asked, "Can you give us the names and phone numbers of a few of your friends who can confirm you were at the Bluebird that evening?"

Charlie consulted his cell phone, went, and grabbed a pad from the kitchen table, wrote down three names and phone numbers, and gave it to Mike with his hand noticeably shaking.

"Would you happen to have Heather's parents' phone number and address?" Mike asked.

"I don't have their address, but I got their phone number in my cell." He looked it up and read it off. Mike pulled out his notebook and jotted the number down.

"We may need to contact you again," Mike said. "We have your home phone number. Can I get your cell number, please?"

Charlie rattled it off, and Mike scribbled the number in his notebook.

"One last question," Rose said. "Can you tell us Heather's car's make, model, year, and color?"

"Yeah, she drove an older four-door white Honda Civic. I don't know the year, but if I had to guess, I'd say it was about ten years old."

Rose asked, "Would you happen to know the license plate number? Are they Kentucky or Tennessee plates?"

"I don't know the plate number, but Heather switched to Tennessee plates since she's been in Nashville for a few years."

"Well, that's it for now, Charlie. Here's my card; call me on my cell if you think of anything that could help us find Heather's killer," Mike said.

"I will, Detective," Cook said, reaching for the card.

"One last thing," Rose said. "I almost forgot. Do you have the house address where Heather lived with her friends?"

"Sorry, I don't. I've never been there. Heather always came here. She stayed with me for a while, thinkin' maybe she'd move in, but

W. D. FROLICK

Heather said I snored so loud that she couldn't sleep. That's when she decided to move in with her girlfriends. I guess I don't blame her. I know I snore like a freight train. I broke my nose playin' football in high school and never got it fixed. Mostly, I got to breathe through my mouth."

"Where did Heather live before moving in with her girlfriends?" Mike asked.

"She lived with a girlfriend in a small two-bedroom apartment in Franklin. When the lease came up for renewal, her friend went back home to Jacksonville, Florida. Since Heather couldn't afford the rent, she decided to try stayin' with me. As I said, that didn't work out, so she moved in with three friends from work."

Mike asked, "Do you know the names of the other girls that rented the house with Heather?"

"I've never met them in person, but Heather talked about them a few times. I remember two first names were Joan and Cindy, and I think the other girl's name is Sandra or Sandy Reardon."

Mike jotted the names down. He turned off the recorder and slipped it back into his pocket with his notebook.

"Thanks again, Charlie. We appreciate your help. I'm curious, what do you do for a living?" Mike asked.

"I'm a songwriter."

"So, you live off your royalties, do you?" Rose said.

"I haven't got any cuts yet, so I don't receive any royalties. I get by with an inheritance from my grandmother, and I work as a handyman. I mow lawns, do minor repairs, paint houses, that sort of thing. My uncle owns the house, so my rent's dirt cheap."

After the detectives had gone, Cook sat in his threadbare recliner. He bent over, put his head in his hands, and began to cry. *If we hadn't had that fight—Heather wouldn't have left, and she would still be alive.* Guilt gnawed at him like a hungry shark! *Maybe if I write a song, I'll feel better, and I think I'll call the song Goodbye Heather.* He picked up his guitar and began to play.

CHAPTER 4

Before leaving, they sat in the car while Mike dialed the first number Charlie had given them. He reached all three of Cook's friends, and they confirmed that Charlie was at the Bluebird Café the night of January 27.

Next, Mike called the desk sergeant and asked him to do a vehicle search under Heather Brown. He provided the make and model of the car that Cook had supplied and asked the sergeant to send out a BOLO once he had the plate number. If they could find Heather Brown's car, it might help the investigation.

Since Charlie Cook had given them the Browns' phone number, their next decision was how to break the devastating news. Using the telephone was not their preferred method, so they decided to take a chance, drive the sixty-five miles to Horse Cave, Kentucky, and speak with Heather's parents in person. After doing a reverse phone search, Mike jotted down the Brown's address, and they headed to I-65.

Less than an hour later, Mike pulled into the driveway of a well-maintained older, white-framed two-story house on Cherry Street. They strolled up to the front door, and Mike punched the bell. Several seconds later, an attractive woman in her mid-fifties with medium-length brown hair and sky-blue eyes appeared in the doorway.

"Mrs. Brown?" Mike asked.

"Yes. I'm Ellen Brown."

Presenting their badges, Mike said, "I'm Detective McMahon, and this is my partner, Detective Sergeant Goodwin, from the Metropolitan Nashville Police Department."

"Is Mr. Brown home?" Rose asked.

"Yes. My husband's getting ready to go to work."

"May we come in and speak with both of you?" Mike asked.

"What's this about?"

"It's about your daughter Heather," Rose replied.

The blood drained from Mrs. Brown's face. She turned and called, "George, please come down, dear. Two detectives want to talk to us about Heather."

"I'll be down in a minute," he yelled.

In less than three minutes, George Brown, in his late fifties, came bounding down the stairs and joined them in the living room. He had a full head of gray hair cut short in a military style, a turned-up pug nose, a clean-shaven face, and pale blue eyes.

When Mr. Brown sat beside his wife on the sofa, Mike said, "Mr. and Mrs. Brown, there's no easy way to say this."

McMahon told Mr. and Mrs. Brown about their daughter's murder, keeping the gruesome details to a minimum.

As soon as she heard the word murdered Mrs. Brows went into shock and began to cry.

For a long moment, Mr. Brown sat silently, trying to absorb what he had just heard. Finally, he asked, "Are you positive it's our Heather?"

"Yes, Mr. Brown," Rose said. "Charlie Cook positively identified Heather from a picture we showed him."

Mike gave them a brief synopsis of their interview with Charlie Cook and about him saying that Heather was on her way home the night of January 27th. He mentioned that Heather had wanted to personally give them the good news about her publishing deal with Frozen North Music. Mike left out the part about the spat, as Charlie had called it. By the time he had finished, Mr. and Mrs. Brown were devastated, and more tears came into their eyes.

After giving them time to compose themselves, Mike asked, "How often were you in contact with your daughter?"

"She`d call every week or so and email us the odd time," Mrs. Brown said between sobs.

"When was the last time you talked to Heather?" Rose asked.

"I think it was just over a week ago," whispered Mrs. Brown.

"Did you find it unusual that you hadn't heard from her since then?" Mike asked.

"To tell the truth, we didn't think much of it because sometimes she didn't call for two weeks," Mr. Brown replied.

"What can you tell us about Charlie Cook?" Rose asked.

"The time we met Charlie in Nashville, he was polite and appeared to be smitten with our Heather," Mrs. Brown said.

"I guess he was okay, but I wish he'd cut and wash his hair. I don't know what Heather saw in him, but I wouldn't interfere. I wanted to say something to her but forced myself to bite my tongue. I wish she would have gotten out of that relationship." Mr. Brown said.

"Charlie said that Heather had decided to break off their relationship, but they had remained friends," Mike said.

"Do you think Charlie had anything to do with Heather's death?" Mrs. Brown asked. "Maybe he was angry she broke up with him."

"Charlie's alibi checked out, and we have no reason to suspect he had anything to do with your daughter's murder. Cook seemed very distraught when we spoke about Heather's death," Mike said.

Rose asked, "Can you think of anyone, other than Charlie, who might have wanted to harm Heather?"

"With Heather living in Nashville for the past few years, we don't know any of her friends or acquaintances, only Charlie Cook," Mr. Brown said.

"Heather was such a nice girl, and I find it hard to believe anyone would want to hurt her. It could be that she was just in the wrong place at the wrong time," Mrs. Brown said.

"You could be right, Mrs. Brown. We don't have much to go on now, but I promise we'll do our best to find your daughter's killer and bring that person to justice," Mike said.

W . D .   F R O L I C K

Mr. Brown asked, "Where is our daughter's body?"

"Currently," Rose said, "her body is at the morgue at 850 R.S. Gass Boulevard in Nashville. If you'd like, I can give you their phone number so that you can arrange to have Heather sent to the funeral home of your choice once her body is released."

"I would appreciate that?" Mr. Brown said.

Rose looked the number up on her cell phone, wrote it down on a piece of her notepad paper, ripped it out, and handed it to Mr. Brown.

"Do you have any other children?" Rose asked.

"Heather was our only child," Mrs. Brown said, tearing up again.

"Sorry," Mike said.

"So sorry," Rose said.

"How old was Heather?" Mike asked.

"She was twenty-two and would have turned twenty-three this November," Mrs. Brown replied, tears rolling down her cheeks.

As they stood to leave, Rose said, "Mr. and Mrs. Brown, you have our deepest sympathy and condolences."

"Thank you, Detective." Mr. Brown said.

Mike and Rose each handed Mr. Brown their card.

"If you have any further questions or think of anything that might help our investigation, Mr. Brown, please call Detective Sergeant Goodwin or me anytime," Mike said.

The mood inside the car was somber. They were almost halfway home before either of them said a word.

Finally, Mike broke the silence and said, "I feel sorry for those poor people. We'd better find that fucker soon because I don't want to have to do this again."

"What are your thoughts on Cook? Can we rule him out?"

"As I told Mr. and Mrs. Brown, his alibi appears solid. I don't consider him a valid suspect at this time. Let's keep him on the back burner and see where the clues lead."

"Okay," Rose said. "Hopefully, something will turn up before the killer strikes again."

CHAPTER 5

B y the time Mike and Rose arrived in the squad room, it was almost five o'clock. They were surprised to find a sum-marised report from Heather Brown's autopsy waiting for them. They were already aware of the details of the murder. The DNA examination from the scraping and clipping of Heather Brown's fingernails found tiny skin particles consisting of seven STR loci of the thirteen STR loci required for a complete match. Toxicology tests turned up negative.

After they had read the report, sounding disappointed, Mike said, "Heather Brown must have put up a fight and clawed at the killer, but partial DNA isn't going to be enough to identify a suspect, let alone arrest anyone."

"That's disappointing," Rose said.

As he placed the report into the murder book, Mike said, "Let's try to get a good night's sleep and pick it up tomorrow."

"Okay," Rose said as she headed toward the door, "see you in the morning."

"Goodnight. Sleep tight."

After Rose had left, Mike sat at his desk, pondering the day's activities. As his stomach began to growl, he realized they hadn't had time for lunch, and he was craving a thick, juicy steak.

He picked up his desk phone and dialed.

"Hi, handsome," Suzanne answered, seeing Mike's number on her cell phone screen.

"Hi, babe, I'm starving and could go for a steak. How about you?"

"That sounds like a good idea."

"Why don't we meet at the Longhorn on Murfreesboro around seven?"

"Great! See you at seven."

After hanging up, Mike glanced at his watch. He figured he had enough time to head home, shower quickly, and change into casual clothes.

His 1200-square-foot, two-bedroom, two-bath condominium was on the twenty-second floor on Church Street in downtown Nashville. He had a great view of the thirty-three-story AT&T building, also known as the "Batman Building." The two-pointed towers resemble the ears on Batman's mask.

When Mike arrived at the Longhorn, Suzanne greeted him with a wide grin. Sitting at the bar, nursing a Bloody Mary, she glanced at her watch. Trying to sound perturbed, she said, "You're late! It's seven fifteen! What the hell kept you?"

Knowing Suzanne was kidding, Mike said, "I went home to freshen up, and I wanted to look good and smell fresh for my beautiful woman. I left at six-thirty, but traffic was still crazy."

"Maybe you should've used your siren," Suzanne said, smiling.

"It never even crossed my mind," Mike said with a chuckle.

Suzanne's wavy blonde hair hung down to her shoulders, kissing her red silk blouse, and her sparkling cat-like green eyes were captivating. She wore a black leather miniskirt with a breathtaking view of Suzanne's long, shapely legs. She wore stylish red cowboy boots that matched her blouse. Suzanne's full, soft, pouty pink lips and snow-white teeth made his heart pound every time she gave him her sexy bedroom smile, the one she was giving him now!

Mike leaned over and kissed Suzanne on the lips, inhaling the fragrance of her exotic perfume.

After he had ordered a Bud, Mike glanced around and said, "I'm surprised. The place looks crowded tonight. Did they say how long we'll have to wait?"

"Should be any minute now. Enjoy your beer, and tell me about your day."

"There's not much to tell, just the same old police stuff. How about you? What's happening with my favorite songwriter and up-and-coming country artist?"

"I had a great rehearsal today. The band was good at the Wildhorse a few weeks ago when I did my showcase, but they're even better now. After a few more practice sessions, we'll be ready to start playing serious gigs."

Before he could reply, a young waiter appeared and said, "Your table is ready. Please come with me."

Mike paid the bartender, leaving a generous tip. They picked up their drinks and followed the waiter.

Once seated, Suzanne said, "I have an appointment with the owners of Frozen North on Monday at ten. They're interested in signing me to a combination publishing and record deal—Frozen North Music for the publishing and FN Records as an artist. They're that new company from Canada. They opened in Nashville a few years ago and are in the process of signing several great songwriters and a select group of talented artists. Everyone down here thinks it's cold up there, so I guess that's why they use the word *frozen* in their name. Their entire place looks like a gigantic igloo. It's the coolest building on Music Row. Pun intended."

Mike smiled and laughed. "That's cool! I'm excited for you, babe. What about Southern Heat Records? I thought they were making a pitch to sign you as well?"

"They are, but when I read their contract, they wanted to choose all my songs. I wouldn't have any say at all, and I should have some say about which songs are best suited for me. FN Records has more flexibility when choosing songs; besides, I prefer the people there. They're down to earth and don't try to impress you with bullshit like Tim Evans, the owner of Southern Heat, does."

"You don't seem to like Tim Evans. What's the problem?"

"I didn't get good vibes when I met him, and I don't trust Tim Evans. I like Dave Franklin and Bill Ormond at Frozen North better. They're friendly and seem like trustworthy, down-to-earth people."

"Speaking of Frozen North, Rose and I plan to go there tomorrow to speak with the owners regarding our murder investigation."

Suzanne looked confused. "How are they involved?"

"They're not involved. In the last few weeks, Heather Brown, the second victim, signed a publishing agreement with them. We're interviewing anyone who knew the young woman."

After looking over the menu, it didn't take long for them to order. They both decided on New York strip sirloin steaks with baked potato and Caesar salad. Mike added a bottle of Red Rock Malbec, a dry red wine from Argentina. When the wine arrived, they toasted to a successful music career for Suzanne and a quick solving of Mike and Rose's new murder case.

Over a leisurely dinner, they covered different subjects and thoroughly enjoyed their quiet time together. When they were ready to leave, Mike took care of the check. After a parting kiss in the parking lot, they agreed to meet at Mike's place. They were looking forward to making love and spending a leisurely night together.

* * *

That same evening, a giant of a man sat at the kitchen table in his cramped two-bedroom musty-smelling basement apartment. The house was in a high-crime neighborhood of the city. He had a yellow legal pad in front of him, and a pen was beside it. Singing the lyrics to the chorus of his new song, he paused periodically to jot down or change words. He put down his pen, picked up his guitar, and began to play and sing.

"I'm gonna kill you, baby, 'cause you lied to me.

You ran off with another guy and thought that you were free.

You're goin' down into the ground, and that will be the end.

I'll live on when you're gone and won't see you again.

Yeah, I'll live on when you're gone and won't see you again.

No, I won't see you again."

When he had finished singing, he jumped up, pumped his fist into the air, and yelled, "Man, what a killer song—'Gonna Kill

You Baby'—that's what I'll call it." He smiled a satisfied smile and drained the rest of his beer.

Checking his watch, he went to the kitchen, grabbed another beer from the fridge, returned to the living room, and sat in his recliner. He picked up the remote control from the small end table beside his chair and switched on the TV.

In a previously recorded interview, a female news reporter, June Murray, talked about the murder victim found floating in the Cumberland River. She was interviewing a detective named Mike McMahon.

The detective said, "We don't know who you are, but we'll find out. We're coming to get you. You can count on it!"

Before signing off, June Murray said, "If you have any information about the Heather Brown murder or the murder of Shannon Greenway, please call our Crime Stoppers tip line. You can remain anonymous if you wish. She gave the number, and it briefly flashed on the screen.

"Good luck finding me, Detective McMahon," he told the TV. Laughing, he picked up the remote control and changed the channel to his favorite program—*Criminal Minds!*

CHAPTER 6

Tuesday morning, Mike sat drinking coffee while reading the *Nashville Star Daily* sports section.

"How did you sleep last night?" Rose asked.

"I slept like a baby."

"That's good to hear."

"How about you?"

"I slept great! Jill stayed over at her best friend Molly's house. They were working on a school project due today, and Molly's mom was driving them to school this morning. Paul and I went out for dinner and returned to an empty house. Need I say more?"

"From the twinkle in your eye and the silly grin on your face, I get the picture."

Looking embarrassed, Rose said, "Enough small talk. Let's get back to the case. Do you have any suggestions as to our next move?"

"Since we've got a two o'clock appointment with the Frozen North people, why don't we pay another visit to NSGI and see if Rita Thompson can find Heather Brown's last address? It might help if we speak with her roommates."

"Good idea. I was thinking the same thing. Maybe Heather's roommates can flag someone who didn't like her."

"It's hard to believe that someone hated her enough to kill her—but you never know. We shouldn't leave anything to chance," Mike said.

When they arrived at NSGI, no one was at the reception desk. Mike was about to go looking for someone when Rita Thompson, looking harried, burst through the door.

Seeing Mike and Rose, she smiled and said, "Good morning, Detectives. I hope you weren't waiting long. Are you looking for me?"

"Yes," Rose said. "We have a few questions that we hope you can help answer."

"Sorry, I'm late. My car wouldn't start this morning, and I had to call AAA to come and give me a boost."

"No problem," Mike said. "Take your time."

After hanging up her coat in the hall closet, Rita sat at the reception desk. "How may I be of assistance?" she asked.

Rose said, "We're still working on the Heather Brown murder case and hope you can help us. We understand from our last visit that Heather didn't update her new address with you. However, we have the name of one of her roommates. Does Sandra Reardon ring any bells?"

"Yes. I'm sure Sandra's a member. Let me check."

Rita typed in the name, and the address and phone number appeared on the screen. She printed the information and handed it to Rose.

"Do you know Sandra Reardon?" Mike asked.

"I met her once or twice but didn't know her well. We've never written any songs together or hung out—that sort of thing."

"When we talked with Charlie Cook, he said that Heather had three roommates, and he mentioned the name Sandra Reardon." Mike flipped open his notebook and said, "Charlie thought the other two girls' first names were Joan and Cindy, but he didn't know their last names. Do you have any thoughts as to who they might be?"

"Gee, Detective, we have so many members; it's hard to know them all. I can type in Sandra Reardon's address to see if their names come up. I haven't had to do this before, but I think our program will allow me to do it. It's kind of like a reverse phone directory thing."

Rita went to work again, and after doing the reverse search by address, all the names came up. She hit print, and seconds later,

Rita handed the sheet to Rose. The other two names were Cindy Wells and Joan Hartman.

Rose smiled and said, "Thanks, Rita. We appreciate your help."

"No problem. Detective."

The house on Woodmont Boulevard was a well-kept yellow-brick bungalow.

Mike pulled the car into the driveway. They got out and strolled up to the front door. Rose rang the bell. A young woman opened the door as Rose was about to ring the bell again. She was attractive and looked to be in her early twenties. She had sparkling brown eyes, short dark hair, and an uncertain half-smile on her face.

Presenting her badge, Rose said, "Good morning. I'm Detective Sergeant Goodwin of the MNPD, and this is my partner Detective McMahon. We're investigating the Heather Brown homicide and understand that she lived at this address—is that correct?"

The young woman looked stunned and confused. It took several seconds for her to find her tongue. "I'm sorry; I thought you were with the Jehovah's Witnesses. They've been canvassing our neighborhood lately. Yes. Heather Brown lived here, and I still can't believe what happened to her."

"And your name is?" Mike asked.

"I'm Sandra Reardon. Most people call me Sandy," she said.

"Do you mind if we come in? We want to ask you and your roommates a few questions about Heather. Are they home?" Rose asked.

"Yes. My roommates and I are in a songwriting session."

"Sorry to interrupt," Mike said. "It's important we speak with all of you."

"Certainly, Detective, I understand."

Reardon led them into a nicely furnished living room where two other females of similar age sat on kitchen chairs with acoustic guitars resting on their laps. Three legal pads with pens and a small digital recorder sat on the large coffee table. Mike and Rose sat on the brown leather couch facing the two young women, and Sandy eased herself onto a wingback chair next to the sofa.

"These are my roommates, Cindy Wells and Joan Hartman," Sandy said, pointing at each girl. Cindy had long, dark hair and big blue eyes; her figure was trim and athletic. Joan had short, red hair, a freckled face, and sparkling green eyes, overdone with thick mascara and eyeliner.

"The detectives are from the Nashville Police Department. They're investigating Heather's murder and want to ask us some questions. Sorry, Detectives, I've forgotten your names."

"I'm Detective Sergeant Goodwin, and this is my partner, Detective McMahon," Rose said.

"Just before you rang the doorbell, I put on a pot of coffee. It should be ready by now. Would either of you like a cup?" Sandy asked.

"If you have enough and it's not too much trouble," Mike said.

"We both drink it black," Rose said.

After Sandy had served everyone coffee and reseated herself, Mike asked, "Do you mind if I record our conversation? It saves a lot of notetaking and finger cramps.

They all agreed, and Mike started the recorder, recording the date, time, location, and names of all those present.

Rose began, "I'm sure you've heard the unpleasant details of your roommate's death by now."

"It was so awful," Cindy said, "We read about it in the paper and watched it on the TV news. It's hard to believe Heather is gone."

"I've had a hard time sleeping," Joan said grimly. "I keep thinking that one of us could be next. When I read what Jeff Stone wrote about the killer possibly targeting NSGI members, it scared me half to death. We all belong to that association. It's gotten so bad that I don't want to leave the house, but I work most nights. I wait tables at the Songwriter's Bar & Grill. We all work there. That's where we met and decided to rent this house together."

"Unfortunately," Mike said, "Jeff Stone is scaring everyone in the city, especially the music community. His job is to sell newspapers, and our job is to catch the killer. That's why we're here. Can you think of anyone who didn't like Heather for any reason? We suspect it could be a big burly man. Does anyone like that come to mind?"

"Heather's ex-boyfriend, Charlie Cook, fits that description. I've never met him, but Heather showed me a picture of him about a month ago," Joan said. "He's as big as a grizzly bear."

"We've already interviewed Charlie Cook," Rose said. "His alibi checked out, and at this time in our investigation, he's not considered a suspect."

"God," Sandy said, "Heather didn't have an enemy in the world. She was nice, always happy, and got along with everyone she met. I can't think of a soul that didn't like her. Who would want to harm Heather?"

"I feel the same way," Cindy said. "I can't think of anyone either."

"Me neither," Joan chimed in.

"Since you all work at the Songwriter's Bar & Grill, I'm wondering if you can recall a large man hanging around that might have looked suspicious—someone who looked like he might be watching Heather a little too closely?" Mike asked.

"Not that I can recall," Sandy said. "Most nights, we're swamped and dead on our feet. I doubt I'd notice if someone were hanging around watching Heather."

Cindy and Joan couldn't think of anyone suspicious either.

Before leaving, Mike and Rose handed out their cards.

"Thank you for your time and the coffee," Mike said.

"We appreciate it," Rose said.

When they reached the car, Mike said, "I'm not saying that was a waste of time, but we didn't learn anything new. It was a rock we had to look under, and now it's time to move on."

"Yeah, I agree." Glancing at her watch, Rose said, "It's almost noon. Let's go to the Songwriter's Bar & Grill for lunch, and if he's there, we can speak with the owner, Frank Fulton?"

"Good idea. I could use some food."

Each detective was munching on a roast beef sandwich and drinking coffee when Frank Fulton joined them at their table. Fulton was in his mid-forties. He had a long brownish-blond ponytail, a light beard, and friendly dark-brown eyes. He almost looked like a younger version of Willie Nelson.

"Hi, Frank," Mike said. "This is my partner, Detective Sergeant Rose Goodwin."

"It's nice to meet you, Sergeant. Mike has told me many good things about you, and I've read about you in the paper and seen you on TV over the last several years."

"Well, Frank," Rose laughed, "don't believe anything you read in the papers these days, particularly if Jeff Stone writes it."

Frank laughed. "Yeah, he's out for blood. Stone hasn't been kind to you in his articles lately. He comes here expecting free drinks and strikes me as an arrogant asshole. Hell will freeze over before Stone gets a free drink in this joint."

"He's pretty cocky and tends to rub people the wrong way. He doesn't seem to like Rose and me or the MNPD. He's a real pain in the ass at the best of times," Mike said.

"I'm sorry I couldn't spend more time with you and Suzanne the last time you were here. We were a little short-staffed that night."

"I understand, Frank—you've got a business to run. Rose and I are the detectives assigned to investigate and solve the murder of songwriters Shannon Greenway and Heather Brown—the 'Guitar String Strangler' case as per our 'friend' Jeff Stone. Did Heather Brown work here with her roommates, Cindy Wells, Joan Hartman, and Sandy Reardon?"

"Yes, that's correct. The murder of Heather and the other girl, Shannon Greenway, was a tragedy," Frank said.

Mike continued. "When we interviewed Heather's roommates, we asked if they knew anyone who might want to harm her. The one person they mentioned was her ex-boyfriend. He's a big man named Charlie Cook. We've already checked him out, and he appears to have a solid alibi for the night Heather Brown disappeared. Since his alibi checked out, we're looking for anyone who may have been stalking Heather."

"With Charlie Cook eliminated, we're out of suspects and can use all the help we can get," Rose said.

"How can I help?" Frank asked.

"Have you ever noticed anyone who might have looked suspicious or out of place hanging around—someone who could have been watching Heather?" Mike asked.

"Not that I can recall. We get a big lunch crowd, and you can hardly move in here most nights. It's usually crowded right up until closing time. It wouldn't be hard to get lost in the crowd. Chances are I'd never notice a weirdo unless he caused a commotion or came up and bit me on the backside." Frank paused briefly. "Although, this guy came in a few weeks ago. He was looking for work as a performer. He was huge with shaggy blond hair and looked like a football player or a wrestler. I thought he said his name was Jerry, but I didn't catch his last name, or maybe he didn't give it. He brought in his guitar, and I wasn't busy then, so I listened to him sing a few of his songs. The guy couldn't play or sing worth a damn, and his songs were awful. It's almost creepy, I feel like I've seen him before, but I can't remember where or when. I tried to let him down easily, but he lost his temper and used a few choice words I wouldn't dare repeat in front of a lady."

"Sounds like a guy you wouldn't want to cross," Rose said. "He could be the lunatic we're looking for."

"Yeah, he was scary. Thank God, I haven't seen or heard from him since."

"If he shows up again, please give us a call. It was nice meeting you, Frank. Thanks for your time." Rose said.

They each handed Fulton a card.

"Frank, we appreciate it," Mike said.

"Sorry I couldn't have been of more help. It was nice meeting you as well, Detective Sergeant Goodwin."

"Please, call me Rose."

"Okay. Rose, it is."

They shook hands, and Fulton got up and went to the bar. Mike paid the tab, and they headed toward the door.

CHAPTER 7

S uzanne arrived at the Frozen North building just before ten that same morning. She had been there once before, several weeks earlier. Having heard one of her songs at an NSGI publisher night, Dave Franklin allowed her to drop off a demo CD of a few songs she had written and sung herself.

Completely renovated, the front of the building looked like a gigantic igloo. The unique entrance gave the impression that you were walking through a tunnel into another world.

As she entered the spacious reception area, a cooler with double glass doors stood on the right wall. It contained a variety of complimentary drinks—juice, soda, and bottled water all labeled with Frozen North Music and FN Records labels. Iceberg Cola had a Frozen North Music label, while Polar Bear ginger ale had an FN Records label—both soft drinks came in regular or diet. A large white freezer, a replica of the original Eskimo Pie model filled with ice cream bars, sat beside the beverage cooler. The red lettering across the front of the freezer read, "The Genuine Eskimo Pie." The original price of five cents had an X through it and the word "FREE" in large red capital letters next to it.

Realistic-looking long white icicles hung from the ceiling. A variety of pictures adorned the walls. Snow-capped mountains, husky dogs and dog sleds, Eskimo igloos, frozen tree-lined lakes, and snow-covered grain fields depicted scenes of a Canadian winter. Suzanne's favorite was the picture of kids playing ice hockey on a frozen pond.

Suzanne thought. *Cool place!*

W . D .   F R O L I C K

Joyce Ormond, the wife of co-owner and vice-president Bill Ormond, smiled as Suzanne approached. She had sparkling hazel eyes, short brown hair, and a smooth, glowing face. She looked to be in her late thirties or early forties. The all-white desk Joyce sat behind looked like a large slab of ice mounted on four icicle legs.

"Good morning, Suzanne," Joyce said, "it's nice to see you again."

"It's nice to see you as well, Joyce," Suzanne said, flashing a radiant smile.

"Bill and Dave are waiting for you in the conference room. It's down the hall, second door on your right."

"Thanks, Joyce."

Suzanne knocked lightly and entered the room. Bill Ormond and Dave Franklin were engaged in a casual conversation. Seeing Suzanne, they stood and welcomed her with warm smiles and firm handshakes.

Bill was in his late forties, and Dave was in his mid-fifties. Broad across the shoulders with muscular arms, Bill seemed as sturdy as a Mack truck. A little shorter than Dave, Bill was bald with a full beard, a round face, and brown eyes. Dave stood a few inches shy of six feet. He had sky-blue eyes, thinning salt-and-pepper hair, a bushy graying mustache, a slim face, and a lean body. They were casually dressed in blue jeans and wore white Frozen North Music golf shirts displaying the company logo—an igloo with a guitar leaning against the entrance and music notes floating through the air. A Canadian and a US flag sat perched on top of the igloo.

"Suzanne, it's nice to see you again," Dave Franklin said. "Would you care for anything to drink?"

"I'm okay, thanks."

Suzanne noticed a few file folders on the table. *Do they contain my contracts?*

Bill Ormond cleared his throat and said, "Suzanne, we're very impressed by the song demos you dropped off a few weeks ago. Your songs are some of the best we've heard in a long time, and your voice blew us away."

"Thank you. I'm so glad you liked my demos, Mr. Ormond."

Dave said, "As you may already know, we're building our roster of in-house songwriters and searching for a few talented artists to sign to FN Records. The showcase you and your band put on a few weeks ago at the Wildhorse Saloon convinced us that you're ready to take the next step in your music career."

Ormond said, "Dave and I have had a discussion, and we're prepared to offer you two agreements. One is a staff songwriter agreement with Frozen North Music, and the other is an artist agreement with FN Records. Suzanne, we believe in your talent, and with the help of our marketing team, we plan to make you a star."

Suzanne smiled. *Is this real, or am I dreaming?*

Franklin said, "We have prepared contracts for you to review, and you can take copies of the agreements for your lawyer's approval. The earlier we get this done, the sooner we can make plans to advance your career. How does that sound?"

"Gee, it all sounds so exciting."

"We hope you say yes," Bill said, flashing a broad smile.

Dave Franklin said, "We've been in Nashville for over two years and have come a long way in that short time. A month ago, we purchased the song catalog of Beetle Bug Music and are now one of the top ten publishers in town. We've signed several up-and-coming songwriters, including your co-writer friend, John Tilley, and Mike Kool, a talented songwriter from New Jersey. Our record label is starting to take off, and we have some great new talent, such as Matt Deacon, Buddy Black, Cindy Clover, and Sommer Rein, a male duo similar to Florida Georgia Line. We have recently inked recording deals with a new bluegrass group called Pickin' Cotton and Rocky Roads, a southern rock band from Alabama. One of our first songwriter/artist signings, Kenny Walker, is doing well. His song, 'Honky-Tonk Shakin','" a co-write with Bill Ormond and Mike Kool, topped out at number twenty-seven on the Music Row chart—not bad for his first single. Kenny is on a radio tour promoting the song as we speak."

Ormond said, "Before coming to Nashville, we first signed Canadian country artist Marven Jones. Marven recorded two albums here in Nashville: *The Nashville Sounds of Marven Jones* and *Tennessee Tears*. Both his albums did well in Canada, and Marven and his wife, Louise, are moving to Nashville soon. We will release Marven's two albums in the US shortly after his arrival."

"Most of our artists are currently out on tour with major acts. When you join the Frozen North family, we aim to make you one of our biggest stars. In the meantime, review the contracts and get back to us as soon as possible," Dave said.

"Sounds great, Mr. Franklin," Suzanne said enthusiastically. She was finding it hard to contain her excitement.

"By the way," Franklin smiled and said, "Mr. is too formal for us. Please call us Dave and Bill."

"Okay, Mr. ... I mean Dave."

They all laughed and shook hands. Suzanne floated out the door with the agreements clutched tightly in her hand.

Out on the street, she felt light-headed, thinking about how Dave Franklin said they aimed to make her a star. That thought sounded crazy to a girl from the small town of Castle Rock, Colorado. Maybe her dream since she was a little girl was about to come true. It saddened Suzanne to think she couldn't share the good news with her mom and dad. Three years ago, her parents died instantly in a head-on collision with an out-of-control eighteen-wheeler. Suzanne and Steve, her older brother, were devastated.

Her father had owned the local drug store, and Steve, a pharmacist, worked for their dad. Suzanne and Steve inherited their parents' investments, house, and business. A few months after their parent's death, Suzanne sold her half of the company to Steve and invested the proceeds. At that time, she was attending Belmont University, majoring in Commercial Music.

After the funeral, when Suzanne returned to Nashville, she couldn't concentrate on her studies. Two months later, she dropped out of school. That's when she decided to try to crack the Nashville music scene as a singer/songwriter. One night, while performing at the Songwriter's Bar & Grill, a ruggedly handsome man named Mike McMahon approached and said how much he had enjoyed her singing. They were instantly attracted to one another. Sparks ignited a fire, and the following evening they went out for dinner, and as the saying goes, the rest is history. She could hardly wait to call Mike with the good news!

Arriving at her gleaming silver Camaro, she sat behind the wheel and speed-dialed Mike's cell. After three rings, he picked up.

Mike smiled when he saw her name on the screen. "Hi, babe, what's happening?"

"Mike," she screamed, "Dave Franklin and Bill Ormond at Frozen North want to sign me as a songwriter and a recording artist! It's all so exciting! I had to pinch myself to make sure I wasn't dreaming."

"That's wonderful! Does it sound like a good deal?"

"I think so. Dave Franklin gave me sample contracts for my lawyer to review. I'm heading there now."

"Good luck, my dear. I'll get back to you later, and maybe we can celebrate tonight."

"Okay. See you later—love you."

"Love you, too."

CHAPTER 8

A fter leaving the Songwriter's Bar & Grill, Mike and Rose drove to the Frozen North building for their two o'clock appointment.

At 1:55 p.m., they walked through the igloo entrance and into the reception area, and Joyce Ormond smiled a warm greeting. After introducing themselves and presenting their badges, Joyce led them to Bill Ormond's spacious office. Bill and Dave stood and smiled as the two detectives entered the room.

Rose said, "I'm Detective Sergeant Rose Goodwin, and this is my partner Detective Mike McMahon." They showed their badges, shook hands, and everyone took a seat.

"I see you're a Montreal Canadiens fan," Mike said, noticing the banner on the wall behind Ormond's desk. It had a large picture of the Stanley Cup, and under it, all the years, the Canadiens had won the coveted trophy—twenty-four in all.

"The best team in hockey," Bill laughed.

Dave chuckled and said, "I'm hoping Boston's going to kick their butts this year, although Boston isn't having a good year."

"He's got the Bruins Stanley Cup picture from 2010-11 on the wall behind his desk," Bill said with a big grin. "Dave's a crazy Bruins fan, and I keep telling him he should be cheering for the Canadiens. So far, I haven't been able to talk any sense into him, but I keep trying."

"As Canadians, I presume you guys must have played a little hockey in your younger days," Mike said.

"Like most American kids grow up playing baseball, basketball, and football, Canadian kids grow up with a hockey stick in their hand. Bill and I played hockey but weren't good enough to make it to the pros," Franklin said.

"I understand you guys came to Nashville from Ontario. How come you don't cheer for the Maple Leafs?" Mike said.

"No way," Bill said, laughing. "In our younger days, I was drafted by the Montreal Canadiens, and Dave was in the Bruins farm system—that's why we cheer for those teams. The one thing we agree on—we don't cheer for the Leafs."

"Well," Mike said, "I hate to tell you this, but the Predators are the team to beat this year. I'm from Dearborn and have always been a Red Wings fan, but now that I live in Nashville, I've decided to cheer for the Predators as long as they aren't playing Detroit. I guess I'll always have a soft spot for the Red Wings. I was at the Predators/Wings game Saturday night when Rose called and asked me to join her where Heather Brown's body was found in the Cumberland River—that's why we're here today."

All this time, Rose sat patiently, listening to the men do their man thing. Not a sports fan, she couldn't understand why they got so worked up over a stupid game.

During a pause in the conversation, Goodwin took the opportunity to break in. She said, "We appreciate you seeing us today, gentlemen."

"Our pleasure," Bill Ormond said, "how can we help?"

"We've been assigned to investigate the homicides of Heather Brown and another young lady, Shannon Greenway. The same maniac may have murdered them," Mike said. "It's possible we could be dealing with a serial killer."

"Yeah, I saw it on the TV news yesterday. I can't even imagine what her poor parents are going through. Heather was young, but she had so much potential as a songwriter," Franklin said.

Rose said, "Yesterday, we drove to Horse Cave, Kentucky, to break the horrible news to her parents. Mr. and Mrs. Brown were devastated."

"We understand Heather Brown recently signed a songwriter agreement with your firm—is that correct?" Mike asked.

"Yes," Bill said, "we thought Heather had a bright future as a songwriter. We inked her to a staff writing deal about three weeks ago and were looking forward to developing her songwriting talents."

"Can you think of anyone who might have wanted to harm her?" Rose asked.

"We haven't known Heather very long, and we don't know any of her friends or associates," Franklin said.

"We originally met Heather at a publisher night at NSGI—that's where we heard a few of her songs. The people there may be able to provide a few names of some of her friends and co-writers," Ormond suggested.

"We were there recently," Mike said, "but at that time, we were trying to find out where she lived and where she was from to notify her next of kin about her death. What you're suggesting makes sense. It might be worth checking out."

McMahon closed his notepad, and he and Goodwin stood, getting ready to leave, when Mike said, "I understand you're interested in signing my girlfriend, Suzanne Taylor, as a songwriter and a recording artist."

"That's right. Your girlfriend is a beautiful and talented young woman, and we'd love to have her join our Frozen North family. If she decides to come on board, our goal is to make her a star. We think she has a promising future in the music business," Franklin said.

"I agree," Mike said, "Suzanne is extremely talented."

After shaking hands, they handed the partners their cards.

Rose said, "Thanks for your time. Please call us if you think of anything that might help our investigation."

"By the way," Mike said, "we like what you've done to your building inside and out. Pardon the pun," as he made air quotation marks with his fingers, "it's a cool place."

"Thanks. Feel free to help yourself to a drink or ice cream bar on the way out. It's a little marketing gimmick we came up with to promote our company," Franklin said.

Mike and Rose each picked up a Polar Bear Cola before leaving the building.

Since they were a few blocks from the NSGI building, they decided to go and see Rita Thompson. When they arrived, she was busy tapping away on her keyboard.

Rita looked up as they approached and said, "Hello, again. I watched it on the TV news last night, and I can't believe Heather is dead. It's so awful! Have you had any luck finding their killer?"

"That's why we're here," Mike said. "We were hoping you could provide a list of names, addresses, and phone numbers of some of Heather Brown's closest friends and co-writers."

"We're trying to determine if anyone knew someone who might, for some reason, want to hurt Heather," Rose said, "Golly," Rita said, "I'd have to think about that. I'll need a day or two to organize a list for you."

"That's fine. Here's my card. When the list is ready, please send it to my email address," Mike said.

"Will do, Detective."

When they arrived at headquarters, Lieutenant Rob Foster asked them to join him in his office.

When seated, Foster asked, "How's the case coming along?"

"Well," Mike said, "to tell the truth, we haven't made much progress. We haven't discovered anyone with a motive who would want to kill either girl. The one thing that doesn't make sense is that all their items were missing, but the killer left their NSGI membership card on each victim. My gut feeling is that he left the NSGI card on purpose. For some unknown reason, he's drawn a treble clef symbol on each victim's forehead, and how he punched and slashed the bodies indicates he's releasing pent-up hate and hostility. Maybe he's targeting NSGI members because he has an axe to grind against that organization."

"This could be a tough nut to crack," Rose said. "At the moment, we don't have much to go on."

"Keep at it—the chief has been on my ass and wants to solve this case ASAP! I just received word that Heather Brown's car was found at a rest stop on I-65 north. An employee noticed it sitting there the past several days, and he thought it was unusual, so he called the highway patrol. When they ran the plate, they confirmed it was Heather Brown's vehicle and contacted us. It's at the crime lab garage on Myatt Drive. Before you arrived, forensics called and said they'd let us know after a thorough search."

"What about video surveillance at the rest stop?" Rose asked.

"The state troopers checked, but the videos are erased every forty-eight hours. Anything that might have been recorded is long gone."

"Shit," Mike said, showing his frustration. "That might have been the break we needed."

Just then, Foster's phone rang. "Lieutenant Foster." He listened for a few seconds. "Okay, thanks, Jim. Forensics didn't find any evidence in the victim's car."

CHAPTER 9

S uzanne's lawyer suggested a few minor changes to the contracts, and after a phone call, the Frozen North partners
approved, and they had a verbal agreement. The arrange-
ments were revised and readied for signing.

Suzanne left her lawyer's office floating on cloud nine. Sitting in
her car, she dialed Mike.

After two rings, Suzanne heard, "Hey, babe. What's up?"

"I just left my lawyer's office, and he found some minor things
he wanted to change. He called Frozen North, and they approved.
Since we've agreed, Dave Franklin said he's scheduling a news
conference for 2:00 p.m. tomorrow at the Frozen North building.
That's when I'll sign the contracts. I'm so excited, Mike. I can hardly
believe this is happening."

"That's great news! Congratulations! Why don't we meet over a
drink at Tootsies around five and then go somewhere for a bite to
celebrate?"

"Okay, sounds good. See you at Tootsies."

McMahon was nursing a beer when Suzanne made her grand
entrance shortly after five. A real head-turner, she looked as sexy
as ever. Suzanne wore tight, faded jeans and a dark-blue turtleneck
sweater. The designer jeans clung to her shapely hips and long, slender legs. Mike smiled as Suzanne approached and sat beside him at
the old oak bar.

"Man, you're looking casually chic tonight, my dear. I feel a little
out of place in this rumpled old suit. Sorry, I didn't have time to go
home and freshen up. I'm starting to look like Columbo, my favorite

TV detective. I guess it's time I got a few new suits. At least my trench coat is in better shape than his." Mike chuckled.

Suzanne laughed and kissed his cheek. "You look fine to me, you handsome devil."

"What would you like to drink, babe?"

"A Miller Lite sounds good."

Tootsie's is a three-story bar with entertainment on each level. They decided to stay on the main floor, drink their beer and figure out where to go to eat.

"I've got an idea. Why don't we head to the Songwriter's Bar & Grill after our drinks? The food's good, and we can catch my friend, John Tilley. He's playing there tonight, and I think he goes on at six."

"Okay. That works for me."

* * *

Frank Fulton greeted them when they entered the Songwriter's Bar & Grill.

"Good evening and welcome," Fulton said, "it's good to see you guys again."

Suzanne said, "It's nice to see you as well, Frank."

"How goes the battle, Frank?" Mike asked.

"Things are great! A little hectic at times, but I'm not complaining. Business is good."

Fulton escorted them to a table in front of the stage. When they were seated, Frank excused himself and headed to the bar.

After they had ordered a couple of beers, Suzanne said, "John Tilley and I wrote a few songs together. He's a staff writer with Frozen North Music, and I think they're considering him for a record deal."

Before Mike could reply, John Tilley strolled onto the small stage, wearing a Songwriter's Bar & Grill T-shirt, faded blue jeans, and black cowboy boots. Tilley was tall and lean with long brown hair that hung under his Frozen North Music baseball-style cap. He was clean-shaven, with sea-blue eyes and a smile as wide as Texas. John Tilley was a good-looking young man.

He picked up his guitar, and with his Texas drawl, he said, "Welcome to the Songwriter's Bar & Grill. I'm John Tilley, and I'll do my best to entertain y'all. I want to start with an original song I co-wrote with a beautiful young woman. Her name is Suzanne Taylor, a talented songwriter, and entertainer. Take a bow, Suzanne." The unexpected attention caused Suzanne's face to redden. She gave a little wave, and the crowd cheered. "The song is called 'Don't Throw Our Love Away.' Come up here and sing it with me, Suzanne. It's a duet, and I won't do the song justice singing it by myself."

Surprised and embarrassed, Suzanne hesitated for a moment. Mike gave her a gentle shove and said, "Go, babe, don't be shy."

Confidently, Suzanne walked up to the stage, took the microphone from John Tilley, and said, "As John mentioned, my name is Suzanne Taylor. We co-wrote this song together and will attempt to sing it for the first time in public."

The crowd began to applaud as John started the melodic intro. A few seconds later, they began to sing and harmonize. The room fell silent.

Three and a half minutes later, as the song ended, the crowd erupted. Everyone clapped, cheered, and whistled loudly.

When Suzanne returned to their table, Mike said, "I've never heard that one. It's a damn good song—great job, babe! It sounds beautiful as a duet. I think the two of you should record it for your first album with Frozen North."

"Yeah, I think I'll talk to them about including it. It could be a hit, judging from the crowd's reaction."

Several people came over, asked for Suzanne's autograph, and said they enjoyed the song.

After the last autograph-seeker left their table, Mike said, "Get used to signing autographs, babe. You'll be hounded for autographs wherever you go when you become a star."

Suzanne blushed. "Gee, do you think so? That would be nice."

Suzanne introduced Mike to John Tilley during a break as they were leaving. They shook hands, and Mike congratulated John on his performance—especially the great job they did on the duet song.

He dropped a twenty-dollar bill into Tilley's tip jar, and they said goodbye.

* * *

Mike stepped out of the shower, dried himself off, and wrapped a towel around his waist. Entering the bedroom, he saw Suzanne waiting for him on his king-sized bed, wearing only a mischievous come-and-get-me smile.

His heart racing, he let the towel drop to the floor. Suzanne could see Mike had already risen to the challenge.

CHAPTER 10

Mike was dead to the world, dreaming about his childhood days in Dearborn when his cell phone vibrated on the night table. Half asleep, he picked it up without checking the screen. He whispered, "Hello." Glancing at the illuminated digital clock on the same night table, it showed 2:24 a.m.

"Sorry to wake you, Detective, it's Sergeant Harding. We have another homicide like the last two—this time at a house on Eden Street. Sergeant Goodwin said she'll meet you there."

Still half asleep, Mike wrote down the address. "Thanks, Sergeant."

Mike dressed in the dark, entered the kitchen, wrote a note, and placed it on the table. He walked to the hall closet, grabbed his overcoat, headed out the door, and took the elevator down twenty-three floors to the underground parking garage. Shivering, he started his car and drove off.

Just as he arrived at the older white-frame bungalow, a light rain began to fall. The cold north wind shook the car and sent a chill throughout his body. In his haste to get to the crime scene, he never thought to bring an umbrella, hat, or gloves. As he exited the car, Mike stuffed his hands into his overcoat pockets, searching for warmth.

Like the Heather Brown murder, a few police officers and a CSU team buzzed like bees near a hive. He signed in with the officer at the entrance to the driveway, ducked under the tape, and hurried to where ME Tony Capino knelt examining the body.

"What do we have this time, Tony?"

The ME looked up and said, "Hi, Detective. We have another murder by the same perp, but it's a male this time. Like the other two victims, the MO is the same."

"Shit! What the hell's going on, Tony?" As Mike took a closer look at the victim, he was shocked at what he saw. *Are my eyes deceiving me?* "That's John Tilley! I can't believe it!"

Tilley's Frozen North cap lay on the pavement a few feet from his body.

"Who is John Tilley?" Capino asked.

"He's a songwriter with Frozen North Music and a friend of Suzanne's. We caught a set of his last evening at the Songwriter's Bar & Grill. Do you know who discovered the body, Tony?"

"One of the first officers at the scene told me the next-door neighbor found him when he returned home from work.

"Do you know where the man is now?"

"He's the guy in front of the house talking with the police officer."

Mike walked up, showed his badge, and introduced himself to the officer and the neighbor. He informed them he was one of two detectives in charge of the investigation. Turning to the man, who looked to be in his mid-forties, he said, "I understand that you're the person who discovered the body, is that correct?"

"Yes. I found John about an hour ago. I told the police officer I was coming home from work when I spotted the driver's door on his truck wide open. I thought that was unusual, so I decided to come over and take a closer look. That's when I found John lying face down in a pool of blood. I could tell he was dead, so I called 911."

"And your name is?" Mike asked.

"I'm Jake Carter. I live next door."

Mike asked a few more questions, wrote down the information, and scribbled the man's name, address, home, and cell phone numbers in his notebook. He handed Carter his card and asked him to call if he thought of anything else.

When he returned, Mike asked, "Did you find any ID on the body, Tony?"

"I only found one thing."

"Let me take a wild guess. Was it an NSGI membership card?

"Bingo!"

"Shit! The MO is the same as the Shannon Greenway and Heather Brown murders. He must have followed Tilley home from the bar and jumped John as he got out of his truck."

"That's the way it looks," Tony agreed. "The poor guy didn't stand a chance."

"The killer is sending us a message. For some unknown reason, he hates NSGI and their members—maybe even Frozen North. The last two victims were signed to that company, and all were members of NSGI. I'm puzzled—why is he drawing a treble clef symbol on their foreheads? I presume he's using it as his calling card. Recently, I watched a movie on TV inspired by a real-life event. The movie was called the *Happy Face Killer*. The psycho murdered eight women on his truck route, and the killer left a happy face drawing near every dead body."

Tony frowned. "It's a real puzzler. Who knows what these psychos think?"

Just then, they heard a familiar voice.

"Hey, guys, sorry I'm late."

As Rose approached, Mike said, "Hey, Goodwin, nice of you to join us."

"Good evening to you too, McMahon.

"It's the same MO as the first two victims," Mike said.

"Has the body been identified?" Rose asked.

"Yes. The victim is John Tilley, a singer/songwriter and a co-writer friend of Suzanne's. Like the others, as you can see, there's a guitar string around his neck, his face is a mess, his chest has several stab wounds, and he has a treble clef symbol on his forehead. The killer is stalking his victims and striking when the timing is right—at night when there's less chance of being spotted."

"The perp must be a strong sucker. Like the other two victims, he almost sliced the poor guy's head off," Rose said grimly.

Once forensics had finished processing the crime scene, Rose and Mike decided to call it a night.

It was 7:30 a.m. when Mike arrived back at his condo, and the note he had left for Suzanne was still on the kitchen table. He threw the paper into the trash can and brewed a pot of coffee. Since sleep was impossible, Mike sat at the table contemplating why he became a homicide detective.

His mother was murdered in their home around this time of year back in 2001. Mike was fifteen at the time. His father, a homicide detective on the Dearborn Police Force, took him to a Detroit Red Wings/Toronto Maple Leaf hockey game that evening. While they were cheering on the Wings, a burglar broke into their home and surprised his mother while sleeping. The police assumed she awoke as the thief rummaged through her jewelry box. Before she could get out of bed, the burglar must have panicked. Instead of running, he smothered her with a pillow. His mother's jewelry and the little cash in her purse went missing. His ten-year-old sister, Joanne, slept through the murder in her bedroom unharmed. The killer was never caught, and the file remains an open cold case.

His dad was devastated after his mother's death. When they couldn't find her killer, he started binge drinking and barely clung to his job. A friend got him going to AA, and with the help of a shrink, he quit drinking. He stayed on the wagon until he retired a few years ago. Mike's father sold his house and moved to Florida, where he purchased a small bungalow on a canal in Fort Myers. He met a few other retired cops and took up golfing. Mike stayed in touch with his father and sister by phone and email. He hoped that one of these days, he and Suzanne could take a trip to Florida and visit his dad.

Mike vowed to become a homicide detective from the day his mother died. He was determined to solve cases like his mother's and bring killers to justice. After graduating high school, Mike enrolled in the Criminal Justice program at Belmont University. Upon graduation, he applied to the MNPD. He was accepted, completing 950 hours of training at the Nashville Police Academy, after which McMahon pounded the beat until an opening came up in the Homicide Unit five years later. He applied and got the job. Detective Sergeant Rose Goodwin became his partner and his mentor.

Mike's thoughts came back to the present when he heard Suzanne stirring. Glancing at his watch, it read 7:58 a.m. He was pouring a second cup of coffee as Suzanne, her hair disheveled, strolled into the kitchen.

"Good morning, sleepyhead," Mike said. "How come you're up so early?"

"I rolled over to put my arm around you, and you weren't there. Then I smelled the coffee and couldn't resist that sweet aroma, so I thought I'd better check it out."

"Here, let me pour you a cup and see if I can wake you up."

Mike picked up the coffee pot, filled a mug, and placed it on the table.

Suzanne sat down, picked up the mug in both hands, and sipped the steaming java. "Tastes so good," she said with a contented smile.

"I got called to another homicide just after two this morning."

"Oh, no, what happened this time?"

"I'm glad you're sitting down. There's no easy way to say this. It was your co-writer friend, John Tilley. He was murdered in the driveway of his residence on Eden Street. The killer used a guitar string—the same MO as the two female victims." Mike decided not to mention the gruesome details.

Suzanne's face turned ghostly white. Her hands began to shake, spilling coffee onto the tabletop. Putting the mug down, she buried her face in her hands and sobbed.

Mike went over, put his arm around her, and whispered, "I'm so sorry, babe—I know you thought a lot of John."

She continued to weep and began to ramble. "I can't believe what you're saying, and I can't believe that John is dead. None of this makes any sense. We just saw him last night. Who would want to kill John?"

"I don't have a clue. Whoever is committing these murders has got to be one sick S.O.B."

"The dream of John and me doing the duet song on my first album has turned into an unbelievable nightmare," Suzanne said as tears rolled down her cheeks.

Mike said, taking her hands in his, "It's such a shame, another senseless killing."

"I'm going to dedicate 'Don't Throw Our Love Away" in memory of John on my first album."

Not knowing what to say, Mike blurted out, "That's very nice. I'm sure John's family will appreciate it."

Suzanne shuddered as the bitter north wind rattled the windows. Suddenly, the room felt as cold as a meat locker. Mike entered the living room and turned on the gas fireplace, hoping it would remove the chill.

"Suzanne, why don't you come into the living room and cozy up by the fireplace? Maybe you could read a good book, rest, and try not to think about John Tilley's death. You can take the day off, and I'll try to get back as soon as possible."

"I can't take the day off," she said, still sobbing, "I've got to be at Frozen North by one. Today is the day I sign the contracts, and I'll have to go home first to get a change of clothes. I must look my best because the local press will be there. *Music Row* magazine will have a reporter and photographer there as well. There might even be some TV reporters. The people at Frozen North have set up a news conference to announce my signing, and I can't let them down."

"Sorry, with all that's been going on, I forgot. Are you going to be okay?"

"I have to be okay. Today is one of the biggest days of my life," Suzanne said, choking back more tears.

"I'm sure you'll do fine. Think of positive things, like how much I love you," Mike said, giving her his dimpled-cheek smile.

Suzanne produced a little smile of her own. She wrapped her arms around Mike and gave him a hug and a tender kiss.

"What would I do without you?" she sobbed. "I'll think about how much you mean to me and how much I love you."

"Good luck today. I'm sure it'll go great! Sorry, but I've got to go." He kissed her on the cheek, slipped on his coat, and headed out the door.

After Mike had gone, Suzanne curled up on the couch and wept until no more tears were left to cry. Gradually, she began to feel a little better.

CHAPTER 11

M ike met Rose in the squad room around 9:00 a.m. He phoned Frozen North, and without giving a reason, he obtained John Tilley's Dallas address and phone number from Joyce Ormond. They flipped a coin, and Rose called Tilley's parents to inform them about their son's murder. Mrs. Tilley answered. After the initial shock and a boatload of tears, she gradually regained her composure.

Rose said, "The state medical examiner's office will contact you and arrange to send your son's body home." Rose expressed her condolences, said goodbye, and hung up. As a mother herself, she could feel Mrs. Tilley's pain.

Her eyes were misty when she turned to Mike and said, "Making that phone call is the worst part of this job."

"Yeah, I know what you mean. I'm glad I didn't have to make that call."

Glancing at her watch, Rose said, "We'd better get moving if we want to get to John Tilley's autopsy on time."

The autopsy took a little over three hours to complete. On their way to the precinct, they stopped for a late lunch at the Songwriter's Bar & Grill.

They arrived in the squad room a few minutes before three, and Mike found the list from Rita Thompson in his email. It contained the names, phone numbers, and addresses of twelve friends and co-writers of Heather Brown. By 5:00 p. m., having talked to everyone, they didn't pick up any leads, and not a single person could think of anyone who might have wanted to harm Heather Brown. It was another frustrating dead end.

* * *

Suzanne arrived at the Frozen North building at 1:00 p.m. Joyce Ormond greeted her warmly and ushered Suzanne into the board-room, where Bill Ormond and Dave Franklin waited with two other people. Dave introduced Suzanne to Joan Watson, Marketing Director, and Mark Bush, Producer. Joan was in her early forties and had short brown hair, a wrinkle-free face, and sparkling almond eyes. Mark Bush, a handsome man in his mid-thirties, stood just over six feet tall. He was a little overweight around the middle, caused mainly by the sugar in his favorite soft drink, Mountain Dew. He had a full head of medium-length wavy dark hair, his face was clean-shaven, and his coffee-brown eyes had a friendly twinkle.

Dave Franklin said, "Welcome, Suzanne. Today is a big day for all of us. We're pleased that you've decided to join the Frozen North family. The contracts with your lawyer's revisions are ready for your approval. We'd like you to sign the agreements before the media circus begins. When the reporters arrive, we can do a mock signing for their cameras. Is that okay with you?"

"That's fine, Dave," Suzanne said with a tired smile. "I presume you haven't heard that John Tilley was strangled in his driveway early this morning, and the killer used a guitar string just like the Shannon Greenway and Heather Brown murders."

It was apparent that no one had seen the early morning TV news or heard about John's murder on the radio. Shock registered on every face. In a split second, the happy mood turned to gloom.

"That's awful. John was a super nice man and a talented song-writer and performer. Whoever's doing this has got to be one sick psycho," Dave Franklin said.

"Yeah," Bill Ormond agreed, "he must be a real lunatic. All these killings are starting to scare the hell out of me. Two of the three murder victims were from Frozen North. Is someone out to get us?"

Mark Bush said, "John was a good friend, and I will miss him. Let's hope the cops catch that maniac soon. You're right, Bill; it's starting to scare me, too."

Tears rolled down her cheeks, and Joan Watson appeared in a daze. Finally, through her sobs, she whispered, "I can't believe John Tilley is dead. Who's doing these horrible things?"

Dave Franklin said, "Even with this devastating news, we've still got to carry on and get through this tragic day as best we can. Suzanne, are you okay with signing the agreements now?"

"I'm good, Dave. Let's do it before the media people arrive."

With the signing and witnessing completed, Joyce carried a bottle of Dom Perignon in a silver bucket filled with ice, placed it on the table, and left. Bill Ormond popped the cork and poured a glass for everyone. Then he raised his glass in a toast. He said, "Here's to you, Suzanne. May you have a successful career with Frozen North Music and FN Records. To John Tilley, Heather Brown, and Shannon Greenway, may you all rest in peace."

They clinked glasses, and Dave Franklin said, "Here's to you, Suzanne, welcome. We're happy to have you on board."

"Thank you, Dave. I'm so excited and proud to be part of the Frozen North team," Suzanne said with a strained smile.

Less than a half hour later, guided by Joyce Ormond, media people began arriving. Reporters and photographers from *Music Row*, *Nashville Scene*, *Nashville Lifestyles*, and *Nashville Music Guide* began filing into the boardroom. Entertainment reporters from two local TV stations and their camera operators strolled in a few minutes later.

Suzanne wore a tailored black pantsuit with a red silk blouse. A beautiful string of pearls hung around her neck—a gift from Mike for her twenty-fifth birthday. She wore a pair of red patent leather open-toed high-heel shoes. Her wavy blonde hair gleamed in the overhead lighting, and eyeshadow and mascara accentuated her beautiful green eyes.

Suzanne sat at the boardroom table when they were ready for pictures, and Bill and Dave stood on either side of her. She pretended to sign the contracts with a pen in hand, and everyone gave their best smile. It took several minutes to accommodate all the media before the question-and-answer period began.

Isabel Berry from *Music Row* asked, "Suzanne, how does signing a recording contract with a Nashville record label feel? I understand other labels, such as Southern Heat Records, were also trying to sign you. What made you choose the FN label?"

"To answer your first question—it feels great! I'm happy to be part of the Frozen North family, and I've dreamed of this day since I was a little girl. As for your second question, you're right; Southern Heat was interested in signing me, and they wouldn't allow me to choose songs for my first album when I checked out their agreement. FN Records are giving me much more freedom to choose songs, which I appreciate. In the end, signing with Frozen North made more sense. I like the down-to-earth feeling I get from all the Frozen North staff. I feel at home here."

Craig Davidson from *Nashville Scene* asked, "Do you know when you'll start working on your debut album?"

"It should be soon. I was hoping to do a single with John Tilley of *Don't Throw Our Love Away*, a duet song we co-wrote together, but with John's sudden death, I'm going to leave that decision up to the record label."

Kevin Clement of channel 5 TV asked, "With the recent murders of Shannon Greenway and Heather Brown and the shocking killing of John Tilley early this morning, are you concerned that a serial killer is on the loose and could target you as well?"

Before Suzanne could answer, Dave Franklin jumped in and said, "Kevin, that's not an appropriate question. Let's not spoil Suzanne's big day by throwing a damper on her party."

After a few more questions about Suzanne's career and expectations, Bill Ormond called an end to the press conference. He said, "It's time to celebrate the addition of Suzanne Taylor to the Frozen North family. You're all invited to stay for food and drinks. As a transplanted Canadian, I'd like to practice my southern dialect. Thank y'all for comin'. Enjoy, eh!"

Everyone laughed.

Several catering staff members entered with platters of *hors-d'oeu-vres* and trays filled with glasses of wine and champagne. They circulated throughout the room while everyone carried on conversations.

The media representatives took turns interviewing Suzanne, Dave, and Bill. By 5:00 p.m., the media crowd had cleared out, and everyone breathed a sigh of relief.

"That turned out better than I thought it would. The publicity should go a long way toward launching your career, Suzanne," Dave Franklin said.

"Gee, I hope so. I'm anxious to complete the album, get out on the road, and start promoting my first single to country radio."

"We can discuss further details and schedules to launch Suzanne's music career starting tomorrow morning. Since we're all tired, why don't we call it a day and start fresh tomorrow at ten," Bill suggested.

"That sounds good," Dave agreed. "See you all tomorrow morning. Have a good evening."

Suzanne walked through the door just before six and found Mike asleep on the living room couch. She planted a warm kiss on his lips, he snorted, and his eyes flew open. Seeing Suzanne, he grinned as he rubbed his sleep-filled eyes.

"Sorry to wake you. I know you didn't get much sleep last night."

"That's okay, babe. I can't think of a better way to wake up. How did your signing go?"

"It went great until some jerk reporter mentioned the murders and asked if I thought I might be a target. Dave Franklin cut him off and told him he was out of line, and he said my news conference wasn't the place to discuss such matters. That reporter scared me, Mike."

"Reporters are always trying to stir up dirt. Don't let him get to you. Rose and I will catch that nut job soon—so don't worry."

"I'll try not to, but I'll feel better once you catch the killer."

"Do you want to go for dinner to celebrate your signing, or would you rather stay home?"

"I'm tired. Let's order Chinese or a pizza and find a good movie."

"That sounds good! After we eat, we can curl up on the couch and watch a movie. TCM has a few Bogie movies on tonight."

"That's great! I love Humphrey Bogart."

* * *

Dave Franklin said good night to Bill Ormond at six o'clock and left for a seven o'clock date-with-a-publisher meeting at NSAI.

Since Bill decided to stay to catch up on some paperwork, Joyce hitched a ride home with Mark Bush. At 8:30 p.m., Bill decided to call it quits. It had been a long day, and he was exhausted. The signing of Suzanne Taylor as a songwriter/artist to the Frozen North group had his adrenaline pumping. The news conference had turned out better than he had expected. Things were going well! Frozen North Music and FN Records were beginning to turn heads on Music Row.

Bill headed out the back door to the parking lot, humming *Don't Throw Our Love Away*, the catchy duet song that John Tilley and Suzanne Taylor had penned.

With all these exciting thoughts racing through his head, Bill pulled out the keys to unlock his new Yukon SUV. Suddenly, he had a creepy feeling that someone was standing behind him. Turning quickly, he saw a gigantic man wearing a black hoodie and a ghostly white clown mask with a red button nose, fake menacing yellow fangs, and thick black eyebrows. The man held a wire in his gloved hands and looked ready to attack. Without thinking, Bill's instincts took over. He kicked the man a solid blow in the crotch, and his assailant let out an agonized scream. Dropping the guitar string, he doubled over, falling to his knees. With both hands, he clutched his genitals in a futile attempt to ease the excruciating pain.

Like he was still playing hockey, Bill body-checked him hard, and the giant toppled backward like a felled redwood. Before his attacker recovered, Ormond unlocked his vehicle and jumped in. Fumbling with his keys, Bill found the ignition switch and turned the key. The doors locked automatically, and the engine roared to life. Ormond put the SUV into gear and punched the gas. Tires screamed, and rubber smoked on the dry pavement as the vehicle fishtailed out of the parking lot.

W . D .   F R O L I C K

T he following day, Mike was at his desk by nine, sipping black coffee and devouring a bagel. His desk phone rang as he was about to pick up the newspaper.

"Detective McMahon,"

"Good morning, Detective. It's Bill Ormond at Frozen North."

"Good morning, Bill. What can I do for you?"

"You may find this hard to believe, but I encountered the 'Guitar String Strangler' last night in our parking lot."

"I believe you. That maniac seems to be everywhere. Tell me about it."

Bill went on to describe the attack and his narrow escape. When he had finished, Mike asked, hopefully, "Did you get a good look at him? Did you see his face?"

"Sorry, I didn't. It was dark, and the guy wore a gruesome-looking clown mask, and a black hood covered his head. Looking at his face, I saw that hideous mask staring back at me. The one thing I do remember, he was a big brute. I was lucky to get away when I did. If I'd hung around, he would've ripped me to shreds and wouldn't have needed a guitar string to do that."

"From what you've said, Bill, you did the right thing. It sounds like your hockey skills came in handy. Lucky for you, you're alive to tell the tale."

"Yeah, I'm glad to be alive. That monster scared the living hell out of me, and I didn't sleep a wink last night."

"You may have made him angry by getting away, and he could be planning another attack against Frozen North soon. To discourage

MUSIC CITY MURDERS   67

another attack, I advise you to inform your people to be extra cautious and to travel in pairs until we catch that maniac."

"I'll inform our people about your suggestion. If this keeps up, I may have to start carrying a hockey stick for protection or buy a handgun and take shooting lessons," Bill said with a nervous laugh.

"That might be a good idea," Mike said. "Call me back if you think of anything else."

"Okay, Detective. Goodbye."

"Goodbye, Bill."

After the call from Bill Ormond, Mike sat thinking about their conversation. As he picked up the paper, he almost choked on his bagel when he read the headline on the front page of the *Nashville Star Daily*.

"GUITAR STRING STRANGLER" STRIKES AGAIN!

By Jeff Stone, Investigative Reporter

On the evening of February 4th, the half-naked, battered, and mutilated body of Ms. Heather Brown, 22, of Horse Cave, Kentucky, was found floating in the Cumberland River opposite Nissan Stadium. Ms. Brown was the second victim of the "Guitar String Strangler." The killer used a steel guitar string to sever the victim's carotid artery and jugular vein. Ms. Brown was an NSGI member and was a recent addition to the Frozen North Music songwriter staff.

The first victim, Ms. Shannon Greenway, 23, was found in the parking lot of her apartment building on the morning of January 21. She was strangled and stabbed, like Heather Brown. Mark Norris and Sharon Myers, two seasoned detectives from the West Precinct, initially caught the case. The Heather Brown murder had the same MO (short for modus operandi) as the Shannon Greenway homicide. When this happens, the police suspect a serial killer could be committing the murders. The case is then assigned to a Homicide Unit responsible for finding and catching serial killers. Catching the killer is now in the hands of Detective Sergeant Rose Goodwin and her "rookie" partner, Detective Mike McMahon.

The third murder happened late Tuesday night (February 7) or early Wednesday morning (February 8). The victim, twenty-five-year-old John Tilley, a singer/songwriter from Dallas, Texas, was found in the driveway of his rented home on Eden Avenue. The MO was the same as the first two murders. Mr. Tilley, like so many young singer/songwriters, came to Nashville seeking fortune and fame. He performed regularly at Tootsies and the Songwriter's Bar & Grill.

The only thing the police found to identify each victim was a laminated NSGI membership card. Is it a coincidence that all three victims were members of NSGI?

Two victims, Heather Brown and John Tilley were recent additions to the Frozen North Music songwriter staff. A Canadian company, Frozen North, opened for business in Nashville about two years ago.

Do we have a serial killer on the loose in Music City? Should you be concerned if you are a member of NSGI or signed to Frozen North Music or FN Records?

When contacted, Chief of Police Bradley Cummings said, "The investigation is ongoing, and it's too early to draw any conclusions. Detective Sergeant Goodwin and Detective McMahon are two of our best detectives, and I'm confident they will catch the killer soon. We will keep the media informed as the case progresses."

Are Detective Sergeant Goodwin and Detective McMahon two of the best detectives? Will they catch the killer soon? Only time will tell.

By the time he finished reading the article, Mike was boiling mad. *That damn Stone—where did he get all the details? It must be from someone in forensics or a police officer who worked all the crime scenes. For some unknown reason, his source didn't tell Stone about the treble clef symbol on all the victim's foreheads. If Stone had known about the symbol, he would have mentioned it. Where does Stone get off calling me a "rookie" after over two years as a detective?*

Rose interrupted Mike's thoughts when she said, "Good morning, Mike."

"Have you seen the front page of the *Nashville Star Daily?*"

"Not yet. What's up?"

"Here, look for yourself," Mike said.

After reading the article, Rose let out a deep sigh. "Where the hell's Stone getting his info so quickly?"

"Your guess is as good as mine. I suspect someone who worked the crime scenes, like a cop or a person from the forensics team."

"Maybe it's Tony Capino," Rose said. "He knows all the gruesome details, but I find it hard to believe that Tony would be Stone's source. If I had to guess, I bet he's paying a forensics tech for the information."

"You could be right," Mike said as he picked up his desk phone and dialed.

After three rings, a voice said, "Jeff Stone."

"Stone, this is Detective Mike McMahon. What the hell are you trying to pull with today's article?"

"What do you mean? I'm just doing my job, Detective. Have you ever heard of freedom of the press?"

"Don't give me that bullshit! You will panic the Nashville music community by saying we have a serial killer targeting NSGI members and Frozen North songwriters and artists."

"Are you saying we don't have a serial killer committing these murders? I thought that's why you and Detective Sergeant Goodwin were assigned the case."

"It's too early to pass judgment on that—and besides, where are you getting all the gory details? Are you paying off someone who's been at all the crime scenes?"

"Detective, you know I'm not obligated to reveal my confidential sources. If you and your partner had granted me an interview and weren't so tight-lipped about everything, I wouldn't have to find other sources."

"That's not going to happen!" Mike yelled, slammed down the phone, and kicked his wastebasket across the aisle.

Rose laughed. "I take it that didn't go too well, and it would help if you didn't let him get under your skin. You know that's what he's trying to do."

Still seething, Mike said, "Yeah, I know you're right, but that Stone is a smug son of a bitch. "Everyone in the music community will be looking over their shoulder, afraid of their own shadow."

"Well," Rose said, "that may not be so bad, especially if it keeps people on their toes, observant and alert. If the killer strikes again, perhaps someone will get his license plate number."

"That would be nice, but I won't hold my breath waiting for that to happen. By the way, just before you arrived, I had a call from Bill Ormond. He came close to being the psycho's latest victim in their parking lot last night. Luckily, Bill got away by kicking the perp in the balls. While his attacker was recovering, he jumped into his vehicle and took off."

"Did he get a good look at the perp?"

"He didn't see his face. Bill said the man had on a demonic-looking clown mask, and he wore a black hoodie. The hood covered his head, but one thing he did notice: the guy was one huge sucker."

Just as Goodwin was about to reply, her intercom buzzed. It was Nancy Allman, Lieutenant Foster's administrative assistant. "Sergeant, Lieutenant Foster wants to see you and Detective McMahon in his office pronto."

Rose looked at Mike and said, "It sounds like we're in for an ass-reaming."

Mike shrugged, laughed, and said, "You don't know that. Maybe he wants to give us a raise knowing how hard we've been working."

Goodwin lightened up and smiled. "If anything, it'll be a demotion back to a patrol car or pounding the pavement."

The lieutenant was on the phone as they entered his office. He motioned for them to take a seat while he continued his conversation.

Foster had been in his current position for the past five years. In his mid-fifties, he had lost most of his hair, and his once bright brown eyes had lost their sparkle. Foster had a small, salt-and-pepper mustache and a long, slender face that had begun to sag from age and the pressure of his job.

He was saying, "Yes, sir, I understand. No, sir, we don't have anything new currently. Yes, sir, we're doing our best and will have more to report in a few days. Okay, goodbye, sir."

Like two laser beams, Foster's eyes focused on Mike and Rose. "I guess you might have suspected that was the chief burning my ass with a hot poker. The mayor called him after reading this morning's paper. He was disturbed by the article, and he's afraid if we don't catch the 'Guitar String Strangler' soon, it will create a major panic in the Nashville music community, and he's concerned it will hurt tourism."

"I think that's already started to happen. I got a phone call from Bill Ormond, the vice president of Frozen North, this morning. He sounded freaked out. Ormond was almost another victim in their parking lot last night and barely escaped the suspected killer."

Mike went on to tell the story. As he listened, Lieutenant Foster's face flushed. The vein on his forehead began to pulse, and he looked like he was about to croak.

When Mike finished, Foster took a sip of water, cleared his throat, and said, "Shit! Too bad that Ormond fellow didn't see his face. All we know about the killer is that he's a big monster."

"The article in the paper could be good or bad depending on how you look at it, Lieutenant," Rose said. "It could be bad if it causes people to panic, but it could be good if people become aware of their surroundings and are more observant. If the killer tries to strike again, someone might see him getting in or out of his vehicle and provide us with a plate number."

"Wouldn't that be nice, Sergeant, but I wouldn't count on that happening any time soon. I know you're doing your best—but you'll have to do better. We're all pressured to find this perp as soon as possible. I know it won't be easy, but you'll have to follow up on every lead, no matter how inconsequential. The chief has asked me to have you work on this case, and this case only, until solved. I'm assigning your other cases to detectives Jefferson and Summerville. That's it! Don't forget to keep me updated."

After leaving the lieutenant's office, they decided to go to the break room, review the case, and plan their next move over coffee.

When seated at a table with their coffee, Mike said, "I think we should try to develop a profile of our killer. Based on a book I read on criminal profiling, there are three types of serial killers— organized offenders, disorganized offenders, and mixed offenders. In most cases, organized offenders are more sophisticated. They're bright and show evidence of planning their crimes. Usually, they are employed and are active socially with spouses, families, and friends. Fantasies drive them, but they keep control and are not impulsive. They tend to prepare and rehearse, targeting specific victims. To maintain victim compliance, they use restraints and bring the tools they need to get the job done. These killers seldom leave evidence behind, and they usually have a dumpsite selected where they can dispose of or hide the body," Mike said.

"Do you think our killer is this type?" Rose asked.

"He shows some of the traits of the organized offender, but he's missing some as well. For instance, the killer seems to be selecting similar victims—all from the Nashville music community. He didn't use restraints on the victims because he killed them quickly. He did bring his tools—the guitar string and a knife to all three murders. However, the killer left the guitar string behind as evidence."

"What are the traits of the disorganized offender?" Rose asked.

"These criminals, for the most part, live alone or possibly with a relative. They are not as smart as the organized offender, and in most cases, are unemployed or work at menial jobs and could suffer from mental illness. They are impulsive and rarely try to gain the victim's confidence. They attack the victim violently without warning. They don't bring any tools and use whatever is handy during the killing—they often leave the crime scene messy. The body is usually left at the crime scene, and they don't appear to worry about leaving evidence behind. Some offenders may even have sexual contact with the victim after the person dies."

"It sounds like our guy could have some of the disorganized offender's traits as well," Rose said grimly.

"You could be right. Sometimes the traits intermingle, and that's where the mixed offender comes in. These killers leave confusing messages at the crime scene, showing signs of planning and sophistication. The crime scene is often cluttered and messy looking, tending to show disturbing violent fantasies," Mike said.

"Based on the three types of offenders you described, our killer falls into the mixed offender category."

"Yeah, he's a mixture of the first two types. Based on the book, most serial killers are male, in their twenties or thirties; for the most part, white serial killers kill white people, and black serial killers kill black people. Organized serial killers may be married, have a family, and be well-liked by friends and fellow workers. Disorganized offenders usually live alone or with a family member because of their mental problems and immaturity. Most serial killers stay in their comfort zone and kill close to home, but exceptions exist. Once they gain confidence, they sometimes expand their geography. Organized offenders, like Ted Bundy, have good social skills and use a ruse to suck in their victims. Disorganized offenders who use the violent attack method do not have good social skills and are uncomfortable carrying on a conversation."

"What other things should we know about these offenders?" Rose asked.

"When it comes to a job, the organized offender customarily has a more stable employment history. They would probably have left with an honorable discharge if they were in the military. A disorganized offender is too unstable to hold a long-term job or finish military service. When it comes to education, organized offenders nine times out of ten have more schooling than a disorganized offender."

"Based on what you've said, our killer is in the middle. Like the organized offender, he's not just killing anyone. His victims are from the music community. He brings his tools—a guitar string and a knife. Like the disorganized offender, the crime scenes are messy and chaotic. Based on the stab wounds and the brutal pounding of the faces of all three victims, he's filled with rage and could be carrying out a violent fantasy."

"I'd say our killer a mixed breed. I estimate he's in his early to mid-twenties, is Caucasian, and is not well-educated. He could be unemployed or has a menial, low-paying job at best. I bet our killer lives alone and is not at all social, and he has a hard time carrying on a normal conversation and does not have any or very few friends," Mike said.

"Now that we've come up with a profile, all we have to do is find that one needle in a haystack," Rose said.

Mike chuckled. "Since our perp is Hulk-like, we can eliminate all the little people in the world."

Rose smiled. "It almost sounds like we're making progress."

"It does, doesn't it?" Mike said with a sigh, releasing the pent-up tension he was feeling. "Getting back to the case, this is what we know. All victims were members of NSGI, and two were associated with Frozen North. Jeff Stone said this could be a coincidence, but maybe not. I have two ideas. One, we go to NSGI and see if they can recall any huge, disgruntled member who may have a grudge against their association. Two, we go back to Frozen North and see if they know anyone who has it in for them. Do you have any better ideas?"

"Not at the moment. I'll let you know if I come up with something."

As they were about to leave the break room, two drug squad detectives smiling from ear to ear, strolled up to their table. Rico

Costa, a new detective in his first year under the wing of veteran Detective Jack Bowman, was in his early thirties and the shorter of the two. He stood about five nine with olive skin, dark, slicked-back hair, deep brown eyes, and a neatly trimmed black mustache. In his late forties or early fifties, Jack Bowman stood around six and a half feet and weighed approximately two hundred and fifty pounds. His gray hair was an old-school crew cut, and Bowman had a long, slim face with a beaklike nose and was arrogant and condescending. He was not Mike's favorite person. They never got along from the day Mike became a detective. He suspected Bowman had wanted his job and was upset when Mike became Rose's partner.

Thank God, Mike thought. *I'm glad I wasn't assigned to work under Bowman.*

Ignoring Rose, Jack Bowman looked at Mike with a taunting smirk. "How's the 'Guitar String Strangler' case coming along, Detective? According to Jeff Stone, it doesn't sound like it's going too well."

"Hey, Bowman," Mike said with a hostile glare, his fists automatically clenching, "It's none of your fucking business how our case is coming along. Why don't you crawl under your rock and get lost or go and arrest a drug dealer?"

"That's not a very good attitude you have there, McMahon. No wonder you're having problems solving the case."

"Who said we're having problems?" Rose asked, showing her annoyance. "Why don't you two take off and let real detectives get to work."

Rico laughed. He glared at Rose and said, "What do you mean real detectives? Real detectives would have the case solved by now."

"Why don't you fuck off, you little prick," Rose shot back, losing her temper. "I don't need your wiseass cracks—green apple."

"Who are you calling a little prick and a green apple?" Rico said, lashing back angrily.

"You, you little asshole," Rose snapped back.

Mike jumped to his feet, his eyes shooting daggers. "Cool it, Rico, don't start anything with Rose you will regret. If you do, she'll kick the shit out of you. That might be embarrassing for a little turd with such a big ego."

Turning to Jack Bowman, Mike looked him directly in the eye. In an ice-cold voice, he calmly said, "Screw off, Bowman, unless you want your beak broken."

Bowman laughed, turned away, and nodded at Costa. "Come on, Rico. Let Jessica Fletcher and her bungling assistant Inspector Clouseau return to spinning their wheels."

On the way out, Costa turned and gave them the middle finger. Mike said, "Rico, that little prick, he's becoming a miniature Jack Bowman. Bowman's training him to follow in his footsteps."

"Don't let them get to you. They know your fuse is short and like pushing your buttons."

"Yeah, I guess I have a short fuse, and I've got to fix that. Easier said than done—it's hard to ignore assholes like Bowman and Costa," Mike grumbled, still fuming.

CHAPTER 13

After their run-in with Jack Bowman and Rico Costa, they decided to go to NSGI. June Murray and her camera operator ambushed them as they left the building.

"Detectives," she said, "can you please spare a minute to update us on the 'Guitar String Strangler' case? Jeff Stone's recent article says you don't seem to be making any progress."

Mike decided to let Rose take care of this one. He was still upset from his conversation with Stone and agitated from their confrontation with Jack Bowman and Rico Costa. McMahon wasn't sure he could keep his cool with June Murray, so he whispered to Rose, "I'll let you handle it."

Rose stopped and politely asked, "What would you like to know, Ms. Murray?"

"The *Nashville Star Daily* said that since you and Detective McMahon are on the case, we have a serial killer on the loose in Nashville. Do we have a serial killer?"

"Although the MOs were similar, I think it's too early to speculate."

"When you say the MOs were similar, are you suggesting we could also have a copycat killer?"

"No. I'm not suggesting that at all."

"Do you have any leads on who the suspect or suspects might be?"

"Again, we are in the preliminary stage of our investigation, and I have no further comment."

"In other words, just as Jeff Stone surmises, you don't have any suspects."

"I have nothing more to say. Have a pleasant day, Ms. Murray."

W . D .   F R O L I C K

Rita Thompson looked up as they approached the reception desk.

"We meet again, Rita," Rose said with a friendly smile. "Who do you see more often these days than us?"

"I read about John Tilley's murder in the newspaper and was shocked. It sounds like the same killer murdered Shannon Greenway and Heather Brown. Are you having any luck finding out who's doing these horrible things?"

"That's why we're here," Mike said. "Can you think of any member who might have a grudge against NSGI? Maybe someone who caused trouble or may have had their membership revoked for some reason?"

Rita paused, deep in thought. "Gosh, no one comes to mind." She hesitated again. "But it could be...Jason Briggs."

"Jason Briggs?" Mike looked puzzled. "Who is Jason Briggs? What about him?"

"Jason used to come to our date-with-a-publisher and date-with-a-demo nights and bring some of the weirdest songs I've ever heard. Every time he got an unfavorable critique, which was pretty much every time, he would get angry with the panel or publisher and rant and rave that they wouldn't know a good song if they heard one. I remember he once said that's just your opinion. Opinions are like assholes; we all got one—and you're a bunch of assholes. It got to the point that it was embarrassing when publishers and panelists were abused like that. After several displays, it got so bad that our board voted to cancel his membership and ban Jason from the building. That didn't go over well with him. I wonder if he's trying to get even with NSGI for canceling his membership. Do you think he could be the killer?"

"Wow! That's quite a story, Rita," Rose said. "Killing NSGI members seems way too drastic for revoking his membership. However, this Briggs fellow might be worth checking out. Do you still have his address and phone number on your computer?"

"I think so."

Rita typed in Jason Briggs, and the information appeared on the screen. She printed a copy and passed it to Rose.

"Thanks, Rita," Rose said, "Once again, we appreciate your help."

After leaving NSGI, they drove straight to the address Rita had provided. The house was in a rundown neighborhood where you didn't walk the streets at night alone or perhaps not even during the day. It was an older, two-story gray frame building with peeling paint that looked like a fish losing its scales. Walking up several steps onto the rickety front porch, they noticed two mailboxes. Apartment "A"—Walter Wallace, Apartment "B"—Howie Murphy, A small sign said, "Jason Briggs, Apartment 'C'—back entrance. Turning around, they retraced their steps and followed the potholed gravel driveway to the rear of the house. A large, faded black metal letter "C" hung loosely on the building to the left of the walkout basement entrance.

Mike placed an ear against the door, and he could hear an acoustic guitar playing an up-tempo rhythm and an irritating male voice belting out weird-sounding lyrics. He knocked loudly.

Abruptly, the playing and singing stopped. When the door opened, a tall, broad-shouldered, muscular young man with a glistening shaved head stood glaring at them. Each earlobe contained a gold stud earring. The surprised look on his blond-bearded face changed into an unpleasant scowl.

"What the fuck do you want? I already gave at the office," he bellowed, then laughed, thinking he was funny.

They ignored his attitude.

"Are you Jason Briggs?" Rose asked.

"Yeah, I'm Jason Briggs. Who the fuck wants to know?"

"Detective Sergeant Goodwin and Detective McMahon of the MNPD," Rose said. "May we come in?"

They flashed their badges.

"What the hell's this about?" Briggs asked. He stood defiantly, his arms crossed in front of his chest, blocking the doorway.

"We're working on a homicide case and interviewing people who might have known the two female victims through NSGI," Rose said politely.

Reluctantly Briggs stepped aside and let them enter.

"It won't take long," Mike said.

Briggs flopped down onto the couch.

"We need to ask you a few questions and clear up a few things," Rose said.

"What kind of things? Oh, I get it. We're goin' to play good cop, bad cop." He let out a smug laugh and glared at Rose.

Rose matched his glare and said, "Cut the smart-ass routine. Maybe you'd prefer to go to the station and do the interview there."

"Are you arresting me?" Briggs asked.

"We're not here to arrest you," Mike said.

"Okay, okay, I give up. I work tonight, and I can't be late. Ask away."

Before asking any questions, Rose obtained Briggs' permission to record the interview. After recording the date, time, location, and names, she began with, "We have three dates—January 21st, January 27th, and February 7th. We need you to tell us where you were on those nights, Mr. Briggs."

"How the hell should I know?"

"Think hard and lose the attitude," Rose barked.

"Where do you work?" Mike asked.

"I work security at the Songwriter's Bar & Grill," he said civilly. "What's this about?"

They ignored his question.

"Were you working on those nights?" Rose asked.

"I don't remember, but if you let me check my schedule, I can tell you."

"Where's your schedule?" Mike asked.

"It's on the calendar on the kitchen wall."

Rose went into the kitchen and returned with the calendar. After a quick check, Rose said, "It looks like your schedule shows you worked those three nights.'

"Did you go to work on those nights?" Mike asked.

"If it's on the schedule, I was at work. I haven't missed a day, or a night, in the last two years."

"Can anyone confirm you were at work on those nights?" Rose asked.

"You can talk with my boss. Frank Fulton, he'll confirm I was there."

"I heard you playing your guitar and singing. Are you a songwriter and a member of NSGI?" Mike asked.

"Yeah, I'm a good songwriter, if I say so myself. I was a member of NSGI until they got high and mighty and canceled my membership," he said, his face flushing with anger, his blood pressure starting to rise.

"Why did they revoke your membership?" Rose asked.

"I was told it was for misconduct. It's a big crock of shit, and NSAI wouldn't give me a refund or even a partial refund."

"What did you do that caused them to cancel your membership?" Mike asked.

"I got a little loud and pissed off at a few date-with-a-demo and pitch-to-publisher nights," he said with a snarl.

"What about Frozen North Music? Have you had any dealings with them?" Rose asked.

"Yeah, those fuckers didn't like my songs at publisher night, and their comments made me angry. They said I used too many clichés, didn't paint enough pictures, and was tellin' and not showin'. What do they know? They're from Canada, live in igloos, and don't know a fuckin' thing about country music, eh? Get it, eh?" he said, laughing at his bad joke.

Rose said, "Would you mind providing a sample of your DNA? Doing a swab inside your mouth takes a few seconds."

"Why do you want my DNA? Oh, I get it. You think I'm the 'Guitar String Strangler,' don't you?" he said, laughing loudly.

"Are you?" Mike asked.

The question seemed to catch Briggs by surprise. He paused for a moment. "I may have a bit of a temper, but I wouldn't hurt a fly." Just then, a cockroach crawled onto the table, and he squashed it with his hand. "You've got the wrong guy. I'm a lover, not a killer." He laughed again, uneasy.

"How did you get swollen and cut knuckles on your right hand?" Mike asked. "I'm sure it wasn't from killing cockroaches."

"No, although I've killed my share of those little fuckers. About a week ago, I threw a rowdy drunk out of the bar because the jerk wouldn't leave peacefully. The asshole took a swing at me, and I had to defend myself, so I pounded the bastard several times before throwing him out on the street," he said, breaking into a silly grin, proud of himself.

"Can we do the swab?" Rose asked again. "If you're innocent, you have nothing to worry about."

"We'll take you to the station, swab you, and keep you nice and comfy until we get the results," Mike said.

"Okay. I got nothing to hide. I'm not your killer. Don't forget. I got to work tonight at six."

"The new DNA-testing-lab-on-a-chip won't take long. If we leave now, you'll be back in plenty of time," Rose said.

When they were in the driveway, Mike asked, "Is this your car?"

"Yep, that's my baby," Briggs said with pride.

The older black car looked to be in excellent condition.

"What year is it?" Rose asked.

"It's a 1969 Chevy Malibu SS—but you'd never know it. I usually keep it pristine, but with the winter weather, I haven't had a chance to wash or clean it for about a month. It would be nice if I had a garage to keep it in."

Mike was thinking, *Jason Briggs is a real whack job. He's a big man! No, Briggs is a huge man! Could he be our killer?*

CHAPTER 14

Rose took Jason's DNA sample and arranged for an officer to rush it to the crime lab.

Since Briggs complained that he was hungry, Rose went to the break room and returned with a ham and cheese sandwich and a can of Coke. She left him in the interview room, locking the door behind her, and headed to her desk to clean up some paperwork and to make a few phone calls.

After dropping Rose and Briggs off at the station, Mike called, made an appointment, and headed to the Songwriter's Bar & Grill to check out Jason's work alibi. When he arrived at the Songwriter's Bar & Grill, Frank Fulton was on the phone, and Fulton waved Mike into his office and motioned for him to take a seat.

Hanging up the phone, Frank said, "It's good to see you again, Mike. What can I do for you today?"

They shook hands, and Mike said, "Thanks for seeing me on short notice, Frank. I want to ask you a few questions about one of your employees. His name is Jason Briggs."

"No problem, Mike. What is it you'd like to know?"

"As you know, my partner and I have been assigned the 'Guitar String Strangler' case."

"Yeah, I've been following it in the *Nashville Star Daily*. The other day I saw your interview on TV."

"I'd like to confirm if Jason Briggs was at work on the nights the murders supposedly took place. The dates are the 21st and 27th of January and the 7th of February."

"Do you suspect Jason had something to do with the murders?"

"Let's say he's a person of interest. NSGI canceled his membership for using foul language and blowing up at a few demo critiques. Maybe he hates NSGI for that reason. The three murder victims were members of that association. It might just be a coincidence, but we've got to check it out to be sure."

Frank pulled out two sheets of paper from the top right hand-drawer. After scanning them, he said, "The schedule shows Briggs was on duty on those dates in January from 6:00 p.m. until closing at 3:00 a.m. The February schedule shows the same for the seventh. He works from six until three, but by the time we tidy up a bit, most nights, Jason doesn't leave until around 4:00 a.m. If he didn't work on those nights, I'd remember because I would've had to call in a replacement."

"Would you have videotapes of those nights on file?"

"We don't use tapes anymore. Recently, we upgraded to a new system with offsite cloud storage. Each security camera records on a micro card. There's no need for a DVR or digital video recorder because we communicate directly with the security camera over the Internet. I use my computer to access the site, type in the dates, and the video is, streamed, on demand, through a Cloud Portal. It plays on my computer monitor. Let me show you."

Mike walked around the desk and stood behind Frank. In a few minutes, the video confirmed that Jason Briggs was at work on the three nights in question.

"Wow, that's a neat system," Mike said. "The technology they have on the market these days is amazing."

"It's not cheap, but it's much better than remembering to keep changing videotapes."

Just before leaving, Mike said, "Jason has some cuts and bruises on the knuckles of his right hand. Do you have any idea how he got hurt?"

"About a week ago, he had to throw an unruly drunk out of the bar. When the guy swung at Jason, he had to defend himself. Briggs hit him a few times before tossing the drunk on the street. That's how he hurt his hand. If you want, I can find the video for you."

"That won't be necessary, Frank. I've taken up enough of your time."

"It won't take long."

"That's okay. Thanks for your help, Frank."

"No problem, Mike. Remember when we talked the other day about the big guy that came in and played me a few songs? It's been bugging me, and now I know why. Because he resembles Jason Briggs."

"That's weird. Does Jason have a brother?"

"He's never mentioned anything about having a brother."

"It might be worth checking out. Thanks again, Frank."

When Mike returned to his desk, Rose said. "The lab just called and confirmed the DNA found under Heather Brown's fingernails was a partial match to Jason Briggs but not enough for a complete match. Since the results were inconclusive, there's no way we can be one hundred percent certain the DNA belongs to Briggs," Rose said.

"We knew that before we sent his DNA to the lab, but it was worth a try. Jason Briggs may have had contact with the victim, but it doesn't prove he killed her. Besides, his alibi checks out. I viewed the videos, and Jason was at work the nights the murders supposedly took place. By the way, where is he now?"

"Briggs is cooling his heels in interview room two. I locked the door. The last time I checked, he had nodded off."

"When I spoke with Frank Fulton, he mentioned that the huge man that sang him a few songs reminded him of Jason Briggs."

"That's odd. Maybe we should ask Jason if he has a brother."

"I'll talk to him and see what he says. Let's keep the soda can and get his prints on file. They might come in handy down the road," Mike said.

Rose's cell phone rang, and she stepped away to take the call.

Mike headed to the interview room, unlocked the door, and sat across from Briggs.

"How are you making out, Jason?"

Looking half-asleep, Briggs said, "How long do I have to stay here? I hope you didn't forget I gotta work at six."

"It shouldn't be much longer."

"I hope not. Frank Fulton doesn't like it when I'm late. I don't want to lose my job."

"Don't worry. You won't lose your job. I went to see Frank Fulton, and he confirmed you worked on the nights in question."

"It's just like I said. I didn't kill anybody. Can I go now?"

"The DNA results were inconclusive, so, for now, you're off the hook. I'll drive you home soon. Do you have a brother?"

The question caught Briggs off guard.

"Do I have a what?"

"A brother. Do you have a brother?"

"My mom and dad died when I was a few years old. I was raised in an orphanage and can't remember a brother or a sister. I always wished I'd had a brother. Sometimes I have dreams of playing with a brother when I was a little kid. Why do you want to know?"

"No reason. Just curious, that's all."

Rose stuck her head in the door and motioned for Mike to step outside. "I just talked with Paul, and he's wondering if I'm going to be able to make our daughter's dance recital—it starts at seven. I told him I was going to try. Because of this crazy job, I've already missed too many of her activities."

"Don't worry; you'll make it. Just go. I'll finish up."

"Okay. Thanks, Mike. See you in the morning."

As McMahon returned to the room, Jason asked, "When can I go home?"

"Just a few more questions," Mike said. "Did you know the two murdered girls, Shannon Greenway and Heather Brown?"

"Yeah, I knew them from NSGI."

Mike asked, "Were you and Heather ever intimate?"

"Do you mean, like, did we ever have sex?"

"Did you?"

Briggs paused, looked away, turned back, and said, "No. We were just casual friends."

"Did you ever write songs with Shannon Greenway, Heather Brown, or Charlie Cook?"

"I think Heather wanted to, but Charlie always had an excuse. He must've thought he was too good to write songs with me. His almighty attitude made me angry. As for Shannon Greenway, she was a conceited bitch. She thought her shit didn't stink. Shannon told me I didn't write the type of songs she liked to write. She said my songs were too weird."

"Okay," Mike said, "I'll drive you home now, Jason."

"It's about time. I can't be late for work."

There's more to the Heather Brown story than Jason Briggs mentioned. He hates other songwriters and NSGI. Maybe we should try getting a search warrant for his vehicle and apartment.

CHAPTER 15

W hen Rose arrived at her desk the following day, Mike asked, "How was Jill's recital?"

"It went great! She did very well, and I know she was pleased I made it. The three of us went out for ice cream afterward, and it was nice to have some quality family time. Thanks again. I appreciate you letting me get away."

"No problem. I'm glad you could make it."

Before getting on with their day, they updated Lieutenant Foster on the Jason Briggs story.

The update completed, as they were about to leave Foster's office, Mike said, "I've got a feeling Briggs wasn't telling us everything about his relationship with Heather Brown. Do you think we can get a warrant to search his apartment and car, Lieutenant? I know it's a long shot, and we're walking on thin ice, but we don't have much to go on."

"You're right, Mike. It's a long shot, and it'll take some convincing to talk a judge into signing a warrant, but I'll give it a try and let you know as soon as I know."

"Thanks, Lieutenant," Mike said.

Their next stop was the Frozen North building. Once again, Joyce Ormond greeted them with a beaming smile.

Joyce said, "Bill and Dave are meeting with Suzanne and a few other staff members in the boardroom."

"I'm sorry, Joyce, I forgot about Suzanne's meeting. We should've called to make an appointment," Mike said.

"Don't worry, Detective. I'm sure they won't mind taking a break."

Joyce took off, and in a few minutes, Dave Franklin and Bill Ormond appeared and asked the detectives to follow them to Dave's office.

Like Bill said, the last time they met, Mike saw the championship picture of the Boston Bruins Stanley Cup victory in the 2010-11 season hanging behind Dave Franklin's desk.

They had just sat down when Joyce appeared with a tray containing four mugs of freshly brewed coffee, cream, and sugar.

"She's the greatest," Bill said after Joyce had disappeared.

As they sipped their coffee, Dave asked, "How can we help you today?"

Rose said, "As you know, the last time we saw you, we were investigating the Shannon Greenway and Heather Brown murders. Now John Tilley's homicide is part of our investigation. You may have seen the article in the *Nashville Star Daily* the other day stating that all three victims were NSGI members and that Heather Brown and John Tilley were recent signings with Frozen North Music."

"Yeah, Dave and I read the article and found the implications very disturbing; everyone here has been distraught by all the murders. As Jeff Stone said, it could be a coincidence, but I'm starting to wonder after I was almost his fourth victim the other night. If this keeps up, no songwriter or artist will want to sign with us—thinking they may be next if they're associated with the Frozen North name," Bill said.

Mike asked, "Can you think of anyone who might have a grudge against your company? It could be anybody—like a songwriter, an artist, or a competitor. To put it bluntly, someone you may have ticked off."

Bill and Dave seemed surprised by the question. They stared at one another with blank expressions.

Finally, Bill said, "Come to think of it, there was this one crazy songwriter we encountered a few times at NSGI. He wrote weird songs and wasn't open to constructive criticism. When we tried to offer him suggestions to improve his songs, he got angry and had a few choice words for us. I heard a rumor that NSGI canceled his

W . D .   F R O L I C K

membership and barred him from the building. I can't remember his name, but he was a big muscular guy with a shaved head and a gold stud earring in each ear."

"Does the name Jason Briggs ring any bells?" Rose asked.

"Yeah, that's the name," Bill said. "He was scary when he got angry."

"I remember him, too. I agree with Bill that he was crazy when he flipped his lid," Dave Franklin said.

"We got his name from NSGI as well. We went to see Briggs yesterday, and he has a solid alibi for the times of the murders. Briggs is a bouncer at the Songwriter's Bar & Grill, and I viewed a video that showed him on the job on the nights in question," Mike said.

"Is there anyone else you can think of?" Rose asked.

"You mentioned competitors. I think we ticked off Tim Evans, the owner of Southern Heat Records when we bought Beatle Bug Music out from under him—and I know we signed a few songwriters and artists he was chasing. When we inked Suzanne Taylor, I know Evans wasn't pleased. Since we moved to Nashville, I'm sure we've put a few noses out of joint. Bill and I are competitive, but we're fair. However, I can't believe anyone would murder to get back at us. That's going way too far," Franklin said.

"Stranger things have happened. When it comes to money, we can't rule anyone out," Mike said.

"Can you think of anyone else?" Rose asked.

They both shook their heads, and with that, the meeting ended.

Since they were already on 16th Avenue, they stopped for a quick lunch at Bobby's Dive Bar. Bobby's, the only live music venue on Music Row, has been in business for over thirty years. It's where aspiring songwriters perform their original songs and network with other songwriters.

While eating, they listened to a few songwriters playing their guitars and singing songs they had written. Most of them were pretty good. *Thank God Jason Briggs isn't one of them*, Mike thought.

When Mike and Rose returned to the squad room, Lieutenant Foster asked them to join him in his office.

"Good news!" he said. "With gentle persuasion, I obtained a search warrant for Jason Briggs' apartment and vehicle. I've dispatched a patrol car to watch his place until you arrive. Call me if he and his car are home, and I'll send a tow truck to haul his vehicle to the crime lab garage. Maybe a thorough check by forensics will come up with evidence that could help our investigation."

"We're ready to roll," Rose said.

Dripping wet, Jason Briggs stood inside the doorway wrapped in a towel. He had just gotten out of the shower and wasn't pleased to see Rose and Mike again.

"What's goin' on?" he asked with a scowl.

Waving the warrant in his face, Mike handed it to him and said, "We have a search warrant for your apartment and your vehicle."

"You guys are pissin' me off. You're like fuckin' cockroaches; I can't get rid of you. I told you yesterday I had nothin' to do with any murder."

"Well, then, you don't have to worry. Do you?" Mike said.

While Mike talked with Briggs, Rose called Lieutenant Foster and asked him to send a tow truck.

When Rose hung up, Jason said, "As you can see, I just got out of the shower. At least let me get dressed."

"Okay, but make it fast," Mike said.

"For your information," Rose said, "we're towing your car to our crime lab garage, where forensics will check it for evidence of Heather Brown's DNA."

"They won't find any evidence 'cause Heather's never been in my car."

"Then you have nothing to worry about," Mike said.

"Shit," Briggs grumbled, "how the hell am I goin' to get to work if I don't have my car?"

"That's not our problem," Mike said. "You'll have to go by bus or take a taxi."

Cursing under his breath, Jason headed to his bedroom.

When Briggs returned to the living room, he was wearing sandals, a pair of faded blue jeans, and a white T-shirt that, in bold red
letters, read, **NSGI SUCKS!**

"How long will this take?" Briggs groaned.

"It'll take as long as it takes," Rose replied. "Make yourself a coffee
and relax in your recliner. We'll call you if we need you."

They were about to start the search when a tow truck rumbled
into the driveway. Mike asked Jason for his keys and took them to
the driver.

The apartment was small. It had two average-sized bedrooms,
one old-fashioned four-piece bathroom, a kitchen with a light oak
table, and four matching chairs. The refrigerator and gas stove were
outdated, and a newer portable microwave and toaster sat on the
counter. The small living room contained a beat-up black leather
couch, a well-worn recliner, and a dusty glass coffee table with a
badly scratched top. The most up-to-date item in the room was
the large flat-screen Sony TV mounted on the wall across from the
couch and recliner.

Slipping on latex gloves, they decided to start in Jason's bedroom
and work together one room at a time.

"What did you think of Jason's T-shirt?" Mike asked.

"If nothing else, it confirms his feelings toward NSGI," Rose said.

"Yeah, you'd almost think Briggs doesn't like them," Mike laughed.

Glancing at the unmade bed, Rose saw that the sheets needed
changing. She inspected the pillows and noticed several long
strands of blonde hair. Calling Mike over, Rose said, "Maybe this
hair belongs to Heather Brown."

"You could be right. It sure as hell isn't Jason's."

Rose placed the strands into an evidence bag, filled out the label,
and signed it.

Mike searched the first three dresser drawers and found only
men's T-shirts, socks, and underwear. He was surprised to find a
woman's bra, panties, and a sheer black negligee in the bottom
drawer.

"Rose," he said with a chuckle, "come take a look. I don't believe these are Jason's unless he's into cross-dressing."

Rose laughed and said, "I don't think they'll fit him." She proceeded to bag the undergarments as possible evidence.

Rose found an open box of Trojan condoms and two sealed packages of Fender steel guitar strings inside the night table drawer beside the bed. Once again, she placed the packages into an evidence bag.

The bedroom closet, second bedroom, bathroom, kitchen, and living room didn't turn up anything interesting. Rose even looked inside the almost bare refrigerator and the greasy oven but came up empty.

After the search, they joined Jason in the living room, where he was sipping on a beer and reading *Music Row* magazine.

Mike said, "We've completed our search and found some items we'd like the lab to check."

"You've been having sex with someone with long blonde hair. Would that someone happen to be Heather Brown?" Rose asked.

Jason's face turned red, and he shouted, "It's none of your fuckin' business who I have sex with."

"It is," Mike said, "if that someone was Heather Brown. You'll have a lot of explaining to do if the lab matches the hair we found in your bed with Heather Brown's."

"Fuck you! Fuck both of you!"

After filling Lieutenant Foster in on the search and the items they dropped off at the crime lab, they headed to the squad room and completed a few reports. Shortly after five o'clock, Mike and Rose parted ways and left for the weekend.

When he arrived at his condo, Mike entered the kitchen and retrieved a beer from the fridge. He found Suzanne sitting in the living room, relaxing on the sofa, reading a book, and sipping red wine.

Before dropping his tired body into his recliner, he bent over and gave Suzanne a soft, tender kiss.

"You look cozy. How did your first day go with the Frozen North gang?"

Suzanne put the book down, took a sip of wine, and said enthusiastically, "It was fantastic! We started listening to songs but didn't find anything too exciting. Dave and Bill are excellent songwriters, and they're willing to write with me. Once the album is completed and released, the marketing team will schedule a radio tour to promote my first single. That will give me a chance to meet the deejays in person. Hopefully, they'll like the song and play it."

"Sounds like the wheels are in motion. I'm sure all the deejays will love you and your song."

"Oh, and they played me some of Marven Jones' songs. I discovered he's from Timmins, Ontario, Shania Twain's hometown. She's still one of my favorite female singers. Marven's voice is unique, and I'm sure it will blend well with mine. Dave Franklin said they want Marven and me to record 'Don't Throw Our Love Away' and plan to release the song as our first single. By doing that, country music fans will get to know Marven and me, and we can tour radio stations together. I still want to dedicate the song to John Tilley."

Suzanne's getting the break she deserves. I hope Rose and I can catch a break and solve the 'Guitar String Strangler' case.

CHAPTER 16

A fter a restful weekend, Monday morning Rose and Mike met in the squad room at eight-thirty and decided to review the case before heading to the Songwriter's Bar & Grill for their eleven o'clock appointment with Frank Fulton.

"So far, Jason Briggs is the closest thing we have to a possible suspect. He seems to hate NSGI and Frozen North. However, the videos you saw ruled him out because he couldn't have been in two places simultaneously." Rose paused. "Unless…"

"He has a brother," Mike said, finishing her sentence. "Maybe he has a twin brother. His twin could have committed the murders while Jason was at work. When I spoke with Frank Fulton the other day, he said the big brute with the awful songs and bad temper that auditioned for him reminded him of Jason. When I asked Briggs if he had a brother, he said he couldn't remember. You never know. Maybe if we did a little digging, we could find out. Briggs said his parents died when he was a few years old, and he lived in an orphanage for half his life. If we can find the orphanage, we could check to see if Jason was there alone or with a brother."

"Since we don't have much to go on, it might be worth checking," Rose agreed.

As they entered his office, Frank Fulton greeted them with a warm smile and a firm handshake.

Mike said, "Frank, we appreciate you taking the time to see us."

"No problem, Mike. It's nice to see you both again."

"Would you two like a coffee? They're on the house."

"That would be great," Mike said.

"How do you take them?"

"We drink them black," Rose replied.

Frank went to the bar and returned carrying a tray. He handed Mike and Rose each a mug and asked, "How can I help you?"

"As you know, we've been assigned to investigate the murders of Shannon Greenway and Heather Brown. Unfortunately, John Tilley is now on the list."

"It's so sad about John Tilley and Heather Brown. John, like Heather, was a great person and a good friend. He had so much talent as a singer/songwriter. I felt he was going places in the music business. I didn't know the other girl, Shannon Greenway. It's a shame they all died so young. I hope you catch that son of a bitch before he kills more people."

"There's nothing we'd like better than to nail his ass to the wall," replied Rose. "We need all the help we can get, and that's why we're here. Did you notice anyone who might have looked suspicious or out of place hanging around the night of John Tilley's death?"

"Not that I can recall."

"Too bad," Rose said. "If you think of anything that might help our investigation, please call."

"I certainly will."

"Thanks for your time, Frank," Mike said, extending his hand.

"Anytime, Mike. Sorry I couldn't help. It was nice seeing you again, Rose. Take care!"

"It was nice seeing you as well, Frank.

As they left Fulton's office, Mike checked his watch and said, "It's almost eleven-thirty, and I'm starving. Why don't we stay for lunch? "

"That's okay with me."

After lunch, Mike's cell phone rang just before they reached the car.

"Detective McMahon," he said. The screen showed Frozen North Music.

"Good afternoon, Detective. It's Dave Franklin."

"What's up, Dave?"

"I thought you might like to know that I received a disturbing distorted voice call from an unknown caller this morning. He said more of our songwriters and artists would die soon. Before he ended the call, he told me to stop signing new talent and fuck off back to Canada. Bill and I are concerned, especially since Bill was almost one of his victims the other night. We've decided to hold off on all new signings until we discover what's happening. We don't want more people getting killed. What do you think, Detective? Do we have cause for alarm?"

"Wow!" Mike gasped. "I'd say someone has got it in for you guys. Any guess as to who it might be?"

"As I mentioned the other day, a few of our competitors aren't too happy that we signed a few songwriters and artists they were chasing. Tim Evans at Southern Heat Records was pissed when we bought Beetle Bug Music, and I know he was counting on signing Suzanne Taylor, and I'm sure our inking her has his nose out of joint. I find it hard to believe Evans would resort to murder to get back at us. If it's Southern Heat, they must have hired someone, and I don't think they employ anyone who resembles Bill's description of his attacker."

"Unfortunately, we don't have proof that Tim Evans is involved, and we can't accuse him without evidence. However, visiting Evans might be worthwhile to check out the vibes."

"Evans and I have locked horns a few times. There's no love lost between us," Dave said, forcing a laugh. "I know he hates my guts, and the feeling is mutual."

"I'll discuss it with my partner and see what she thinks. I'll get back to you." Mike hung up and whistled softly.

Once he had filled Rose in on Dave Franklin's call, they decided to detour and visit Tim Evans.

When they arrived at the reception desk, an attractive young woman in her mid-twenties greeted them. She had short black hair, round brown eyes, and a pleasant smile. There was a name plaque on her desk that read Debbie Eastman.

"Hello," Rose said, "I'm Detective Sergeant Goodwin of the MNPD, and this is my partner, Detective McMahon." They showed their badges. "We'd like to speak with Mr. Tim Evans, please."

"Do you have an appointment?"

"No, we don't," Mike replied. "Is that a problem?"

"Mr. Evans is busy and prefers to meet by appointment only."

"If you could please tell him, it's imperative that we see him now, and we'll only take a few minutes of his time," Rose said.

"Okay, I'll see what he says." She picked up the phone and buzzed his office. "Mr. Evans, there are two detectives here to see you, and they say it's important they speak with you now."

She listened for a few seconds, looked up, and said, "He wants to know what it's about."

"Tell him we'll let him know when we see him," Mike said.

"They'll let you know when they see you. Okay, I'll show them in."

After hanging up the phone, she said, "Please follow me."

Debbie led them into a plush office with expensive dark mahogany furniture. The walls contained framed platinum and gold records, pictures of celebrities from the entertainment industry, and a few politicians. Mike spotted a picture of Tim Evans with the former mayor, George Donavan, during the ribbon-cutting ceremony for the opening of Southern Heat Records. Standing in front of a red ribbon, the mayor held a pair of scissors in his left hand while the two men smiled for the camera as they shook hands.

Tim Evans was a small, thin man who looked to be in his early sixties. He was bald, with a diamond earring in his left ear. His narrow, piercing black eyes viewed them from an oval face with bushy black eyebrows and a neatly trimmed salt-and-pepper beard.

Evans stood and greeted the two detectives with a limp, fish-like handshake. They showed their badges and introduced themselves.

"Please be seated," he said. "To what do I owe the pleasure, Detectives?"

Rose said, "We're investigating the recent murders of Shannon Greenway, Heather Brown, and John Tilley. All of them were songwriters and members of NSGI, and Heather Brown and John Tilley were staff writers at Frozen North Music. I presume you've heard about the killings in the local media."

"Yes, I've read about the murders in the newspaper and saw clips on the TV news. How does it concern me?"

Mike came right to the point. "Frozen North Music recently signed Heather Brown and John Tilley to their songwriting staff. It might be a coincidence, but Dave Franklin and Bill Ormond think someone has a grudge against Frozen North and is out to get them."

"So, you think we're killing off our competitor's songwriters?"

Mike looked straight into his beady eyes and said, "I didn't say that."

"You seem to be implying that, or why else would you be here?" he said, his face flushing, anger enveloping him.

Rose said, "It's our job to check out everyone who might have a reason to get back at Frozen North."

"What reason would I have?"

"We understand Frozen North scooped you on a few deals lately. The big one was Beetle Bug Music, and they also signed several songwriters and artists you were chasing," Mike said. "Artists like Suzanne Taylor."

"Let me get this straight. Do you think we would be stupid enough to kill off our competitor's songwriters and artists? I'll admit there's no love lost between the Frozen North people and me. I admit that Dave Franklin and I have had a few disagreements, and I told him in a heated moment that I wished he and his partner would fuck off back to Canada—and yes, they did scoop us on several deals and signings, but to go around killing off their songwriters is crazy. That's the most incredible thing I've ever heard!"

"Again, I didn't say that. You're putting words in my mouth," Mike said.

Rose said, "Frozen North received a threatening phone call this morning from someone disguising his voice. He said if they keep signing new songwriters and artists, more of their people will die. Like you, he told them to fuck off back to Canada."

"Do you have any evidence proving we're involved? If not, then I suggest this meeting is over. I'll have my attorney present the next time you wish to speak to me. Now, excuse me; I have work to do."

Once they were back in the car, Mike said, "What do you think, Rose? Evans seemed a little hostile and uptight."

"Yeah, he got upset quite easily. It could be his nervous personality, or he could be hiding something."

"I got that same impression."

When they returned to the office, Mike dialed Dave Franklin. Joyce Ormond answered and put him through.

"Dave Franklin."

"Dave, it's Detective McMahon. My partner and I visited Southern Heat Records and spoke with Tim Evans. He admitted that you two didn't have a good relationship. He also said that in a heated moment, he told you to fuck off back to Canada. We can have all the suspicions in the world, but without evidence, there's nothing we can do. We'll have to wait and see if anything else turns up. In the meantime, let us know if you get any more threatening phone calls."

"Okay, will do. Thanks."

After hanging up, Mike turned to Rose and said with a chuckle, "It looks like Southern Heat is trying to melt the Frozen North."

Rose gave him a strange look and managed to keep a straight face. She smiled and said, "Maybe Frozen North is trying to freeze out Southern Heat."

They laughed, easing the tension.

"Yeah, I know—bad jokes," Mike said.

CHAPTER 17

Suzanne spent the day listening to demos and writing songs with Dave Franklin and Bill Ormond. Things had gone better than expected, but the long day mentally drained her.

When Suzanne arrived home, she found Mike stretched out on the sofa, snoring loudly. She kissed him lightly, and he snorted. His eyes blinked open, and it took him several seconds to realize where he was and to get his brain functioning.

"Hi," he whispered drowsily, "I guess I dozed off. What time is it?"

"It's a little after eight. Sorry, I shouldn't have woken you. You look exhausted. Did you have a rough day?"

"No, that's all right; I'm fine. I had a good day, and I'm just a little tired. How was your day?"

"It was super! We listened to demos, and I wrote two great songs with Dave and Bill. We should be ready to start on the album in a week. I'm drained but excited by how well things are shaping up."

"Are you anxious to start recording?"

"I can hardly wait! There's a state-of-the-art studio at the back of the Frozen North building. Mark Bush will be producing my album. From what I've heard, he's one of the best producers in Nashville."

"Sounds like things are moving in the right direction. I'm sure your album will turn out great."

"I can't wait until it`s finished. By the way, did Dave Franklin call you today?"

"Yes, he did. Why do you ask?"

W . D .   F R O L I C K

"While we were listening to demos, he got an upsetting phone call. Someone threatened to kill more Frozen North songwriters and artists. I'm scared, Mike. I could be on his list."

"Don't worry. I'm sure it's some harmless crackpot who reads the newspaper and wants to stir up a little shit."

"I can't help but worry. That call has me freaked right out."

"There's no reason to panic, babe. Two of Nashville's best detectives are on the case."

Suzanne smiled and said, "I hope you're right and are not saying that just to make me feel safe?"

"I'd never do that. Try to relax. I'll protect you."

"Okay, I believe you," Suzanne said as she picked up a book about the history of Nashville. In high school, history had always been one of her favorite subjects.

A few minutes after she started reading, she said, "Hey, it says here that Nashville's earliest settlers back in the late 1700s celebrated with fiddle music and something called buck dancing after arriving on the shores of the Cumberland River. Nashville's first 'celebrity' was the famous frontiersman and Congressman Davy Crockett. Did you know that Davy Crockett told colorful stories and that he played the fiddle? This book is so interesting, don't you think?"

"Yeah, it's fascinating," Mike mumbled behind his newspaper.

"And listen to this! Back in the 1800s, Nashville became a national music publishing center. A musical group named the Fisk Jubilee Singers from Nashville's Fisk University went on the first around-the-world tour by a musical act. It says their efforts helped fund the school's mission to educate formerly enslaved people after the Civil War. The Fisk Jubilee Singers put Nashville on the map as a global music center. When the group played for the Queen of England, the Queen commented that the group was from the 'Music City.' I'm guessing that's how Nashville became known as 'Music City.' Neat stuff, huh?"

"Yeah, great stuff, my dear," Mike said before returning to the *Nashville Star Daily* sports section.

"Mike, listen to this. In the year 1897, a group of Confederate veterans chose Nashville as the place to hold a big reunion. The event was held in a tabernacle later known as the Ryman. It says the Ryman became the Grand Ole Opry's home, nicknamed the Carnegie Hall of the south. In 1925, WSM radio launched a broadcast called the Grand Ole Opry. I can't wait to sing on the stage of the Grand Ole Opry. Too bad it's not at the Ryman anymore. Did you know they have a circle of wood from the Ryman in the new Opry building that you can stand on when you sing?"

"Uh-huh."

"Did you know that Tootsies began as Moms? In 1960, Hattie 'Tootsie' Tatum bought Moms and renamed it Tootsies Orchid Lounge. The orchid part of the name comes from the painter who painted her building orchid—the rest is history. And get this! Willie Nelson got his first songwriting job after playing at Tootsies. Over the years, Tootsies had several movie scenes filmed there. Songs such as 'What's Tootsie Gonna Do When They Tear the Ryman Down?' and 'The Wettest Shoulders in Town' are all about Tootsies. Patsy Cline, Mel Tillis, Kris Kristofferson, and Waylon Jennings were a few of its early customers. Over the years, Tootsies has become one of Nashville's most famous tourist attractions. Gee, this is all so interesting."

"Uh-huh.'"

"Mike," Suzanne scolded, "you're not even listening to me. I bet you haven't heard a single word."

"Sorry, what did you say, babe?"

"I said I bet you haven't heard a single word. You men hide behind your newspapers and pretend to be listening, but you're only interested in sports, sports, and more sports."

"Guilty as charged, Your Honor!"

Mike got out of his recliner, went to the couch, and hugged and kissed Suzanne.

"Forgive me, babe," he said with a sheepish grin.

"Okay, I forgive you," she said, jabbing him in the ribs with her elbow.

"Ouch!" Mike said, pretending to be hurt.

Suzanne laughed. "Don't let it happen again, or next time I'll poke you harder."

Suzanne appears to be feeling happier and safer. Too bad I'm not!

CHAPTER 18

Suzanne awoke to the aroma of freshly brewed coffee.
Mike was busy preparing a breakfast fit for a queen: scrambled eggs, toast, crispy bacon, blueberry pancakes, and freshly squeezed orange juice.

As she entered the kitchen, Suzanne looked puzzled. "What's the special occasion?"

"Happy Valentine's Day," Mike said with a big grin. He walked over, put his arms around her, pulled Suzanne's body into his, and hugged her tightly—giving her a long, tender kiss.

"Wow! What a wonderful way to wake up." She turned around and dashed out of the room, leaving Mike confused.

When Suzanne reappeared, her right hand was behind her back, and she had a beaming smile on her beautiful face. She handed Mike an envelope and said, "Happy Valentine's Day, sweetheart."

Mike opened the envelope, read the verse, and said, "It's lovely." He found a gift certificate for five hundred dollars from Bruno's Men's Shoppe. "I guess you're hinting that I need a new suit, huh? Thanks, my dear." He grabbed Suzanne and kissed her again.

As their lips parted, she laughed and said, "Wow, what a kiss! I'm not hinting. I'm telling you, Detective, it's time for a new suit."

Mike said, "We should eat while it's still hot. I've got a surprise for you, but it can wait until after breakfast."

Suzanne faked a pout and asked, "Do we have to wait?"

"Yes. I want to keep you in suspense. It won't take long."

When they finished eating, Mike left the room and returned quickly. He had both hands behind his back and said, "Close your eyes, and don't you dare peek."

Suzanne closed her eyes, shifting from one foot to the other, wondering what the big mystery was.

"Okay, you can open your eyes now."

He handed her an envelope. She opened it and removed the card. As she read the beautiful verse, her eyes began to moisten. When she had finished reading, happy tears rolled down her cheeks.

"Thank you," she said, dabbing at her eyes with a tissue, "it's lovely."

"Close your eyes again." A few seconds later, he said, "Okay, you can look now."

When Suzanne opened her eyes, Mike was kneeling, holding a small red velvet box. When he opened the lid, a beautiful diamond sparkled brilliantly in the overhead lighting.

"Suzanne Michelle Taylor, I love you with all my heart and soul and want to spend the rest of my life making you happy. Will you marry me?"

Suzanne's mouth dropped open—she was speechless. Again, her eyes moistened with tears of joy. Then she screamed, jumping up and down, "Yes, Michael John McMahon, I will marry you. I will marry, marry, marry you!"

Mike stood up and slipped the ring onto Suzanne's finger. It was a perfect fit.

"I've been thinking, now that we're officially engaged, why don't you move in with me? You'll be on the road promoting your first album and doing gigs, and you won't be using your apartment much. Why pay rent for nothing? What do you think?"

"I was wondering when you were going to ask," Suzanne said with a big grin. "I'll give my notice tomorrow, and I can be out in sixty days."

"Why wait! We can move you in this Saturday. You'll have sixty days to figure out what you want to do with your furniture. If you don't wish to sell it, you could store it until you decide."

"Okay, that sounds like a plan."

Previously, Mike made reservations at Valentino's Ristorante on West End Avenue. The atmosphere was ideal for celebrating their engagement and Valentine's Day.

They arrived at Valentino's at 6:30 p.m. The host escorted them to a table for two in a quiet corner, and after they were seated, a waiter appeared, and Mike ordered a bottle of Pinot Grigio. A few minutes later, the waiter returned, opened the bottle, and poured them each a half glass. After a toast to their engagement and a future together, Mike said he was famished. They studied the menu, and when they were ready to order, Mike waved the waiter back to their table. He chose veal scaloppini with smoked mozzarella, rosemary, sun-dried tomato sauce, mashed potatoes, and sautéed spinach for his main course. Suzanne ordered Valentino's specialty—veal shank braised with vegetables, fresh herbs, tomato sauce, and overstuffed risotto.

Suzanne couldn't stop glancing at her beautiful diamond throughout the delicious meal.

CHAPTER 19

After the excitement of his engagement, the wonderful dinner, and a night of the best lovemaking Mike had ever experienced, his spirits should be soaring—but that was the furthest thing from the truth. He sat at his desk, sipping coffee and thinking about the case. *I can't see any concrete evidence. Every lead Rose and I follow ends up a dead end. This case is getting frustrating. I know everyone above us in the chain of command is losing patience. Why did I ever choose this profession? I should have known better after seeing what life as a homicide detective did to my father and mother. There was always tension in our home. If it weren't for what happened to my mother, I'd be doing something else with his life. Stop feeling sorry for yourself, McMahon. Get a grip! You've made your bed. Now you'll have to lie in it. Get this case solved before it drives you crazy.* A vision of the bungling Inspector Clouseau flashed through his head.

Rose interrupted Mike when she said, "A penny for your thoughts,"

Preoccupied, Mike didn't notice her arrival.

"You scared me half to death, Rose! Don't go creeping up on me like that."

"Boy aren't we jumpy this morning," she laughed.

"Sorry. Everything we work on keeps going nowhere, and this case is driving me crazy. The good news is I asked Suzanne to marry me yesterday, and she said yes."

"That's great news, Mike! Congratulations! I'm so happy for you and Suzanne. You're such a romantic. Of all days, you chose Valentine's Day. Have you decided on a date yet?"

"To tell the truth, the subject never came up. I'll leave that decision up to Suzanne."

Mike blushed as Rose gave him a hug and a peck on the cheek. Embarrassed, he said, "Let's update the boss. We need to tell him about the phone call Dave Franklin received and our visit with Tim Evans at Southern Heat Records.

Lieutenant Foster thanked them for the update and said, "Keep your noses to the grindstone. The chief and the mayor are getting impatient. I don't know how much more of this my ulcer can take. Keep me informed. Now get the hell out of here and go find the killer."

Just as Rose returned to her desk, her phone rang.

"Detective Seargent Goodwin."

"Good morning, Detective. It's Jim Clark at the crime lab."

"Good morning, Jim," Rose said. "I hope you're calling with good news."

"The good news is the garments and hair tested positive for Heather Brown's DNA, and the guitar strings match the killer's brand. We went through the car with a fine-tooth comb but found nothing. I'll send you a report later today."

"Okay, thanks, Jim."

Rose looked at Mike and said. "We have a match to Heather Brown's DNA from the hair and clothing. It looks like Briggs didn't tell us the whole story."

"Let's pay him another visit and find out why he lied to us."

Forty minutes later, looking spaced out, Jason Briggs opened the door.

"I can't believe it." He scowled. "You two again. Don't you know it's the middle of the night for me? I worked last night and didn't get to bed until after five this morning. Thanks to you, I don't have my car, and it takes forever to get to work and back."

"We hate to disturb your beauty rest, Jason, but we've got to talk," Mike said.

"What's this ab…?"

Before he could get it out, Rose asked, "Why did you lie to us, Jason? You were sleeping with Heather Brown. It's time to level with us and tell the truth."

Mike said, "Let's start from the beginning, and no more crap about her being a casual acquaintance."

Briggs raised his hands as a gesture of surrender and said, "Okay, okay. I'll tell you—but I swear I didn't kill her. We met at NSGI several months ago. For some reason, we took a shine to one another. We started flirtin'. One thing led to another, and once a week, we got together for sex. Heather was still datin' Charlie—she just wanted to have a little fun on the side. That was fine with me. I didn't want to get involved in a relationship. She'd tell Charlie she was goin' to NSGI to co-write, and then she would come here instead. We'd get high on pot, have kinky sex, and then she would leave. That's the whole story—the whole truth. I lied when I said we didn't write a song together. We wrote one song. 'Cheatin' Can Be Fun' is what we called it." He let out a nervous laugh.

"Did anyone tell you that you've got a twisted sense of humor, Jason? Now let's get serious. How do you explain the DNA the lab found under Heather's fingernails? It pretty much matched yours," Rose said.

"I didn't kill her! My DNA must have gotten under her fingernails when we had sex. Heather would get so wild that she tore the skin off my back with her long fingernails." He took off his T-Shirt and showed them the healing scratch marks.

"Shit," Mike said, "why didn't you tell us the last time we were here?"

"If I told you, you'd think I killed her. I guess I wasn't thinkin' straight."

"Damn right, you weren't thinking straight. How could you kill Heather when the video showed you were at work the night of her suspected murder? If you didn't kill her, do you know who did?" Rose asked.

"Honestly, I have no idea....unless Charlie found out about us and decided to make her pay."

"All right, Jason, you're off the hook for now," Mike said.

"It's about fuckin' time," he said. "Now, if you don't mind, I'd like to go back to sleep. A growin' boy needs his beauty rest. I got to work tonight." He stretched, yawned, and headed back to his bedroom.

When they reached the car, Mike said, "Something about this scenario is bugging me. Whatever it is, we're damn well going to find out."

"Yeah, I know what you mean. When we think we're getting somewhere, we keep drawing blanks," Rose sighed.

Mike picked up a French Merlot on his way home that evening. Before dinner, he opened the wine and poured two glasses. Just as they clinked glasses, Mike's cell phone rang. Without checking the screen, he answered, "Detective McMahon."

"Good evening," a distorted voice said, "I hope I didn't catch you and your sweetie at a bad time. How is the case coming along? You're not having much luck catching me, are you? I wanted to let you know that this is just the beginning, so you'd better keep an eye on your lovely Suzanne." He let out a garbled, chilling laugh.

Mike hollered, "Who are you, you fuck? How did you get this number?" He heard another bizarre laugh, and the line went dead.

"Who was that?" Suzanne asked, concerned.

"Don't worry, it's just a prankster with an obscene phone call," Mike lied, his face flushed from anger.

"Then why are you so upset?" Suzanne asked, worry written on her face.

"It's just that these prank phone calls make me angry. Forget about it. Let's enjoy our evening."

"Okay," she said, not looking or sounding too sure.

"The TCM channel is running a series of Peter Sellers movies, and tonight we can watch my favorite, *The Pink Panther*, followed by *A Shot In The Dark*."

Mike was thinking, *Maybe Jack Bowman was right—I'm starting to feel like the bungling Inspector Clouseau. What kind of game is the killer playing? Who will be his next victim? The stakes are mounting, and I'm feeling the pressure like never before. Lives are on the line—and one of those lives could be Suzanne's!*

Mike tried, but he couldn't erase that disturbing phone call from his mind. His thoughts were in another world, and the movie was a blur in the background.

CHAPTER 20

T he following day, Mike insisted on driving Suzanne to Frozen North. He told her to call when she was ready to come home, and he would pick her up.

As he dropped her at the front entrance, Suzanne couldn't understand why Mike was overprotective. Then like a bolt of lightning, it hit her! *He didn't receive an obscene phone call—the call was from the killer! The "Guitar String Strangler" was taunting him. No wonder Mike was so agitated.*

Mike got to the squad room later than he had planned. By the time he arrived, Rose was at her desk. Smiling, she looked at her watch and, with a touch of sarcastic humor, said, "Good afternoon, Detective McMahon. Did someone sleep in this morning?"

Mike barked, "I've got enough problems without you getting on my case."

"My, my, aren't we grouchy this morning."

"Sorry. I didn't mean to snap at you. I detoured and dropped Suzanne off at the Frozen North building this morning. I got a call last night from the maniac hinting that Suzanne could be his next victim. I'm not taking any chances with her life. I'm frustrated, and my nerves are on edge."

"I can see why you're so jumpy. It sounds like the psycho wants to kill someone soon, and we don't have the faintest idea who this nut job is."

"He must use burner phones. If he calls again, there's no way we'll be able to trace or triangulate it to get his location. No doubt he's purchased several burner phones and destroys each one after he uses it once. This maniac is no dummy. Like Jason Briggs, I bet he watches cop shows."

"Yeah, I agree. The UNSUB is smarter than we think. His next target could be anyone associated with NSGI or Frozen North, and there's no way of knowing who the next victim might be. I suspect the NSGI card is a red herring he's using to throw us off. I've got a feeling that it's all about Frozen North," Rose said.

"That's why I'm so concerned about Suzanne's safety. The lunatic hinted she could be next."

"I think we'd better update the boss about your phone call. He won't be too happy if we don't keep him in the loop."

After meeting with Lieutenant Foster, they decided to clean up some paperwork and catch up on a few phone calls.

One of the phone calls Mike made was to Dave Franklin.

When Franklin came on the line, Mike said, "Dave, it's Detective Mike McMahon. I had a call last night from someone who could be the serial killer. He said he was going to kill more music people soon. It could be a crank caller, but I don't think we should take any chances. Please ask your people to be on guard. We must take this threat seriously. I suggest they travel in pairs, if possible. I think that might discourage the killer from trying anything."

"This is freaking me out," Franklin said. "I'll let everyone know immediately. Thanks for the heads up."

As Mike hung up his desk phone, his cell phone rang. "Unknown Caller" came on the screen.

"You lunatic," Mike shouted, clearly frustrated. "I'm going to get you, you sick bastard."

"Calm down, Detective, or you might have a heart attack," the garbled voice said. "I'm calling to see how you slept last night. Did you have any nightmares? I slept like a baby."

Mike took a few deep breaths and exhaled slowly. "What are you trying to prove? Why are you killing innocent people? You've got to have some warped reason in your sick mind."

The distorted voice gave another one of his crazy laughs and said, "Do I need a reason? Maybe I like killing for the sake of killing. Have a good day, Detective."

Before Mike could reply, he was gone. "Shit, shit, shit," he yelled, pounding his fist on the desk.

"I presume that was the perp," Rose said. She frowned, her face sullen.

"Yep, that was him! He's starting to get to me. He knows I'm frustrated, and he's trying hard to get under my skin."

"From the sound of it, I'd say he's succeeding."

"I know I shouldn't get so upset, but my short fuse is one of my downfalls when dealing with psychos like him."

"I guess there's no way we'd recognize his voice if we recorded it," Rose said.

"No. It's too garbled, and there's no way we'd recognize it."

Rose saw the exasperation written on Mike's face. She said, "We'll have to keep at it, and sooner or later, we'll catch a break."

"I won't hold my breath waiting for that to happen." Just then, Mike's cell phone rang. Without checking the screen, his frustration at a peak, he yelled, "What the fuck do you want now, asshole?"

"I want you to pick me up for dinner. Having a bad day, are we, Detective?" Suzanne said.

"Oh, my God, I'm so sorry, babe; I thought you were someone else."

"Who did you think I was—the 'Guitar String Strangler'?"

"Has Dave Franklin talked with you?"

"Yes, he has, but I figured it out after you dropped me off this morning. I knew that call last night wasn't an obscene phone call."

"Let's talk about it over dinner. Hang tight, and don't wait on the street. Stay inside. I'll pick you up in twenty minutes."

Suzanne was waiting on the street at the front entrance.

"Why were you waiting on the street? I told you to wait inside the front entrance. Are you trying to get yourself killed?"

"You don't have to treat me like a child," Suzanne countered. "It's still daylight, and I think you're overreacting."

W . D .   F R O L I C K

"I'm sorry for yelling, but you've got to start taking this seriously."

"I am taking it seriously."

"I don't think you are, and we can't take any chances. I'd rather err on the side of caution—there's no telling what that idiot will do. I love you, and I don't want to lose you."

They drove in silence until Mike pulled into the parking lot of The Southern Steak House on 3rd Avenue.

Finally, Mike said, "I hope you don't mind a steak tonight."

"What a nice surprise. Steak sounds great! I'm so hungry I could eat a horse."

CHAPTER 21

*T*he night was black as the devil's soul. Suzanne could sense some-one was behind her. Thinking it was Mike, she didn't appreciate him sneaking up on her. She was about to turn around and give him a blast when she suddenly felt the cold wire slip around her neck. Next, a chilling whisper pierced her ear. "I got you. It's your turn to die, Suzanne." She tried to scream; her mouth opened, but nothing came out. The wire began to tighten, and she felt the excruciating pain as it sliced into her flesh. The last thing she remembered was the obnoxious stench of body odor, his foul breath, and cigarette smoke.

In a panic, Suzanne awoke, screaming, "No, no, don't kill me!" She sat straight up, her heart pounding, feeling like it was about to leap out of her chest. Her entire body began to shake, and tears flowed down her cheeks like a mountain stream.

Dead to the world, when Mike heard Suzanne scream, he sat upright, and it took him a few seconds to realize what was happening.

Now wide awake, he whispered, "It's okay, babe, you're with me." Wrapping his arms around her, he cradled Suzanne and held her tightly. "Don't cry, babe. You're safe."

Suzanne placed her head on his chest. "Oh, Mike," she sobbed. "He was strangling me with a guitar string

"Calm down, babe. You had a nightmare, and no one is strangling you."

"God, it seemed so real!"

Mike held Suzanne until she stopped shaking and crying. Even though she was exhausted, it took an hour before she drifted off to sleep.

It was 4:21 a.m., and Mike's mind was racing like a runaway train. *That bastard, now he's getting to Suzanne. If this keeps up, she's going to become a basket case. Somehow, we've got to catch him before he kills again.*

That morning at eight-thirty, Mike delivered a sleepy Suzanne to the Frozen North building. When he arrived at his desk, he felt like a herd of stampeding elephants had run over his body. The black coffee didn't help. He had a migraine headache, and his mind was in turmoil.

Rose wore a long face when she entered the squad room and looked unhappy.

"Why the sad face?" Mike asked, squinting from his jabbing headache.

"I'd rather not go into it if you don't mind," she said dejectedly.

"Wow, it must be something big to take away your beautiful smile. Is the 'Guitar String Strangler' starting to get to you, too?"

"I wish it was that simple."

"Now you've got me curious. I won't stop hounding you until you tell me what's going on," Mike said, swallowing two extra-strength Tylenol tablets with a sip of coffee.

Rose said, exasperated. "Paul wants a divorce! I should've seen it coming but kept pretending nothing was wrong. For the last few years, I sensed he wasn't happy. We tried counseling, but that didn't seem to work. He told me he was in love with someone else and wanted out of our marriage. I'm concerned about how Jill will react when we tell her the news. I love my job, but it's been hard on our marriage and home life."

Paul Goodwin was one of Nashville's most prominent criminal defense lawyers. Their marriage was a contradiction. While Rose tries to catch and convict criminals, Paul tries to get them off. Although they were on opposite sides, when it came to their jobs, their marriage seemed to work—until now.

Mike sat there, his mouth wide open, looking like he was catching flies. After the initial shock had worn off, he said, "God, that was the furthest thing from my mind. I always thought you and Paul were the perfect married couple. It's a real shocker! Please let me know if I can do anything to help you get through this. You know Suzanne and I are here for you."

"Thanks. I'll have to take it one day at a time and deal with it as things unfold. I know you and Suzanne will be there for me. I appreciate it! If you don't mind, I'd like to change the subject."

Lieutenant Foster appeared and said, "It's happened again. We have another homicide with the same MO—another guitar string murder. I just received the news that a female victim is in her car in a parking lot near the Songwriter's Bar & Grill."

It was beginning to feel like the movie *Groundhog Day*, with the heartbreaking gruesome scene repeating itself.

When they arrived at the crime scene, a patrol car was already there, and the officers had sealed off the area. They showed their badges and signed in. Forensics was in the early stages of searching for evidence in and around the victim's car.

The door on the driver's side was wide open, and a tech was starting to take pictures. They could see a female with short brown hair slumped over the steering wheel from where they stood. A chubby, dark-haired, middle-aged woman stood talking with a police officer a short distance from the vehicle. They decided to go over and see if she was the person who had discovered the body.

The name on the patrol officer's badge was Smith. "Officer Smith, I'm Detective Sergeant Goodwin, and this is my partner Detective McMahon. We're in charge of the investigation. Is this the person who discovered the body?"

"Yes," Officer Smith said, "I was just about to take her statement. Now that you're here, I'll let you handle it."

"Thanks," Mike said.

Rose took out her notebook and asked the distraught-looking woman her name.

"My name is Olga Kerchev," she said, almost choking on her words.

"When did you discover the body?" Rose asked.

"Maybe one hour, I come to clean Songwriter Bar. I park my car. I see a woman asleep in car. Look in window. Woman dead. I run Songwriter Bar—call number 911. I wait. Police come. Ask me to stay. Give how you say?"

"Statement. Did the police ask you to stay and give a statement?" Rose asked.

"Yes. Statement."

"Did you see anyone else around when you discovered the body?" Mike asked.

"No, see anyone."

Before they let her leave, Rose jotted down her address and phone number. She gave Olga Kerchev her card and asked her to call if she thought of anything that might help their investigation.

Arriving on the scene, ME Tony Capino said, "We meet again, Detectives. I hear we have another murder victim by the same perp. I haven't worked this hard in a long time. Maybe we'll get lucky and find a print. God knows you two could use a break in this case."

"Amen to that, brother," Mike agreed. "We're tired of banging our heads against a brick wall."

"Let's go and see if we can identify the latest victim."

Before he began to search for identification, Tony examined the body and estimated that the victim had been dead for several hours. Like the other victims, the MO looked the same. The victim's lifeless blue eyes were open and almost bulging out of her head. Even with all the damage to her face, it was apparent she had been a pretty young woman. For the fourth time, all Tony found was an NSGI membership card. The name on the card was Kandi Kane.

"Who the hell is Kandi Kane?" Mike asked. "I don't think she's associated with Frozen North."

"Her name sounds like an exotic dancer, but she's a new recording artist with Southern Heat Records. I read an article about her in *Music Row* a few weeks ago," Rose said.

"You read *Music Row*?" Mike asked, surprised.

"Yeah, I'm a closet country music fan," Rose laughed. She had a sheepish grin on her face.

Mike chuckled. "There's nothing wrong with being a country music fan in Nashville."

Rose said, changing the subject, "Since the victim was associated with Southern Heat, it eliminates them as suspects."

"What about Frozen North? Do you think they would try to get back at Southern Heat?" Mike asked.

"I suppose anything's possible, but I can't believe they would stoop to murder. Although, I guess you can't rule anything or anybody out when money is involved. The common thread appears to be NSGI. Perhaps it was a coincidence that the last two victims were associated with Frozen North," Rose said.

Mike looked bewildered. "Nothing seems to make any sense, and the killer changes direction when it looks like he's establishing a pattern. The common thread appears to be a membership in NSGI."

W . D .   F R O L I C K

After spending three hours at the crime scene, Rose and Mike returned to the squad room feeling depressed and more confused than ever. After obtaining the Boston address and phone number for Kandi Kane's parents from Debbie Eastman at Southern Heat Records, Mike lost the coin toss and made the call he dreaded the most. Mrs. Kane cried nonstop for a few minutes after Mike broke the heart-wrenching news. When the call ended, Mike's eyes filled with tears, and he gulped before speaking to Rose.

"We'd better collar that fucker before he kills someone else. I don't want to make a call like that ever again."

They briefly met with Lieutenant Foster, filling him in on all the gory details. After hearing what they had to say, the lieutenant was not in a good mood. He said, "I'm expecting another call from Chief Cummings, and I'm not looking forward to that conversation. We need to solve this case before my ulcer starts to bleed again," Lieutenant Foster said as he swallowed an antiacid tablet.

Rose said when they were back at their desks, "Just when we thought we had figured things out, he went and threw us a curveball."

"It appears to be NSGI that he's targeting—unless he's got a grudge against all three of them. As I said before, I'm not ruling anything out."

Just then, Mike's cell phone rang. The screen read "Unknown Caller."

He took a deep breath and calmly asked, "What the fuck do you want now, asshole?"

"Do I have you frustrated, 'rookie'? It sure sounds like it."

"You think calling me 'rookie' is funny, don't you, you sick fuck. Well, this 'rookie' will catch you sooner or later and nail your sorry ass to the wall. You won't be so cocky when sitting on death row at Riverbend awaiting a lethal injection."

"You'll have to catch me before that ever happens."

"Oh, we'll catch you. You can count on that!"

"I told you the killings were just getting started. I'm sure I threw you off by killing Kandi Kane. With a name like that, she should have been a stripper, not a singer/songwriter. You may have noticed I used a 'G' string. Get it—'G' string—stripper." He laughed hysterically at his sick joke. "Where's your sense of humor, Detective? I didn't even get a chuckle out of you. You don't have any clues, do you? Maybe I should provide a few, so you don't give up hope."

The killer's weird sense of humor reminds me of Jason Briggs.

Trying to calm himself, Mike took another deep breath and said, "I'm listening."

"I'm only going to say this once. Maybe you should write it down." He paused a moment. "What starts as one then splits in two, you look like me, I look like you. Did you get that, Detective? It shouldn't be too hard for a smart guy like you to figure it out. Good luck in solving the puzzle." He laughed and hung up.

Mike looked at Rose and said, "Now the lunatic is playing mind games, and he gave me a puzzle to solve. What starts as one then splits in two, you look like me; I look like you?"

Rose stared at him frowning, a blank expression on her face—thinking. Mike could almost hear the gears grinding. Suddenly, a light came on, and Rose smiled and said, "I think I've got it. A fertilized egg starts as one—if it breaks in two, what happens? Twins or possibly identical twins are the result of the egg splitting."

"Do you think that's what he means? Is he a twin or an identical twin? If so, who is he, and who is his brother? He may be giving us this hint to mislead us. He's smarter than we think. If he's misleading us, we could spend valuable time spinning our wheels with more dead ends and more dead bodies."

"But what if he's telling the truth and has a twin brother? We'd be crazy not to investigate it. What else do we have to go on?"

"It's probably a waste of time," Mike said. "But you're right; what else do we have to go on?"

"The first person that comes to mind is Jason Briggs. Does he have a twin brother?" Rose asked.

"Yeah, I was thinking the same thing. Even the asshole's weird sense of humor sounds like Jason Briggs. Maybe we should find out. The place I'd like to start is the Songwriter's Bar & Grill."

Mike phoned ahead, and Frank Fulton was in his office when they arrived.

"Thanks for meeting with us again, Frank," Mike said. "I'm sure you heard about the latest murder in the parking lot across the street last night."

"Olga Kerchev, our cleaning lady, called and woke me this morning. She was all in a flap, and I could barely understand her words. Her Russian accent is hard to understand, but it's almost impossible to know what she's saying when the poor soul gets excited. I managed to understand what she was trying to tell me. Olga was so distraught I told her to go home after she was done with the police and not to bother cleaning today."

"We have reason to believe the killer might have a twin brother. One brother could be acting alone, or they could both be involved in the murders. Would you happen to know if Jason Briggs has a twin brother?" Mike asked.

Frank paused, scratched his head, and seemed to ponder the question. "To tell you the truth, I don't know. As I said, the last time you were here, he never mentioned a brother. However, the crazy songwriter who came in for an audition reminds me of Jason."

"We asked Briggs the other day if he had a brother, and he said he didn't know. He told us his parents died when he was very young and can't remember ever having a brother, but he didn't seem sure." Mike said.

"Was Jason on duty last night?" Rose asked.

"Yes, he was."

"Could we view your videos from last night?" Mike asked.

"Sure, no problem," Frank said.

To make it easier, he turned the monitor around, so Rose and Mike could view the screen from their chairs in front of his desk. Frank walked around to join them and brought up last night's video.

As they scanned the video from early evening until closing, Mike and Rose could see that Jason had been there the entire time. They spotted Kandi Kane chatting with some people at the bar. Around eleven thirty, the video caught her walking out the front entrance. Next, an outside camera showed her on the sidewalk. Several frames caught a hulking figure dressed in a black hoodie following Kane as she left the building and started across the road. Because his back was to the camera, his face was not visible, but the man's size was like Bill Ormond's description.

"Frank," Mike asked, "could you please play back the last few seconds—where the huge man came into view." Frank did as Mike asked. "That's it. Could you pause it there? Thanks."

"Do you see that, Rose? If I didn't know better, I'd say that's either Jason Briggs or his twin."

"We know he was in the bar, so it can't be Jason," Rose said.

"Whoever he is, he must have been waiting for her and followed Kandi Kane to her car. At the crime scene this morning, I noticed the light above her vehicle was out, so it would've been pitch black in that area, making it harder to spot the killer," Mike said.

They thanked Frank for his time, shook hands, said goodbye, and left.

W . D . F R O L I C K

Saturday morning, Mike and Rose attended the autopsy of Kandi Kane. After the autopsy, they decided to take the rest of the weekend to recharge their batteries and clear their heads.

Because of the unexpected autopsy, Mike and Suzanne postponed her move until Sunday morning. Suzanne would be bringing her newly adopted cat with her. When she found him roaming the street near her apartment building, the flea-bitten little gray and white kitten appeared malnourished and homeless. Suzanne bathed, fed him, and named the kitten Oliver after Oliver Twist, the orphan child from the Charles Dickens novel. She read the book in high school, and it became one of her all-time favorites.

He couldn't believe how many pairs of shoes and all the clothes Suzanne possessed. She filled half of Mike's large walk-in and guest bedroom closets. For her car, Mike had managed to rent an underground parking space from an older woman who no longer drives.

They finished the move by four and were too exhausted to cook, so they ordered Chinese food. After eating, Mike and Suzanne spent the evening watching *Gone with the Wind* on the couch. Suzanne managed to stay awake throughout the movie, but Mike and Oliver fell asleep within the first thirty minutes.

* * *

Monday morning, Mike sipped coffee while Rose talked to her husband, Paul.

After hanging up, she said, "I didn't get much sleep. We stayed up half the night discussing our relationship. Paul said he did a great deal of thinking and realized he was too hasty in asking for a divorce. He said he broke it off with the other woman and would like us to try again. He wouldn't tell me who she was, but I suspect it might be a fellow attorney from the law firm next door. We both agreed to go back to counseling and take it one day at a time. At least that's a step in the right direction."

"That's good news, Rose. If you can work things out and save your marriage, that would be great for everyone, especially Jill. Good luck!"

"Enough about me and my problems; we'd better get back to work and plan our next move."

Mike had just opened the *Nashville Star Daily,* and the headline hit him like a blast of TNT.

The bold headline almost jumped off the front page.

"GUITAR STRING STRANGLER" STRIKES AGAIN

By Jeff Stone, Investigative Reporter

The strangled and brutalized body of Kandi Kane, 24, from Boston, Massachusetts, a newly signed recording artist with Southern Heat Records, was found yesterday morning in her car, slumped over the steering wheel in a parking lot near the Songwriter's Bar & Grill. Ms. Kane is the fourth victim in a series of murders that appear to be the work of a psychopathic serial killer. Once again, the killer strangled the victim using a guitar string.

The previous victims: Ms. Shannon Greenway, 23, of Chicago, Illinois, Ms. Heather Brown, 22, of Horse Cave, Kentucky, and Mr. John Tilley, 25, of Dallas, Texas, were members of NSGI.

Heather Brown and John Tilley were staff song-writers at Frozen North Music.

Our original assumption was that the killer had a grudge against NSGI and Frozen North Music. That theory may prove unfounded since Ms. Kane was a recording artist with Southern Heat Records, and all the victims were members of NSGI.

A PR spokesperson from the MNPD said that the detectives were making progress but would not provide any details.

Are the detectives making progress? Do they have any leads or suspects?

The killer will strike again if they don't catch him soon. Who will be next?

The music community is teetering on the edge of panic. If you're a member of NSGI, should you be looking over your shoulder? Darn right, you should!

"Well," Mike said, "our 'friend' Jeff Stone is stirring up more shit. I'm sure once the mayor and Chief Cummings read his article, all hell will break loose."

"You're right about that," Rose agreed. "Let's get out of here before we get called on the carpet."

"Good idea. Let's go see Jason Briggs."

Briggs was dead to the world when Mike beat on his door. Still half-asleep, he got out of bed and slipped on a white T-shirt, gray track pants, and a pair of black sandals.

Mike pounded harder.

"Hold your horses," Briggs yelled.

As soon as they saw him, his glazed red eyes indicated he was still high on something.

"What the hell?" Briggs said when he saw the two detectives.

"Jason," Rose said emphatically, "we need to speak with you."

"What do you want now?"

Mike barged past him and said, "Sit down, Jason, before you fall."

Unsteady on his feet, Briggs stumbled backward, landed on the sofa, and stared into space. The sweet smell of marijuana filled the room and their nostrils.

Mike came right to the point, "Do you have any brothers?"

Briggs looked dazed and confused. "Do I have any what?" he mumbled.

"You heard me! Brothers," Mike repeated. "Do you have any brothers?"

Briggs spoke very slowly, "How the hell should I know?"

"Why wouldn't you know?" Rose asked.

"My parents died when I was two or three, and I spent half my life in an orphanage. I can't remember my parents, and if I had a brother, I can't remember him either."

"Do you have a birth certificate?" Mike asked.

"Yeah, of course, I got a birth certificate."

"Could you get it for us, please?" Rose asked politely. She sounded like the good cop.

Jason got up and staggered down the hallway toward his bedroom. When he returned, he handed it to Rose.

In her notebook, she jotted down: Jason Donald Briggs, July 23, 1990, Montgomery, Alabama.

Mike asked gruffly, "Do you remember the name of the orphanage?" He sounded like the bad cop.

Briggs rolled his eyes. "How could I ever forget that wonderful place? It was called Happy Hills, just outside Montgomery, on several acres, but it was more like Crappy Hills." Briggs started to giggle, still feeling the effects of the pot.

"With your permission, I'd like to call Happy Hills and ask them a few questions about the time you spent there," Rose said.

"Go ahead. I don't care. I got nothin' to hide."

Goodwin called information and received Happy Hills' phone number; she wrote it down, then dialed. After three rings, a receptionist answered, and Rose explained who she was and why she was calling.

"Just a minute, please. I'll put you through to our administrator, Mr. Tucker," the female voice said.

"Hello, George Tucker here. How may I help you?"

"Good day, Mr. Tucker. I'm Detective Sergeant Goodwin of the Metropolitan Nashville Police Department." She went on to tell him what she required.

"Sorry, I can't release any information without written permission from Jason Briggs. I'll fax you the form. Once you receive it, after completing the request, have it signed by Jason Donald Briggs, witnessed, and faxed back. When I receive it, I'll send you the information." They exchanged fax numbers and hung up.

After explaining her conversation with George Tucker to Briggs, Rose said, "That's it for now, Jason. We'll be back when the form is ready for signing."

"You can go back to sleep now," Mike said as they headed toward the door.

"Nah, I'm up now. I got to work tonight. Think I'll have a beer and write a song."

Before starting the car, Mike called and made an appointment with Tim Evans at Southern Heat Records.

Rose said as they sat in his office, "The reason we're here today, Mr. Evans, is to follow up on the murder of your recording artist Kandi Kane. We are very sorry for your loss, and you have our sincere condolences."

"Thank you, Detective. Kandi was one of the most promising new artists in the music business, and we were planning big things for her. It makes me angry to think some deranged person is doing these horrible things on our streets. I hope you catch him soon."

"That's why we're here. Can you think of anyone who might have the motive to kill Ms. Kane?" Mike asked.

"I'm sure Dave Franklin mentioned me when two victims were from Frozen North. Now I'm going to mention him and his company. There's no love lost between us. If he thought I had something to do with killing their songwriters, maybe they're looking for revenge. Perhaps they killed Kandi or arranged to have her killed."

"To tell the truth," Rose said, "I don't think either you or they are involved in the murders. The common thread appears to be that all the victims were NSGI members."

"Have you had any problems with any other competitors?" Mike asked.

"We've had our differences with other companies, but nothing serious enough to result in murder. Based on what you've said, the NSGI membership is the common denominator in this whole mess."

"If you come up with anything you think might help our investigation, please call us," Rose said.

They shook hands, said goodbye, and left.

The form from Happy Hills was waiting for them when they arrived back in the squad room. Rose filled it in, called Jason, and they returned to get his signature.

Mike faxed the form to George Tucker when they returned to the station.

After updating Lieutenant Foster on their day, Mike and Rose packed it in and headed home.

Paul was taking Rose and Jill out to dinner. It looked like he was trying to make things work. Rose had her fingers crossed, but they still had a long way to go.

Mike picked Suzanne up at the Frozen North building. They decided to grab a quick bite and see the newly released *Star Wars* movie. They were both ready for an escape from reality. Suzanne wanted to forget about music, and Mike wanted to forget about murder.

CHAPTER 24

T he following day, Mike dropped Suzanne off at the Frozen North building, kissed her goodbye, and headed for the squad room. The previous evening was enjoyable and relaxing, and he was feeling positive with renewed energy. When he arrived at his desk, even Rose was in good spirits. That ended when Mike's cell phone rang and flashed "Unknown Caller."

"What do you want now?" Mike barked.

"Good morning to you as well, Detective," the distorted voice said.

Mike forced himself to calm down. "It was a good morning until you called," he said.

"It's nice to hear a civil tone for a change. I'm curious. Have you solved the puzzle?"

"Even if we did solve your fucking puzzle, why would I want to tell you?"

"There you go getting nasty again. Guess I'll have to give you another murder to try to solve. Heaven knows you haven't done too well on the first four." He let out another one of his irritating laughs.

A dial tone hummed in his ear as Mike was about to speak.

"Sounds like another call from our perp," Rose said.

"Yeah, he sure knows how to spoil what I thought would be a good day."

Just then, they heard a ring across the room.

Walking to the fax machine, Mike pulled out two sheets of paper, a cover page with Happy Hills Orphanage and a second page containing information about Jason Donald Briggs.

As he returned to his desk, Rose asked, "Well, don't keep me in suspense. What does it say?"

Mike began to read aloud. "Jason Donald Briggs was born July 23, 1990, at Baptist Medical Center South, Montgomery, Alabama. Parents, Janis Anne Briggs and Allan Edward Briggs. Sibling, Gerald Walter Briggs. Admission date, September 20, 1993. Janis Anne Briggs and Allan Edward Briggs deceased on August 15, 1993. That's odd. Both parents died on the same day. I wonder what happened to them."

"Maybe they were in a car accident. Let's try to find out," Rose said.

She sat down at her computer and brought up the website of the *Montgomery Advertiser*. Rose clicked on the Archives tab and typed August 15, 1993. A choice of pages came on the screen. She checked the first page and several other pages but found nothing. Then it dawned on her. If the parents died on August 15, the news wouldn't hit the paper until a day later. She retyped August 16, 1993. The headline on the front page read:

"MURDER/SUICIDE IN MONTGOMERY."

The article said that on August 15, 1993, after hearing a loud argument followed by gunshots, neighbors called the police. When the police arrived, they found two victims without vital signs on the living room floor of the Briggs residence. The evidence indicated that Allan Edward Briggs had shot and killed his wife, Janis Anne Briggs, and then turned the gun on himself. Their two young boys were found asleep in their bedroom unharmed. The article said the boys were placed in a state-approved Foster Care Facility but did not give the name of the foster home. At press time, the police were still investigating.

"Well," Rose said, "at least now we know Jason has a twin brother named Gerald. What we don't know is, are they, identical twins?"

"Let's find out," Mike said.

Mike went online, found the Montgomery Police Department website, wrote down the phone number, and dialed.

Four rings later, a female voice said, "Montgomery Police Department," McMahon identified himself and explained the reason for his call.

"Please hold, and I'll transfer you to our Homicide Unit."

"Homicide, Detective Joe Brock speaking."

"Detective Brock, this is Detective Mike McMahon from the Metropolitan Nashville Police Department." He told Detective Brock the reason for his call.

"Leave it with me, Detective, and I'll get back to you shortly."

Mike gave Detective Brock their fax number, and within an hour, he received a report outlining details of the police investigation. The information mentioned Gerald Walter Briggs and Jason Donald Briggs were in a foster home run by Peter and Joan Coburn at 1985 Scenic View Drive in Montgomery.

"We know the boys are twins, but are they, identical twins? I suggest we check with the hospital to find out what their records show," Rose said.

"That's a good idea, Goodwin."

Rose googled the hospital's website, found the phone number, and dialed. After three rings, a recorded message began to play, going through all the options. When she heard the voice say, "Records Department, press five," she punched in the number.

"Records Department," a cheerful voice said, "Jenny speaking, how may I help you?"

"Hello, Jenny, I'm Sergeant Detective Goodwin of the Metropolitan Nashville Police Department. I'm calling regarding a case we're working on, and I would appreciate your help."

Rose went on to explain what she needed.

"One moment, please." When Jenny returned, she said, "On July 23, 1990, Mrs. Janis Anne Biggs gave birth to identical twin boys."

"Thank you, Jenny," Rose said and hung up.

"Bingo," Mike said when Rose gave him the news. "Our next move is to contact Peter and Joan Coburn."

"Let's hope they're still in business," Rose said.

"There's only one way to find out," Mike said.

After calling information, Mike wrote down the phone number and dialed.

After three rings, a female voice answered.

"Hello."

"Good morning," Mike said pleasantly. "Mrs. Joan Coburn, please?"

"I'm Joan Coburn."

"Mrs. Coburn, I'm Detective Mike McMahon with the Metropolitan Nashville Police Department. A case my partner and I are working on requires locating the whereabouts of Mr. Gerald Walter Briggs. We understand he was a resident at your foster home starting in September 1993. Is that correct?"

"Yes. Gerald, or Jerry as we called him, was with us for several years. Unfortunately, he ran away when he was sixteen, and we haven't seen or heard from him since. The police search turned up nothing, and it was like he had vanished from the face of the earth. Sorry, that's all I can tell you."

"What type of a child was Gerald? Was he hard to handle, get into trouble, that sort of thing?"

"Jerry was a handful and didn't get along with the other kids, bullied them, and got into fights. Once, when he was fourteen, he stole a purse from an older woman and pushed her to the ground. She went to the hospital for a gash on her forehead and received several stitches. Thankfully, the woman didn't press charges because of his age. Jerry got off with a warning from the police, and they asked us to keep a close eye on him. A few years later, after his sixteenth birthday, he ran away. I know this is a horrible thing to say, but I was relieved when he took off."

"Okay, thank you, Mrs. Coburn. I appreciate your time. Before I go, I have one more question. A newspaper article in the *Montgomery Advertiser* said that the twin boys went to a state-approved foster home after their parent's death. I presume they meant your home. Did Jason Donald Briggs ever stay with you?"

"Yes, he stayed with us for a few days. However, we were already overcrowded. Unfortunately, they had to separate the boys, and Jason ended up at Happy Hills orphanage."

"Thank you for your help, Mrs. Coburn. Have a nice day."

Mike hung up and stared at Rose. His face lit up, and he said, "We know where Jason is. Now, all we need to do is find Gerald or Jerry, as Mrs. Coburn called him. I've got an idea. It may be a long shot, but it's worth a try."

Using his computer, Mike accessed the FBI National Criminal Information Center (NCIC) and typed in Gerald Walter Briggs. Several seconds later, mug shots with front and side profiles and his fingerprints came up. The pictures looked like Jason Briggs. In the mug shots, Gerald did not wear earrings, had long blond hair, and was clean-shaven.

His criminal record showed that on April 9, 2009, in Atlanta, Georgia, Gerald Walter Briggs was charged with involuntary manslaughter after beating another man to death in a bar fight in a dispute over a girl. He claimed self-defense, but on September 24, 2009, Briggs was found guilty and sentenced to six years in the Georgia State Prison. After serving four years, Gerald Walter Briggs became a free man on November 12, 2013. The early release date was due to good behavior and previous time spent in custody awaiting trial.

"Very interesting," Rose said after Mike gave her the details.

Mike printed the information and said, "The sixty-four-thousand-dollar question is—where is Jerry Briggs now?"

CHAPTER 25

T he following morning, Mike made a call to the Georgia State Prison. After obtaining the name and phone number of Gerald Briggs' parole officer, he made another call. A brief conversation with the parole officer informed him that Gerald Briggs, in the last year of his three-year probation period, had requested a transfer to the state of Tennessee. Because he would be joining a family member, his brother, Jason Briggs, the transfer was approved quickly. The new parole officer in Nashville was a man named Myron Starkey. Mike dialed the number.

After the second ring, a deep voice said, "Myron Starkey."

"Good morning, Mr. Starkey. I'm Detective Mike McMahon of the MNPD. My partner and I are working on a case that requires the address and phone number of one of your parolees, Gerald Donald Briggs?"

"I understand from reading the newspapers and watching TV that you're working the 'Guitar String Strangler' case. Would Gerald Briggs have anything to do with your case?"

"We're not sure. Briggs is a person of interest at this point in our investigation. Has he given you any trouble?"

"So far, Jerry has been a model parolee. If all goes well, he'll be finished his parole in June."

"Is he working anywhere?"

"Yes. A few months ago, I helped Gerald get a job at the Shine 'n Polish car wash."

"Do you have his home address and phone number?" Mike asked.

"Just a minute, and I'll get them for you."

After receiving Briggs' address, cell, and home phone numbers, Mike thanked Starkey and hung up.

"Well, well, maybe we're getting somewhere," Mike said with a smile.

"Yeah, I'm starting to think you're right. Guess we'd better go visit Mr. Jerry Briggs."

"If what Starkey said is right, he should be at the car wash this time of day. Let's start there," Mike suggested.

They arrived at Shine 'n Polish at 9:45 a.m. Since it was a sunny day, the car wash was busy.

As they came through the front entrance, a slender, bald, smooth-shaven, middle-aged black man sat behind a desk in a small office to their right. He wore neatly pressed black dress pants and a white golf shirt with the car wash name and logo embroidered in red.

Since the door was open, Rose rapped on the doorframe. "Are you the manager?"

He looked up from his paperwork and smiled. "Yes, I'm Derk Ryder, the manager. How can I help you?"

They showed their badges and introduced themselves.

"We're looking for Gerald Briggs or Jerry Briggs. We understand that he works here," Mike said.

"Yes, he does. Jerry works on pre-wash, where the cars enter the building."

"We'd like to speak with him, please," Rose said. "Does Gerald get a break soon?"

"His morning break is normally around ten thirty, about a half-hour from now. I can relieve him if you need to talk with him now."

"Thank you. Would you mind if we use your office, Mr. Ryder?" Mike said.

"No problem. I'll send Jerry around in a few minutes."

Ten minutes went by, and there was no sign of Gerald Briggs. They walked to the back of the building, and just as they had suspected, he wasn't there.

Seeing Ryder with a hose in his hand, Mike asked, "Did you send Briggs to your office?"

Nodding toward an empty parking spot, Ryder said, "His truck is missing. When I told him two detectives wanted to speak with him in my office, he must have panicked and taken off. Sorry, I didn't see him leave."

"It's not your fault," Rose said, "we should have known better and come here ourselves."

"What kind of truck does Briggs drive?" Mike asked.

"He drives an older white Chevy pickup with a dent in the front fender on the driver's side."

"Do you know his plate number?" Rose asked.

"Sorry, Detective, I don't."

"Okay, thanks," Rose said.

"What's our next move?" Mike asked as they approached the car. "Where would he go if he's feeling guilty about something?"

"I doubt he'd go home," Mike said.

"You're right—assuming Jason and Jerry are in contact, he's probably gone to Jason's."

"It's worth a try. Let's go see," Mike said.

When they arrived at Jason's address, his black Malibu was in the driveway, but there was no sign of Gerald's truck. They drove around the area and spotted a beat-up white Chevy pickup with a dent in the driver's side front fender a few blocks from Jason's place.

"Bingo," Mike said. "It looks like he suspected we might check Jason's driveway."

Mike parked a few houses from Jason's address, and they proceeded cautiously on foot. Reaching the back door, they pulled and racked their Glocks. When they were ready, Rose nodded, and Mike hammered on the door.

"Open up! MNPD," Mike yelled.

"Go away!" they heard Jason scream.

Mike hammered on the door again.

"Don't force us to break down the door," Rose yelled.

As Mike was getting ready to pound on the door again, Jason's scowling face appeared in the doorway.

As they barged past him, they saw another identical unhappy face—Jerry Briggs. Instead of a shaved head, he had long blond hair pulled back into a ponytail.

Mike said, "I think you both had better sit down. We need to ask you some questions."

The brothers just stood there, defiantly glaring at the two detectives. "Sit down," Mike shouted, pointing to the couch.

Finally, they complied.

Glancing at Jerry, Jason laughed and said, "Is it time to play good cop, bad cop?"

"Cool it," Mike barked. "You only speak when answering our questions."

"You must be the bad cop," Jerry laughed.

Mike ignored him.

"Jason, You said you didn't have a brother," Rose said.

"You caught me," Jason said with a smart-ass smirk. "This is my twin brother, Jerry. I didn't know I had a brother until he found me a month ago."

"Why didn't you tell us when we were here the other day?" Mike asked.

"I didn't think it was any of your business. And I still don't think it's any of your fuckin' business," Jason growled.

"Jerry, why did you run from the car wash when Mr. Ryder said we wanted to talk with you?" Rose asked.

Jerry shifted uneasily on the couch, looked at the floor, lifted his head, and glared back at Rose.

"I don't like cops, and I don't trust cops."

"Why do you say that?" Mike asked.

"Cops are always tryin' to pin somethin' on you for somethin' you didn't do."

"What type of something are you talking about, Jerry?' Mike asked.

"You know—anythin'. The cops are always lookin' for a patsy to take the fall for somethin'."

"Is that why you ran?" Rose asked. "Or is there something you're afraid of that you're not telling us?"

"No, there's nothin' else. I'm on parole, and I can't afford to mess up. I'm due to come off parole in a few months, and there's no way I wanna go back to jail for somethin' I didn't do."

"What specifically are you thinking that you didn't do?" Mike asked.

"Like those murders, where the killer used guitar strings. You're goin' to try to pin them on me. Well, I didn't murder anybody, and just because I got a record, you're thinkin' I would be a good patsy."

"We told Jason if you're innocent, you've got nothing to worry about," Rose said.

"Yeah, I don't believe that. I know guys in prison who cops framed."

"Where were you on the nights of the 20th and 27th of January, the 7th and 17th of February?" Mike asked.

"How the hell should I know? I don't keep a daily diary. I could've been home writin' songs, watchin' TV, or out drinkin'. Maybe I was at a movie."

"You said you could've been writing songs. Are you a songwriter like your brother? Do you belong to NSGI?" Rose asked.

"Yeah, I write the odd song. No, I don't belong to that shit organization. I can't afford the one hundred and fifty bucks it costs to join, and I wouldn't want to join anyway after what they did to Jason."

"Have you ever tried to pitch your songs to publishers or record companies like Frozen North Music or Southern Heat Records?" Mike asked.

"Yeah, I've tried to pitch to most publishers in town, but none of them will take unsolicited material. You can't even get past the receptionist. If you try to leave any demos, they throw them in the trash. They all say they're lookin' for hit songs but won't even listen to see if you got a hit song. That's a fuckin' contradiction. I'll tell you right now. They wouldn't know a fuckin' hit song if it jumped up and bit them on the ass," Jerry said. His face turned red, and anger flashed in his eyes.

Jerry not only looks like Jason but speaks like him, too. It sounds that Jerry, like Jason, hates how the music industry operates, Mike thought.

"You said you don't know what you were doing on those nights. Is that correct?" Rose asked.

"Well, I know I wasn't out killin' people, that's for sure. You'll have to take my word that I was home writin' songs or watchin' TV. Sometimes I stay up late and watch movies or reruns of my favorite cop shows—like *Dragnet,* and I love *Criminal Minds.*"

Mike looked at Rose; she glanced back, and they both shrugged. They knew there wasn't any evidence to charge Jerry with anything, and without probable cause, they had no grounds for a search warrant. Things were at another roadblock—at least for now.

The twins lit up and smoked a joint as soon as the detectives left. When they had finished, Jerry headed back to work.

A few days earlier, Jason asked Jerry to move in with him. By splitting the rent, they would save money, and they could drink beer, smoke pot, write songs and watch cop shows together. It was time to make up for all the years they had spent apart. After all, they were family.

CHAPTER 26

M ike's phone rang Thursday morning while drinking coffee and talking with Rose. It was the crime lab.

"Detective McMahon."

"Good morning, Detective. It's Scott Parsons from the crime lab. I wanted to inform you that we lifted a few fingerprints from the top of the driver's seat in the victim's car. After running the prints through IAFIS, we came up empty. Sorry, Mike, maybe we'll have better luck next time."

"Okay, thanks, Scott."

The IAFIS stands for Integrated Automated Fingerprint Identification System. It holds the fingerprints and histories of 70 million criminals in the master file, 31 million civil prints, and the fingerprints of approximately 73,000 known and suspected terrorists processed by the United States or international law enforcement agencies.

"The crime lab found a few prints on the top of the driver's seat, but nothing came up in IAFIS," Mike said.

"Well, that eliminates Jerry Briggs for now," Rose said, looking and sounding disappointed.

"If those prints were Jerry's, they'd be in the system. Our UNSUB doesn't have a record, and those prints could belong to a friend who rode in Kandi Kane's car. God, this case is going nowhere fast. When we think we're getting a break, we end up back at square one," Mike said, frustration etched on his face.

"Yeah, it looks like we just hit another brick wall."

At that moment, Mike's cell phone rang, and the screen showed "Unknown Caller."

"What the hell do you want now?" he snapped.

"Good morning, Detective," the familiar garbled voice said.

"It was a good morning until you called." Mike could feel his blood pressure rising.

"Gee, you don't sound happy today, Detective. Maybe you should take a few cheer-me-up pills," he laughed. It was obvious he was doing his best to taunt Mike.

"What's on your mind, asshole?"

"I don't think you and your partner could solve the puzzle. You're chasing your tail like a dog going in circles, and you'll never catch me that way. Maybe you need another hint."

"I'm all ears," Mike said, his voice calmer.

"Listen carefully. What starts as one and then splits in two? You look like me, I look like you—but looks can be deceiving." Another laugh and he was gone.

"What did he say this time?" Rose asked.

"That fucker is still playing mind games. The jerk gave me the same puzzle, but added looks can be deceiving. What the hell does that mean?"

"I haven't got the slightest idea. If it's not twins, then what else could it be?" Rose said, baffled.

The *Nashville Star Daily* was on Mike's desk. When he picked it up, he wasn't surprised to see another story by Jeff Stone. This time the article was a little smaller, and the headline was not quite as large. However, it was on the front page and caught your attention.

"GUITAR STRING STRANGLER" CALLS NASHVILLE STAR DAILY

By Jeff Stone, Investigative Reporter

Yesterday evening I received a phone call from the "GUITAR STRING STRANGLER." A device disguised his voice, but his message was loud and clear.

He said, and I quote: "The two detectives assigned to track me down are getting nowhere fast. They don't know who I am, even after I provided hints to help them find me. It makes me laugh at the incompetence of the MNPD. If they don't catch me soon, someone else will die. I'm getting the urge to kill again."

The caller went on to tell me things that only the killer would know. What he told me is much too gruesome to repeat in print. He asked me why I hadn't mentioned the calling card he had left on all the victim's foreheads—a treble clef symbol. I told him my source had not informed me that he had left a calling card. When I asked him the meaning of the treble clef symbol, he told me there was no real meaning other than his victims were in the music business.

When asked if he was targeting members of NSGI, he wouldn't give me a direct answer. He skirted the question, saying he had reasons but would not elaborate.

Are you safe if you're not part of the music scene in Nashville? Only the killer knows for sure.

Was this a crank call? Maybe, but it sounded like the real deal.

Before hanging up, he told me he liked the name "Guitar String Strangler."

Will he call again? Stay tuned—we'll let you know if he does!

When they had finished reading the article, Mike tossed the newspaper onto Rose's desk and said, "This time, Stone's letting the killer stick the knife in for him. Now everyone knows about the treble clef symbol the psycho draws on the foreheads of all his victims. The psycho's not shying away from the limelight. Next thing we know, he'll be on TV interviewing with June Murray."

Rose chuckled at Mike's last comment and said, "If he goes on TV, let's hope he isn't wearing a mask. From the sounds of things, it's almost like he's begging to get caught."

"The problem is, someone else could die before that happens," Mike said, dejected.

"When the mayor and our bosses read the new article, they'll hit the roof. Next thing you know, they'll be forming a task force or bringing in an FBI profiler team—just like on Jerry's favorite TV show, Criminal Minds, Rose said jokingly. "Of course, in real life, no such team exists. The team on Criminal Minds makes for interesting TV, but we know it's a complete fantasy."

Mike laughed, saying, "I don't think we need the FBI. We've already created the killer's profile."

"All we have to do is catch that monster. And that won't be easy since we don't have any clues," Rose said.

"Maybe not, but I feel we're getting close."

* * *

That night, after he had killed again, he felt invincible! The "Guitar String Strangler" smiled as he read Jeff Stone's article. He was thinking. It looks like the Nashville music community is panic-stricken, and those stupid detectives don't have a fucking clue. Wait until they find the body of my latest victim—it'll be a real mind-blower!

I look forward to reading Jeff Stone's next article and calling Detective McMahon.

The killer plucked a cold beer from the refrigerator and placed it on the kitchen table. He went into the living room and retrieved his guitar. He thought. I'm in the mood to write a new song, and maybe I'll call this one "You'll Never Catch Me." He took a long swig of beer, picked up his guitar, and began to play.

CHAPTER 27

Rose and Mike spent Friday updating the murder book, typing reports on the week's interviews, and in meetings with Lieutenant Foster and Chief Cummings. They reviewed the case from top to bottom and brainstormed ideas to determine the killer's motives. In his psychotic mind, they concluded that the killer despises the music community. Perhaps he was trying to get even for some unknown reason, believing they were responsible for causing him an injustice of some kind. Nothing else seemed to make any sense.

* * *

Saturday morning, Mike dropped Suzanne off at the Frozen North building. She had a 10:00 a.m. session to record vocals for her new album, and she told him to pick her up around five.

Mike returned to his condo to relax before making a sandwich for lunch. At one o'clock, he drove to Regal Hollywood Stadium 27 for the one-thirty showing of the new movie *Split*. Since Suzanne had not expressed interest in seeing the film, he felt it would be a perfect time to view it. The movie was getting good reviews. It told the story of a man with twenty-three personalities who suffered from dissociative identity disorder (DID). He was interested in the subject and thought it might be helpful in his work to know more about DID.

McMahon enjoyed the movie. James McAvoy, the lead actor, was brilliant.

Mike picked Suzanne up at five, and they spent the weekend relaxing and hanging out at home.

* * *

Monday morning, Rose asked, "How did you sleep over the weekend?"

"Most nights, I sleep like a baby, but lately, I keep tossing and turning, and it takes a while before I drift off. I can't stop thinking about the case. What are we missing? I keep drawing blanks. How about you? Have you got any ideas?"

"Not really. I agree we're missing something."

Mike was about to speak when Lieutenant Foster walked up and summoned them into his office.

As they followed him, Rose whispered, "Foster doesn't look happy. Something must be up."

"You're right! "Be prepared for an ass-kicking," Mike whispered back.

They waited while Lieutenant Foster washed an antacid pill down with water.

"Your killer has struck again. There's another body in a parking lot on 17th Avenue behind the Southern Heat Records building. All I know is, this time, it's another male victim. The chief and the mayor will be stirring up a shit storm when they hear the news. Jeff Stone will have a field day writing about how incompetent we are, and the music community will be in full panic mode, hounding us to catch the killer. You two had better get your asses over to the crime scene."

As the detectives stood to leave, Lieutenant Foster gulped down two antacid pills and said, And don't forget to keep me updated."

"Yes, sir," they said in unison.

Mike said on their way to the crime scene, "Foster isn't looking too good, and I think the pressure of this case is stressing him out big time."

"He's not the only one feeling the stress from this case. If we don't catch the killer soon, we might be assigned to desk jobs or sent back to pounding the pavement," Rose said, shuddering at the thought.

"Yeah, it's getting to me as well. No wonder I have a hard time sleeping. If this keeps up, I'll probably develop an ulcer like Lieutenant Foster."

A forensics team buzzed like bees around a hive when they pulled into the parking lot behind Southern Heat Records. After signing the logbook, Goodwin and McMahon joined the huddle of techs and the ME at the crime scene.

When he saw the two detectives, Tony Capino looked up and said, "It looks like we've got a fifth murder by our psycho serial killer."

Rose gasped as she looked at the victim. "Oh, my God. It's Tim Evans."

"Who is Tim Evans? Tony ask

"Tim Evans is the owner and president of Southern Heat Records," Mike replied.

"The MO is the same as the other murders. But there's a big difference. The victim's wallet, credit cards, and money are still on his body, and I didn't find an NSGI membership card," Tony said.

"That's odd when we thought we were getting somewhere—he throws us a sweeping curveball. All the other victims were members of NSGI, and that seemed to be the common denominator. This murder blows that theory all to hell," Rose said.

"The killer is trying to confuse us, and he's succeeding," Mike replied.

"If I recall correctly, didn't he say in Jeff Stone's article that his next killing would be a real shocker?" Rose said.

"Yeah, that's what Stone said," Mike agreed.

"It looks like he delivered," Rose said. "Killing the president of a major record label is a real shocker, and this is bound to spook the Nashville music community into full panic mode."

"Every big-shot music executive will be looking over their shoulder," Mike said. "I wouldn't be surprised if they started hiring bodyguards."

"That might not be a bad idea," Rose said.

"How long do you think he's been dead, Tony?" Mike asked.

"Based on the body's condition, he's been dead for approximately twelve hours. That would put the time of death somewhere between nine and ten last night. He must have worked late, but it's hard to believe he'd be here on a Sunday evening."

"I agree," Rose said. "He must have had a good reason."

"Some people don't need a reason because they're workaholics," Mike said.

"Tony, do you know who found the body?" Rose asked.

"I believe it was the victim's receptionist when she came to work this morning."

"Is she still around?" Rose asked.

"I think she's inside the building."

They found Debbie Eastman sitting at her desk, bawling like a baby.

"We're so sorry to bother you at such a trying time, Debbie, but we must ask you a few questions. Are you able to talk to us now?" Rose asked gently.

Still sobbing, Debbie nodded and whispered, "Yes, Detective, I'm okay."

"Take all the time you need," Mike said softly.

When she looked more composed, Rose said, "We understand that you found Mr. Evans. Is that correct, Debbie?"

She dabbed at her eyes with a tissue, gulped a few times, looked up, and whispered, "Yes. When I came to work this morning, I found Mr. Evans lying near his car."

Before Rose could ask another question, Debbie broke down again and began to tremble. When she finally stopped shaking, she wiped her eyes with a tissue and said, "Sorry, go ahead, Detective."

"Do you remember what time that was?" Rose asked.

"It was around eight-thirty."

"What did you do when you found Mr. Evans lying in the parking lot?" Mike asked.

"When I saw what that monster did to him, I ran into the building as fast as possible and locked the door. I went into the bathroom and got sick. As soon as I felt a little better, I called 911."

"While in the parking lot, did you happen to notice anyone else there?" Rose asked.

"No. I was horrified and afraid. I didn't stop to look around."

She began to cry once more.

Feeling her angst, Mike asked, "Debbie, are you okay?"

"I think so. I called my sister, Angel, and she's coming to get me. I'm going to stay with her for a few days. I don't want to be alone."

"Good idea," Rose said. She asked Debbie for her home and cell numbers, jotted them down, closed her notebook, and slipped it back into her coat pocket.

"If you think of anything that might help our investigation, please call," Mike said.

They handed Debbie their cards and left.

Their first stop after leaving the crime scene was Lieutenant Foster's office. He was on the phone when they arrived, listening more than he was talking. When he finally hung up, Foster said, "That was the chief. He wanted an update on the case and asked me to call him back as soon as I spoke with you two. Just a minute." He paused, grabbed his water bottle, picked up an antacid tablet, and gulped it down. "Okay, I'm ready. Tell me what happened this time."

Mike nodded at Rose, indicating that he wanted her to talk.

Rose began. "The MO at this crime scene was the same as the previous four murders."

After she had finished with the update, Lieutenant Foster leaned back in his chair. Suddenly he shot forward, crossing his arms on his desk, and glared at the two detectives. He raised his voice and said, "This case appears to be going nowhere fast. It's driving everyone crazy. I want to think I've assigned the two best detectives to find the killer and bring him to justice. However, I'm beginning to have my doubts. Are you making any progress? I'm losing my patience, and you're making me look bad. I'm running out of excuses. I don't know what to tell the chief when I call him back."

Foster had caught them entirely off guard.

Mike stammered, "We're…we're working on a few leads, and I think…I think we're getting close. This perp is as slippery as an eel and smarter than a fox, but sooner or later, he's bound to slip up and make a mistake—that's when we'll collar him."

"Well, it had better be before he kills again," Foster said, the vein on his forehead beginning to pulse. "Now get out of here and go find that fucker!"

CHAPTER 28

T he next day, when Mike picked up a copy of the *Nashville Star Daily*, the headline read as he expected.

"GUITAR STRING STRANGLER" BREAKS PATTERN—KILLS MUSIC ROW EXECUTIVE

By Jeff Stone, Investigative Reporter

Hold on to your hat, folks! The "Guitar String Strangler" deviated from killing songwriters and recording artists who are NSGI members, and this time he murdered a well-known Music Row executive.

Early yesterday morning, the strangled (with a guitar string) and badly mutilated body of Tim Evans, President, and owner of Southern Heat Records, was discovered by his receptionist, Ms. Deborah Eastman, on her way to work. Mr. Evans, 62, was found lying near his car in the parking lot behind his building on 17th Avenue. Tim Evans established his record/publishing company in the year 2000. Over the years, he signed several new country artists and songwriters who went on to fame and fortune, propelling Southern Heat Records to numerous chart-topping hits. Recording artists such as Tracey Lark, Johnny Jacobs, Terry Compton, and others have won CMA awards under the Southern Heat banner.

At first, it looked like the killer targeted NSGI members and Frozen North songwriters and recording artists. Southern Heat Records appears to be his new target. The previous murder of Kandi Kane, a Southern Heat recording artist, and now Tim Evans shows the killer has taken a new direction. Who will be number six? I don't think anyone in the Nashville music community is safe.

I received another phone call from the suspected killer last night. He told me he was only getting started. He said the cops were spinning their wheels and had no clues about his identity. The suspected killer said he'd given the detectives in charge of the investigation hints, but they couldn't solve the puzzle. Before hanging up, he said, and I quote, "If you think the Tim Evans murder was a shocker, just wait and see who will be next."

Like his first four victims, the killer left his calling card, a crudely drawn treble clef, on the forehead of Mr. Evans.

"Holy crap," Mike said, handing the newspaper to Rose.

When Rose finished reading, she said with a forced laugh, "It looks like Jeff Stone is trying to speed up our return to a desk job or patrol car."

"Yeah, the jerk's not helping, that's for sure."

Mike's cell phone rang. "Unknown Caller."

Try to stay calm, Mike.

He let the phone ring several times while gathering his thoughts and composure.

"What do you want now?" Mike said calmly, even though he was boiling mad inside.

"Gee, Detective, I can't believe you`re beginning to sound civil. For once, you're not yelling and calling me obscene names." He laughed and continued. "Do I have the right number?"

"Are you calling to gloat and rub salt into my wounds?" Mike was surprised at how calm he sounded.

"I can't believe it's you, Detective. Are you on tranquilizers? Maybe you're smoking weed to calm your nerves because you sound so relaxed."

"I've decided you're not worth getting worked up over," Mike said.

"What do you think of my latest conquest?"

"Well, to tell you the truth, I think you're still a sick, demented lunatic. You need help. Why don't you stop by and turn yourself in? I know a few good shrinks who would love to crawl into your psycho brain to see if they can find out what makes it tick."

"Now you're getting nasty again. So, you think I'm a psycho, do you? That's not nice. You've hurt my feelings, 'rookie.' You wish I would turn myself in, don't you? I'm sorry to disappoint you, Detective. That would be too easy. You're going to have to earn that measly salary of yours."

Mike said, "I don't think you've got any feelings."

"I sure do have feelings. Every time I kill someone, I feel great!"

"How do you feel when you talk to me?" Mike asked.

"When I call you, I feel great when you yell and get upset. Today, I'm not so sure. Being nice doesn't suit you. I'm sure you'll get upset if I tell you who the next victim will be, but I'll keep it to myself. I know you'll be startled when you find out. Goodbye, Detective. Have a nice day—if that's possible."

Before Mike could say another word, the killer was gone.

"I can't believe you carried on a conversation with that maniac without yelling and screaming at him," Rose said, sounding amused.

"I can't believe I did either. I wanted to scream, but I figured I'd get upset, and my blood would boil. I decided I didn't want to give that maniac the satisfaction."

"What did he want?"

"He gets his jollies by trying to get me angry and frustrated, and I think he was disappointed that I sounded civil for a change. He said we would be startled when we found his next victim."

CHAPTER 29

Marven Jones and his wife, Louise, flew into town the night of the Tim Evans murder. Until they found an apartment, Frozen North had booked them into a suite at the Embassy Suites Hotel on Broadway. It was a short distance from the hotel to the Frozen North building, so the following morning, Marven and Louise decided to walk and take in the sights of Music Row.

Suzanne could hardly contain herself in the car with Mike that morning.

"This is the day I meet Marven Jones and his wife, Louise. Marven loved 'Don't Throw Our Love Away' from the first time he heard it. We're going to start rehearsing the song today before recording it for my album," Suzanne said, her face glowing with excitement.

As they pulled up in front of the building, Mike said, "Good luck, babe." He kissed Suzanne goodbye, then said, "I hope everything goes well with your rehearsal. Have a great day! I love you."

Before leaving the car, Suzanne gave Mike a peck on the cheek and said, "I love you, too."

Suzanne greeted Joyce Ormond with a pleasant smile and an enthusiastic good morning.

Joyce lit up and said, "This should be an exciting day for you, Suzanne. You're going to meet Marven Jones and his wife, Louise. They're super nice people, and I know you will love them. Everyone is waiting for you in the studio."

"Thanks, Joyce. I can hardly wait to get started. I love Marven's voice, and I think 'Don't Throw Our Love Away' will be a big hit."

"I feel the same way," Joyce said, smiling warmly. "As they say in show biz, break a leg."

All smiles, Suzanne floated down the hallway. As she entered the recording studio, she saw the familiar faces of Dave Franklin, Bill Ormond, producer Mark Bush, and engineer Jesse Potter. In his mid-thirties, Marven Jones, with a neatly trimmed black beard, was the handsome new face in the crowd. He wore a Frozen North baseball-style cap, a white long-sleeved shirt, blue jeans, and highly polished black cowboy boots. Marven's pretty wife, Louise, sat next to him. She was slim with short brown hair and sparkling hazel eyes. She wore a pink long-sleeved blouse, blue jeans, and white sneakers. Louise looked to be in her early thirties.

"Good morning, Suzanne," Dave Franklin said. "I'd like you to meet Marven Jones and his lovely wife, Louise."

After shaking hands and exchanging pleasantries with Marven and Louise, Suzanne said hello to everyone and sat beside engineer Jesse Potter. She had met Jesse once before. He was in his mid-twenties, tall and slim, with long shoulder-length black hair, dark-brown eyes, and an infectious smile.

Suzanne let out a huge sigh. Her dream was about to begin!

Bill Ormond said, "Suzanne, we had the musicians in the other day, and they laid down tracks in the key that you and Marven agreed on. Let's listen before you start rehearsal and see what you and Marven think."

Jesse started the playback, and they listened intently.

When the track finished playing, Dave Franklin asked, "Well, what do you think?"

Marven and Suzanne looked at one another with broad smiles.

"It's fabulous! I can't wait to get started," Suzanne said.

"They did a great job," Marven commented. "I love recording in Nashville because the musicians are the best in the world."

"Do you guys want to give it a go?" producer Mark Bush asked.

Marven picked up a lyric sheet and said, "Suzanne, I'm ready if you are."

Suzanne smiled and said, "Let's do it, Marven."

Jesse followed Marven and Suzanne into the vocal room, adjusted the microphone, and returned to the control room.

Jesse asked, "Are you good to go?"

They both nodded. The music began to play in their headsets and through the speakers in the control room. As the intro finished, standing side by side, Suzanne began to sing.

"The day I met you, darlin', sparks began to fly."

Marven: "They soon became a blazin' fire burnin' in our eyes."

Together: "As time passed, the fire died, put out by the rain."

Together: "Let's hope and pray it's not too late to fall in love again."

Suzanne: "Don't throw our love away."

Marven: "Don't go and leave me, baby."

Together: "Don't throw our love away 'cause it would drive me crazy.".

Together: "'Cause it would drive me crazy.

Together: "Don't throw, don't throw, don't throw our love away."

After singing the second verse, chorus, bridge, and chorus, the song ended with everyone smiling.

* * *

Tuesday afternoon, when Rose and Mike returned to the squad room from the Tim Evans autopsy, Lieutenant Foster asked them to join him in his office. They were surprised to see Chief Cummings sitting in their boss's chair.

Chief Cummings, an African American, was a forty-year veteran of the MNPD. He had worked his way up in the Patrol and Planning and Research Divisions, which had served him well as an Administrative Assistant to former Chief Ron Graham. He was trim and average height in his early sixties, with receding gray hair and a clean-shaven oval face. His rimless glasses made him look like a college professor. He appeared calm outside, but inside, his stomach churned. He cleared his throat, took a sip from a water bottle, and gave Mike and Rose an icy glare. Then, in a harsh tone, he said, "What the hell's going on with the 'Guitar String Strangler' case? I was hoping you'd have that son of a bitch collared and in jail by now. Do you have any suspects, or are you spinning your wheels as Jeff Stone suggested?"

Mike glanced at Rose, and Rose looked back at Mike for a split second. She turned to the chief, stared directly into his eyes, and said, "Every suspect we thought had a motive turned into a dead end. This perp is no dummy. So far, he hasn't left so much as a fingerprint until the Kandi Kane murder. After checking the prints forensics found in her car, nothing came up in the registry. We're not even sure the prints belong to the killer. They could be from someone who rode in her car—like a friend, and forensics didn't find any clues at the Tim Evans murder scene. The UNSUB broke his pattern of killing NSGI members when he murdered a Music Row executive. He may be crazy, but he's crazy like a fox."

The chief sighed deeply and said, "Based on what I've read in the paper, he's getting cocky. He's making the MNPD look like a bunch of morons. Everyone is getting on my ass. The mayor hounds me daily, and I'm getting calls from scared executives in the music community. I don't like it when I have trouble sleeping, and this case is giving me insomnia."

Lieutenant Foster spoke up when the chief paused and said, "Chief, I know we're all frustrated with this case, but these two detectives are working their tails off. It's not from a lack of effort. Sooner or later, the perp will slip up, and that's when they'll collar him."

"Let's hope he slips up soon, or I may have to contact the FBI to do a profile on our suspect. Maybe it's time to think outside the box. I want you two to go back and rethink every one of the murders. You may have missed some tiny detail. Turn over every stone until you figure this thing out. We're running out of time. That's all!" Chief Cummings said, thoroughly exasperated.

In the squad room, Mike said, "Since we're not qualified profilers, I think we should keep the profile of the suspect we came up with to ourselves."

"I agree. There's no sense getting into any more trouble than we're already in."

They reviewed each murder, hoping to find a clue they had missed. Nothing new surfaced. Frustration was at an all-time high!

Mike's cell phone rang. It was Suzanne.

"Hi, babe, what's up?"

"Hi, sweetie. I want to let you know I'll be working on the album for a few more hours. "

"When you're ready, call, and I'll pick you up."

"That's okay. I'll take a cab home."

Mike opened his mouth to protest, but Suzanne was gone.

When Mike got home, he put two meat pies into the oven and made himself a tossed garden salad. He grabbed a beer from the refrigerator, and when the meat pies were ready, he dug in. After eating and cleaning up, he fed Oliver. Mike grabbed another beer and retired to the living room. Dropping down onto the couch, he powered on the TV.

The announcer said, "That's the world news. Here's June Murray's report on something a little more local."

"Thanks, Peter. Today, I received an anonymous phone call from someone speaking in a distorted voice claiming to be the 'Guitar String Strangler.' He asked me to pass along a message to our viewers. He said the killings were not over, and he would have a stunning surprise soon. When I asked him to be more specific, he said, 'If I told you, it would spoil the surprise.' Before I could ask him another question, he was gone. If the call was from the 'Guitar String Strangler,' we'd better take him seriously. For reasons unknown, he appears to be targeting members of the Nashville music community. His first three victims, Shannon Greenway, Heather Brown, and John Tilley, were NSGI members. Brown and Tilley were staff songwriters at Frozen North Music. The fourth victim, Kandi Kane, was also an NSGI member and a recording artist with Southern Heat Records. The latest victim, Tim Evans, owner and president of Southern Heat Records, was not a member of NSGI."

"When contacted, Police Chief Bradley Cummings would only say that the MNPD is working tirelessly to find the killer and bring him to justice. When asked if the police had any suspects, he only said, 'I have no comment.'

We will keep you updated as this story unfolds. That's it for now. Back to you, Peter."

Mike turned the TV off, his mind in chaos. *What did he mean by a stunning surprise?*

CHAPTER 30

Mike felt exhausted, so he stretched out on the sofa. It didn't take long before he drifted into a restless sleep and began dreaming.

The cemetery was overflowing with friends, relatives, neighbors, the Dearborn Police Department, and surrounding police forces.

The priest said his mother was in a better place, in God's loving hands. Mike didn't understand. How could his mom be in a better place when she was dead?

When the prayers ended, Mike, his sister, Joanne, and their father, with tear-filled eyes, each placed a red rose on the casket, said a final goodbye, turned, and slowly walked away.

Mike's dream ended abruptly when his cell phone shrilled.

It must be Suzanne! What time is it?

His watch showed 10:15 p.m.

Half asleep, he reached for his phone, and without checking the screen, he sleepily whispered, "Hi, babe. Are you still in the studio? Are you ready to come home? Do you want me to pick you up?"

"No, Detective, I've already picked her up. She's at my place and not ready to go home yet," the familiar distorted voice said.

Startled, Mike sat upright—instantly awake.

"What the fuck! If you've harmed Suzanne, you're a dead man."

"Don't worry, Detective, she's still alive. I thought I'd let her hear my latest song in the morning. It's called 'Suzanne', and I wrote it just for her. I want to write a few songs with Suzanne so she can put them on her first album in heaven," he said, laughing hysterically.

Taking a few deep breaths, Mike tried to control the panic gripping him like a vice. He said in a calm, controlled voice, "Are you fucking with me? I don't believe she's there."

"It sounds like you don't trust me, Detective. Please take my word. Suzanne is here."

Losing his patience, Mike yelled, "You idiot, I wouldn't trust you or take your word to save my life."

Once more, Mike heard that all too familiar laugh. "Well, maybe you'd better start—if you want to save your lovely Suzanne's life."

"I don't believe she's there. If she is, let me speak with her."

"Suzanne's taking a nap right now. She's out like a light from the sedative I gave her. I don't think we should disturb her—let Suzanne sleep. I'll call you in the morning. Pleasant dreams, Detective. I hope you sleep well." He gave another blood-curdling laugh and hung up.

Mike picked up the empty beer bottle and hurled it across the room, smashing a picture on the wall and sending shards of glass flying everywhere. When Oliver heard the breaking glass, he jumped off the sofa and made a mad dash to his favorite hiding place—under Mike's bed.

Mike's blood was boiling, and rage consumed him. His head pounded so hard he felt like it could explode any minute. He ran into the bathroom, shook two extra-strength headache tablets out of the bottle, and gulped them down without water. Staring at himself in the mirror, he screamed, "Fuck, fuck, shit, shit, shit—I should have picked her up."

Calm down and think—the clock is ticking—you'd better find Suzanne fast, or she'll be victim number six.

His stomach rebelled at the thought of it! Dropping to his knees, he brought up in the toilet bowl. Feeling a little better, he rinsed his mouth, splashed cold water onto his face, toweled it off, and rushed back into the living room. Mike picked up the phone and dialed Rose. It took four rings before a sleepy voice answered.

"Hey, Mike, what's up?"

In a panic-stricken voice, he yelled, "That maniac kidnapped Suzanne. He called me a few minutes ago. I think she's still alive, but for how long, I don't know. We've got to find her fast."

"Calm down, Mike. Let's meet in the squad room in thirty minutes."

"Okay, but hurry!"

When Mike arrived at his desk, he took several deep breaths and began to think.

Who is this nut job? How did he get my cell number? It's on my card. It must be someone I gave my card to since the murders began. It can't be the Briggs brothers; they're no longers suspects. It certainly can't be any of the Frozen North people or anyone at Southern Heat Records now that Tim Evans is dead. Then who can it be? Suzanne had called a taxi. It must be the taxi driver! Who drives a taxi that might have my card? I don't have a fucking clue.

Rose interrupted Mike's thoughts as she dashed into the squad room out of breath.

Suddenly, he yelled, "I've got it!"

"What have you got?' Rose asked, still breathing hard.

"The taxi driver. The taxi driver must be our killer."

"What...what taxi driver?"

"Suzanne was working late in the studio and told me not to pick her up. She said she was going to take a cab home."

"Do you know what taxi company picked her up?"

"She always uses Music City Taxi."

Mike looked up the number, grabbed the phone, and dialed.

"Music City Taxi," a male voice answered on the third ring.

"This is Detective McMahon of the MNPD. We're investigating a possible abduction. Can you tell me if your records show a pickup at the Frozen North building on 16th Avenue this evening?" He gave the dispatcher the address.

"Give me a minute, and I'll check."

Mike shifted uneasily in his chair and drummed his fingers on the desk. The dispatcher's few minutes to return on the line felt like an eternity. Finally, he heard, "We received a call for a pickup at that address around eight-thirty, but when our driver arrived, there wasn't anyone there."

"What? Are you sure?"

"Yes, Detective, I'm very sure. Sorry, that's what the driver told me. Since no one was at that address, I dispatched him to another call."

"Okay. Thanks. Shit!" Mike shouted, slamming the phone down.

"Sounds like another dead end," Rose said.

"I was sure it was the taxi driver. Who else could it be? I know damn well Suzanne wouldn't get into a car unless she trusted the driver."

"If the killer works for Music City Taxi, he might have heard the dispatcher and beaten the other driver to the address. Suzanne wouldn't know the difference, and she'd get in the cab thinking it was the driver the company had dispatched," Rose said.

"You could be right. Maybe the killer lurked in the area, got there first, and whisked her away. He could have been on break or just gone off duty. That way, the dispatcher wouldn't have a clue."

"If that's the case, the killer must drive for Music City Taxi," Rose said.

"I'll call them back and see if the dispatcher can tell me if any driver was on break or went off duty around the same time Suzanne requested a pickup."

Mike dialed Music City Taxi once more.

"Music City Taxi," the same voice said.

"It's Detective McMahon. I have another question. Did any of your drivers go on break or come off duty around when you dispatched a pickup to the 16th Avenue address I gave you?"

"It might take a few minutes to check. Do you wish to hold? If not, I'll get back to you as soon as possible. Is it the number I see on my screen?"

"I prefer to hold, and please hurry. It's a matter of life and death."

"Okay. I'll put you on hold."

Once more, Mike started drumming his fingers on his desk while Rose shifted in her seat, her face pale from concern.

It felt like forever before the dispatcher came back on the line. "Two drivers went off duty around that time," he said.

"Do you know the names of those drivers?" Mike asked, trying his best to stay calm.

"Let me look—yes, I have them right here. One was George Gray, and the other was Chuck Connors."

"Was there anyone else?"

"No, Detective, just those two."

"Do you know the drivers personally?"

"Yeah, I do."

"Can you describe them to me?"

"George Gray is an African American, about five-ten with a shaved head. He has a full beard, and I'd guess he's about thirty-five. Chuck Connors is white. He's huge, about six and a half feet, with a black ponytail and a goatee. I'd say he's in his early to mid-twenties."

"Are you sure Chuck Connors is his real name? Have you ever heard the name Charlie Cook?"

"He's always been Chuck Connors, as far as I know. I've never heard the name Charlie Cook."

"What about his driver's license? What name is on it?"

"As far as I know, it's Chuck Connors."

"Do you happen to have a home address for Chuck Connors?"

"Hold on, and I'll look it up."

When the dispatcher returned on the line, he gave Mike a familiar address—it was Charlie Cook's.

Mike thanked the dispatcher and hung up.

"Bingo," he said. "I bet Chuck Connors is Charlie Cook."

"What? What are you talking about?"

"It might be a coincidence, but it sounds like Charlie Cook is using the name of the movie actor who played *The Rifleman* in the TV series back in the black-and-white days. If I recall correctly, Chuck Connors was a big man, and I think he stood around six and a half feet."

"Are you saying that Charlie Cook is our killer?"

"He could be. I bet he's been watching reruns of *The Rifleman* and came up with the name that way. We're wasting valuable time. Let's get our asses over to Charlie Cook's place."

The siren wailing, Mike took off like he was on the Indy 500 track.

"Why would he use an alias?" Rose asked.

"I have no idea. Maybe Charlie Cook has a twin brother, just like Jason Briggs."

"I find that hard to believe. If Charlie does have a twin, why aren't their last names the same?"

"How the hell should I know?" Mike snapped, clearly frustrated.

"How do you know it's him? He was at the Blue Bird Café the night Heather Brown died," Rose said. "Cook's alibi checked out."

"Yeah, he was there on January 27th, just like he said. He has witnesses who verified his story," Mike said.

"Then how could he have killed Heather Brown?"

"What if he killed her a night or two before January 27th? Since forensics figured she had been dead for about a week, a day or two wouldn't make that much of a difference. It's not an exact science about the time and day she died. It's an educated guess; that's all. It must be Charlie. Cook lied to us. We took his word when he said Heather left for home on January 27th. He could've followed her on the 25th or 26th. Charlie must have killed Heather Brown at the Rest Stop on I-65 and tossed her body into the Cumberland River. By doing that, he bought himself extra time to plan his alibi. I don't think he counted on anyone finding the body so soon," Mike said.

"Wouldn't you know we've been spinning our wheels all this time thinking it couldn't have been Charlie because of his alibi? When you showed him the picture of Heather Brown, he looked devastated. Cook could win an Academy Award with his performance," Rose said.

"Yeah, he could." Suddenly, the movie *Split* flashed into Mike's head. "But what if he's got a split personality, and Chuck Connors is one of his personalities?"

"I never thought of that."

CHAPTER 31

W hen Suzanne regained consciousness, she had a splitting headache, her whole body hurt, and she felt like she might throw up. *If I get sick, with duct tape covering my mouth, I'll choke on my vomit.*

As her eyes began to focus, Suzanne realized she was lying on a smelly floor covered with thin carpeting in a small living room. She could make out a couch, a glass coffee table, and a recliner chair. A large-screen TV hung on the wall opposite the sofa. Suzanne shuddered and let out a muffled scream as a small rodent ran across her legs and disappeared under the couch. She could hear someone snoring loudly a short distance away, off the hallway from the living room.

How did I get here? Vaguely, she remembered a cab pulling up in front of the Frozen North building. The driver, a monstrous man, opened the back door. A large hand covered her nose and mouth as she was about to get onto the back seat. The unpleasant smell of chloroform was the last thing she remembered.

Suddenly, it hit her like a lightning bolt. Panic and terror enveloped her. Her mind started racing, and questions began to pop into her head. *Where the hell am I, and how long have I been here? What time is it? Why am I still alive? There must be a reason! Oh, my God, is he going to kill me? He must be the Guitar String Strangler.*

Suddenly, the snoring stopped, and Suzanne heard him moving. After a few loud snorts and some mumbling, the snoring resumed.

Her fingers and feet began feeling numb from the duct tape on her wrists and ankles. Tears formed in her eyes and began to rain

W . D . F R O L I C K

down her face. As she sobbed, she began to tremble. *Why was I so stupid? I should have let Mike pick me up. Now I may never see him again. Where are you, Mike? Save me! Please, please, save me!*

* * *

"Maybe we should call for backup," Rose suggested.

"We don't have time. Every second that ticks by could mean life or death for Suzanne. We can assess the situation when we get there and call for backup if we need it."

"Okay. Let's do it!" Rose said with conviction.

The rest of the way, they rode in silence. Mike parked the car in front of the house. The driveway contained three vehicles. One was a newer gray Ford F-150 pickup truck, and one was an older blue Chevrolet Impala four-door sedan—Charlie's car? The third vehicle was a Music City Taxi taxicab.

Silently, they slinked along the side of the house, turned the corner, and crept up to the back entrance. Racking his Glock, Mike put his ear to the door. At first, all he could hear was the pounding of his own heart. Listening intently, he thought he heard a muffled sound.

Mike whispered, "I hear something. I think someone's crying, and it could be Suzanne."

Then a booming voice screamed, "Shut up, bitch. I'm trying to sleep. Keep it up, and I'll come in there and strangle you with my bare hands."

"Shit," Mike said, "I wish we'd brought a battering ram."

He raised his right foot and kicked the door, and it cracked a little, but the lock held. Mike raised his foot and kicked again, but the door still did not open.

"Fuck," he said.

Mike backed up a few steps and charged the door with his shoulder. It crashed open, and he stumbled inside, Rose on his heels. With their guns and flashlights pointed straight ahead, it took a few seconds for their eyes to adjust to the bright room. What they saw wasn't what they were expecting. Charlie Cook/Chuck Connors stood behind Suzanne with a guitar string wrapped around her neck.

"Don't come any closer, or Suzanne will die," he yelled.

"Charlie, it's over; no one needs to get hurt. Let her go," Mike said.

"My name's not Charlie; it's Chuck—Chuck Connors," he bellowed, irritated.

He looked like Charlie, but there was something different about him. His voice and mannerisms didn't fit the Charlie they had interviewed after Heather Brown's murder. This man was aggressive, as if he was someone else. He pronounced his words differently—more articulately than Charlie Cook did. Doctor Jekyll turned into Mr. Hyde.

In a soothing tone, Rose said, "Okay, Chuck, no one has to get hurt."

For a brief moment, his aggressive personality changed.

"Jeez, you came too soon. I was going to write a few songs with Suzanne in the morning," he said, sounding like a disappointed kid who couldn't go to Disney World.

"If you let her go, Chuck, I'm sure Suzanne would like to write a few songs with you. You can do it now," Mike said.

"No, I can't. You've gone and spoiled my plan."

"What plan was that, Chuck?" Rose asked soothingly.

"As I said, I wanted to write a few songs with Suzanne in the morning."

"Why wait until morning? You can write the songs now. If you kill her, you won't hear the songs on her album," Mike said, stalling for time. "Let Suzanne go, and we can sit down and talk about it. No one needs to get hurt."

While he kept Chuck distracted, Rose gradually shifted to her left, trying to get a side-angle shot at Chuck.

"It's too late for that. I must kill Suzanne," he said, his disappointment turning into rage.

With his gun trained on Chuck's forehead, Mike said, "No, Chuck, it's not too late. Let Suzanne go, and we can sit down and talk about it. No one has to get hurt."

Mike didn't want to shoot for fear of hitting Suzanne. He sensed what Rose was trying to do and prayed she had a better angle.

While all this was happening, Suzanne's eyes were bugging out of her head. Mike could taste the fear she was radiating.

Without warning, Chuck sneezed and released the guitar string with his right hand, instinctively putting the hand to his mouth. Before he could re-grip the guitar string, Suzanne slid slightly to her left, exposing more of Chuck's large frame. Rose fired. The bullet hit his right shoulder, and Suzanne tumbled to the floor to his left. Like a giant redwood, Chuck fell backward, smashing his head on the coffee table and sending shards of glass in all directions. He was out colder than a mackerel.

While Rose held her gun on Chuck, before he regained consciousness, Mike cuffed Chuck's hands behind his back.

Blood was oozing from the wound in Chuck's shoulder. Rose ran into the bathroom and returned with a towel. She pressed the towel onto the wound to try to stop the bleeding. Under the lights, she could see the injury was not as severe as she had thought. The bullet had grazed him, causing a flesh wound, and there was no significant damage. After the bleeding subsided, Rose stood up and kept her pistol trained on Chuck while Mike attended to Suzanne.

A short time later, he opened his eyes, and Chuck became Charlie.

"Hi, detectives," he said as he glanced around the room. "What happened?" Feeling the pain from his aching head and throbbing shoulder, he grimaced and asked, "Why did you shoot me?"

"Because you kidnapped Suzanne Taylor and tried to kill her with a guitar string," Mike replied.

"What? I wouldn't do that," he said, looking bewildered.

"What's your name?" Rose asked.

"You know my name. It's Charlie Cook."

"When you held Suzanne with the guitar string wrapped around her neck, you said your name was Chuck Connors. Do you know who he is?" Mike asked.

"No. I don't have a clue. You must have me confused with someone else."

"Right now, you need medical attention. You're wounded, and you may have a concussion. We'll have to sort this out later," Rose said.

"Ouch!" Suzanne yelled as Mike ripped the duct tape from her mouth. He used his pocket knife and cut the tape from her wrists and ankles. Mike could make out a red ligature mark around her neck, but there were no cuts or bleeding. Suzanne would have a stiff neck for a while and some bruising, but nothing serious that time wouldn't heal.

Suzanne flexed her fingers, trying to get the circulation flowing again. It felt as if sharp needles were jabbing into them. She staggered as she tried to stand up.

Seeing she was still a little shaky, Mike wrapped Suzanne in his arms to help keep her on her feet. He kissed her softly and said, "How are you, sweetie? Are you okay? Did he hurt you?"

"Other than a migraine headache, a sore neck, and a body that hurts all over, I'm fine...I think. My feet are still tingling like they're half asleep." Then the reality of the situation hit her. The dam burst, the floodgates opened, and Suzanne began to shake. "Thank God," she sobbed, "you and Rose figured it out and got here just in time. I thought for sure he was going to kill me."

"It's okay, babe; you're safe. I couldn't let the future Mrs. Michael John McMahon not be here to marry me and have our children."

Suzanne managed a half-smile through her tears and whispered, "Oh, Mike, I love you so much it hurts. What would I do without you?"

Catching Suzanne's humorous pun, Mike smiled and said, "I love you, too, but it doesn't hurt me as much as it's hurting you. I can't imagine my life without you, sweetie."

As Mike kissed Suzanne again, Rose gave a subdued laugh and said, "Why don't you two get a room."

They both laughed, releasing their tension.

"Good idea, Rose," Mike said. "We might just do that."

"We were lucky he sneezed when he did," Rose said.

"Yeah," Suzanne said, "I think he was allergic to my perfume or hairspray."

"Thank our lucky stars he was," Mike said.

While Mike continued to cling to Suzanne's trembling body, Rose called for an ambulance. Charlie, his head still groggy, lay on the floor in silence.

Five minutes later, they heard the wail of a siren.

"That was fast," Rose said.

Two MNPD police officers burst through the door with their guns drawn a few minutes later.

"Put your hands up," the first officer shouted.

"What's going on here?" the second officer asked.

Rose, Suzanne, and Mike complied by putting their hands above their heads.

"We're MNPD detectives," Rose said.

"Careful," the first officer said. "Show us your badges."

They produced their badges, and once the officers were satisfied, pointing at Charlie, the older officer asked, "Who's the ape on the floor?"

"The suspect called the 'Guitar String Strangler,'" Mike said.

"No shit," the same officer said, "We got a call from the house owner complaining about a disturbance in his tenant's basement apartment. We thought we were coming to a domestic situation or a burglary call, and we had no idea—congratulations!"

"I guess the landlord heard me breaking down the door," Mike said. "I'm sure the noise woke him up."

"I've called for an ambulance to take the suspect to the hospital. He's got a slight shoulder wound and a possible concussion," Rose said. "Could you two go with the ambulance and watch him until an officer is assigned to guard him?"

"Okay," the younger officer said. "We'll look after it."

"We'll follow shortly and take the victim to emergency to be checked by a doctor," Mike said.

Charlie Cook, you are under arrest for kidnapping and attempted murder," Rose said. She read him his Miranda rights and said more charges were pending.

"Do you understand what I just said?" Rose asked.

Charlie nodded and said, "Yes, I understand."

Rose wasn't sure he did understand. He still looked spaced out.

Just then, an ambulance arrived, and in less than a minute, two paramedics rushed in carrying their bags and a collapsible gurney.

After attending to Charlie's shoulder wound, they cleaned and patched the cut on the back of his head and gave him a sedative. The two officers helped the struggling paramedics lift the gigantic body onto the gurney.

Rose explained the circumstances to the paramedics and asked, "Where are you taking him?"

"We're going to Nashville General." the female paramedic said.

"Okay," Rose said. "These two officers will follow you, and we'll catch up later."

Rose called dispatch and informed the dispatcher of the situation. She told him they would need a police officer sent to Nashville General to guard the suspect and another two officers to secure the crime scene. She gave the dispatcher Cook's address and said she and Mike would wait until the officers arrived.

"No problem," he said, "I'll take care of it."

It took twenty minutes for the officers to arrive at Charlie's apartment. As the officers began securing the crime scene, Mike, Rose, and Suzanne left for Nashville General Hospital.

After the emergency room doctor examined Suzanne, he said, "Your neck is badly bruised and will be stiff and sore for a few days, but you should be back to normal soon."

The doctor gave her a few tablets for her migraine headache and said it was okay for her to leave.

Patched up, sedated, and hooked up to intravenous, Charlie fell asleep. He rested comfortably with his left wrist cuffed to the metal bed railing. He had sustained a mild concussion and needed several stitches to close the three-inch gash on the back of his head.

While Cook slept, a young police officer sat on guard outside the door to his room.

CHAPTER 32

H aving had very little sleep the following day, Mike and Rose were bleary-eyed when they arrived in the squad room. The coffee they were drinking did little to clear their foggy heads.

Their first stop was Lieutenant Foster's office. They informed him about Suzanne's kidnapping and the suspect's wounding and capture. On hearing the news, he was elated. Foster picked up his phone and called Chief Cummings with the good news.

When he had hung up, he said, "Chief Cummings was relieved to hear the great news. He asked me to congratulate you on a job well done." Smiling broadly, he said, "Congratulations! Well done, detectives."

"Thank you, Lieutenant," Rose said.

"Thanks," Mike said.

"You've made us all proud with your hard work and dedication. We can all breathe a sigh of relief. The mayor will be pleased to hear of the suspect's capture. Unfortunately, Sergeant Goodwin, since you fired your weapon and wounded the suspect, the rules state that you will be on administrative duty until the Office of Professional Accountability can fully investigate the shooting. Based on what you've told me, you had no choice, and your quick thinking saved Suzanne Taylor's life. For now, you're off the case. However, I'm confident you will be cleared of any wrongdoing and will be back on the job soon. I'll speak with the chief and see if we can resolve this matter quickly."

"I did what I had to do under the circumstances. There's no doubt in my mind that I did the right thing. If given a choice, I'd do the same thing again," Rose said with conviction.

"I'm sure you did the right thing. Let's hope OPA sees it the way we do."

"I'm sure they will," Mike said.

Looking at Mike, Lieutenant Foster said, "It's unfortunate that it took the kidnapping of Suzanne to figure out who the killer was. Thank God she wasn't badly hurt."

"We were lucky to figure it out and get there in time. Because the suspect wanted to write songs with Suzanne in the morning, that delayed things long enough for us to save her life." Mike said.

"What's your take on the suspect?" Lieutenant Foster asked.

"As you know, after Heather Brown's murder, we interviewed Cook, and his alibi was solid. We had no reason to consider him a suspect at that time. It wasn't until last night's crisis that we put all the pieces together. When he's Mr. Nice, he's Charlie Cook. When he's Mr. Killer, he's Chuck Connors. If he's acting and sane, he's one hell of an actor."

"It sounds like you're on to something, Detective."

"I've done a little reading on the subject, and the medical term is dissociative identity disorder. People suffering from DID experience different emotional and neurological symptoms–such as memory loss, depression, anxiety attacks, delusions, suicidal thoughts, severe headaches, and a few others. Violent, self-destructive behavior that conflicts with normal behavior is another symptom of DID. Amnesia and losing track of time are a few other things that can happen to a person with this problem. I'd be willing to bet that Charlie Cook suffers from DID. Recently, I went and saw the movie Split. It told the story of a man suffering from DID. In the film, he had twenty-three different personalities. Near the movie's end, his worst personality turns him into a murdering monster. If Cook suffers from DID, he could have several personalities," Mike said.

"You could be right. I think I'd better call the DA. The DA may want to petition the court for an assessment. If the assessment finds

Cook suffers from DID, a good defense lawyer will plead insanity and push to commit him to an institution. If that happens, there's no way he'll go to prison."

At that moment, Lieutenant Foster's phone rang.

"Lieutenant Foster," he said. "Yes, it's great news." He listened a little longer and said, "I'll inform them. Yes, we'll be there. See you in the morning."

He said goodbye and turned to Rose and Mike. "That was Mayor Hardy. The chief informed him of the suspect's capture, and he's arranging a news conference for 10:00 a.m. tomorrow in the council chambers. I want you both to be there by nine-thirty. I'll need you to help field questions about the case and the suspect's capture. I should have a search warrant within an hour. I want Detective McMahon to join the forensics team at Cook's apartment to see if any incriminating evidence can tie him to the other murders. We'll have his car towed to the crime lab garage and have forensics thoroughly search it. He might have kept some of his victims' items as souvenirs, and I'm guessing he may have transported Heather Brown's body in his vehicle. If they find anything that ties him to the other victims, it will solidify our case and give the DA what he needs to get a conviction. I'll authorize forensics to work all night if they must. I want a report on what they find before the news conference in the morning. We've got him for kidnapping and attempted murder, but I also want to nail him for the other homicides."

An hour and a half later, with the search warrant in his hand, Mike joined the forensics team at Charlie Cook's apartment, leaving Rose bored and brooding at her desk.

At two-thirty, the search completed, Mike headed to the station to update Lieutenant Foster on their findings.

After Mike had finished his update, Foster smiled and said, "Good work! We have the evidence we need to nail that son of a bitch. Why don't you and Sergeant Goodwin go home and relax? You deserve a little downtime. I'll see you both at the news conference in the morning."

"Sounds good, Lieutenant," Mike said. "See you in the morning."

After informing Rose of the good news, she said, "It's been a couple of hectic weeks. I need to recharge my battery and spend time with my family."

"Yeah, I feel the same way. I'd better get home and see how Suzanne is coping. She will need rest and time to get over her traumatic experience and might even need to see a shrink. See you in the morning and don't worry, you didn't do anything wrong. By shooting Cook, you saved Suzanne's life. That'll all come out in the interview, and you'll be back on the job in no time."

"I hope you're right. Thanks for the vote of confidence. I needed that. See you at City Hall. Take care." Rose put on her coat and headed for the door.

When Mike arrived home, Suzanne was fast asleep, with Oliver curled up at her feet.

He left the bedroom, headed into the living room, and stretched out on his recliner. Within five minutes, he fell into a deep sleep.

His mother was sitting in the bleachers. His dad couldn't make it because of a murder investigation. His mom cheered loudly, "Mike, Mike, Mike." He almost felt embarrassed as she made more noise than the other parents combined.

Each team had won two games in the best-of-five series for the Dearborn Little League championship. The score was five-five. The bases were empty with two outs in the bottom of the ninth as Mike stepped into the batter's box.

The pitcher wound up, and the first pitch zoomed past him. "Strike" screamed the umpire. The second pitch was outside for ball one. The third pitch was a curveball, and Mike swung wildly and missed by a country mile. "Strike two," the umpire yelled. The fourth pitch was low for ball two, and the fifth was out of the strike zone, high for ball three. The count was three balls and two strikes. Mike knew the pitcher didn't want to walk him with their cleanup hitter on deck. He figured he was going to get a fastball. The pitcher went into his windup and let it fly. It looked to Mike as if the ball was traveling at warp speed. Just before it reached home plate, he took a mighty swing. To his surprise, there was a loud crack as the ball hit the sweet spot on his bat. His head came up as the ball flew over the left-field fence. I can't believe I hit a home run and won the game and the championship. He tried hard to contain his excitement.

As he rounded the bases, his mother's screams and cheers from his teammates and the other parents rang in his ears. "That's my boy! That's my boy! Way to go, Mike," his mother hollered loudly. When he reached home plate, his entire team and coaches were there to greet and mob him. It was the best moment in his young life. His biggest regret was that his dad wasn't there to share the proud moment with him and his mom.

At 5:15 p.m., Mike awoke to the sound of the shower running. In less than ten minutes, Suzanne appeared in a pink bathrobe with a white towel wrapped around her head. She looked tired and drawn, and her neck still showed the red ligature mark.

He smiled and asked, "How are you feeling?"

"I've felt better. My neck is stiff, and my body still aches. At least I know I'm alive. Believe it or not, my headache is gone," Suzanne said, forcing a faint smile.

"You look great!" Mike lied. "You'll be as good as new in a day or two. I spoke with Dave Franklin today and filled him in on what happened. He said to wish you a speedy recovery and to take all the time you need before returning."

"I want to return to working on my album in a few days. I think my voice is okay."

"To be sure, you should take at least a week off before returning to the studio. By the way, you should know, as a witness, OPA will ask you to provide a statement regarding Rose's shooting of Charlie Cook. You may have to testify at a hearing if it goes that far. Until they determine it was a justified shooting, Rose is on administrative duty. Your statement and mine should be enough to reinstate her to active duty."

"If it weren't for Rose's quick action, I'd be dead. And I'll damn well tell them that!"

Mike laughed. "That's my feisty girl. You're almost starting to sound like your old self again. I picked up a bottle of your favorite wine on the way home. Why don't we spend a quiet evening reading or maybe we can watch a movie? I checked, and the *Coal Miner's Daughter* comes on at seven on TCM."

Suzanne's face lit up. "That's one of my all-time favorite movies. Sissy Spacek played Loretta Lynn and won an Academy Award for best actress, and Tommy Lee Jones played her husband, Mooney Lynn. I can't wait to see it again. We can relax and veg out. I'm sure you need the rest as much as I do, and the movie will help get our minds off things."

"A little R&R after the last few days sure won't hurt."

Meanwhile, at Nashville General Hospital, Charlie became Chuck again!

CHAPTER 33

T he morning was bright and sunny. The local morning show's
weatherman predicted a high of 55 degrees. Maybe spring
was just around the corner.

Mike awoke feeling relaxed and rested.

After breakfast, he kissed Suzanne goodbye and headed to the
elevator. He arrived at City Hall at 9:25 a.m. and caught up to Rose
as she entered the council chamber.

"Good morning, Rose," he chirped.

"Good morning, Mike. I trust you had a restful night."

"It was the best night I've had in a long time. How about you?"

"I can't complain. I was home to meet Jill when she got off the
school bus. I'm sure I built up a few brownie points with Jill and Paul.
I feel stress-free for the first time since I can't remember when. By
the way, how is Suzanne making out?"

"She sleeps a lot, but she's starting to feel a little better. She's
eager to return to the studio and start working on her album again.
I'm sure it will be good therapy for her, and it should help to get her
mind off her recent traumatic experience."

"I'm glad to hear Suzanne's feeling better. Catching the killer
helps to relieve the pressure for all of us."

"That's for sure. I think my blood pressure is returning to normal,"
Mike laughed.

Directly before them, Mayor Tyler Hardy conversed with Chief
Cummings and Lieutenant Foster. They were all smiling, laughing,
and looking relaxed.

June Murray from Channel 2 news stood talking with her camera operator while another reporter from Channel 5 TV, Drake Davidson, was also there with his cameraman. The news conference was going out live on the two local TV stations. The council chamber was filling up quickly as more and more media people arrived.

Mike felt a tap on his shoulder. When he turned around, he was staring at a silly grin on the face of Jeff Stone. The bangs of his medium-length brown hair almost covered his mischievous blue eyes, and it looked like he had not used a razor in several days.

"Congratulations, Detective McMahon," Stone said, not sounding sincere. "You and your partner got lucky and finally caught the serial killer."

Stone caught Mike off guard. He smiled and said, "Yeah, you could say that. There's an old saying by a man named Thomas Jefferson. I believe he was the third president of the United States of America and the author of the Declaration of Independence. It goes something like this, 'I'm a great believer in luck, and I find the harder I work, the more I have of it.'" With that, Mike turned and walked away. Jeff Stone stood there frozen, unable to utter a single word.

Rose, who was close by, overheard their conversation and couldn't help but snicker. She was still smiling as they joined the mayor and their two bosses. That was the first time she had seen Jeff Stone speechless.

"Good morning," the chief said with a friendly smile. "I hope you both had a pleasant evening. How is Suzanne making out, Mike?"

"We enjoyed a quiet evening, and Suzanne's feeling much better. Thank you, Chief."

"Best evening I've had in a long time," Rose chimed in.

After they all shook hands, Mayor Hardy said, "Congratulations, Detectives! I had a sound sleep last night after I heard the good news—hopefully, we can breathe a lot easier now thanks to your hard work."

"I agree, Mr. Mayor; we can all breathe much easier. I received the crime lab report earlier this morning, and I'm pleased to say that they found evidence that links the suspect to all the murders. Heather Brown's blood and hair particles turned up in the trunk of his car. They found wallets, credit cards, and driver's licenses of Shannon Greenway, Heather Brown, John Tilley, and Kandi Kane in a metal box under his bed. They didn't find any items belonging to Tim Evans. He left all of Evans' identification on his body for unknown reasons. They found a clown mask, a serrated hunting knife, and a red market under a pile of socks in a dresser drawer. In his closet, they found several burner phones in a shoe box. With all this evidence, it should be a slam dunk for the DA to get a conviction," Lieutenant Foster said.

"That's great news!" Mayor Hardy said.

Hardy stood just over six feet tall with sandy hair and bright brown eyes. The rumor circulating in town was that he was considering running for governor in the next state election.

The mayor took his seat perched above everyone at the front of the council chamber. The four police representatives sat directly below him. The chief sat in the middle with Lieutenant Foster on his right. Rose sat next to Foster, and Mike sat on the chief's left. Everyone had a microphone.

At exactly 10:00 a.m., Mayor Tyler Hardy said, "Good morning, everyone. I'm pleased to inform you that the MNPD has a suspect in custody. We believe he is the perpetrator known as the 'Guitar String Strangler'—the serial killer who has terrorized our city and the music community for several weeks. Thanks to the hard work and dedication of Detective Sergeant Rose Goodwin and her partner Detective Mike McMahon, we can all breathe easier. At this time, I would like to turn the proceedings over to Chief Cummings for his comments, following which the floor will be open for a brief question and answer period. Thank you! Chief Cummings."

The chief cleared his throat and said, "Thank you, Mayor Hardy. I want to thank you all for being here today. It's been a stressful time for our city, not knowing where the killer would strike next. Unfortunately, it took five murders and almost a sixth before we could track him down. Thanks to the tireless efforts and bravery of

Detective Sergeant Rose Goodwin and Detective Mike McMahon—here with us today—they tracked down and captured the suspect before he could kill again. I'd also like to thank their commanding officer, Lieutenant Rob Foster, seated to my right, for his superb efforts in coordinating the investigation and informing me of ongoing developments as the case progressed. On behalf of the MNPD and myself, I would like to express our heartfelt sorrow and condolences to the victims' families. It's hard losing a loved one at any time, let alone from a senseless killing by a deranged individual. Before we open the floor to questions, I suggest we keep things orderly. Please raise your hand, and I will pick you one at a time. I ask that you identify yourself, the media you represent, and to whom you wish to direct your question. Thank you!"

Hands shot up like arrows.

The chief pointed to a woman seated in the front row. She stood and said, "I'm June Murray from TV News 2. Detective Seargent Goodwin, can you provide the name of the man you have in custody?"

"Yes, his name is Charlie Cook, and he also goes by the name of Chuck Connors."

"That name sounds familiar. I believe I read that he was the boyfriend of murder victim Heather Brown. Wasn't he cleared because his alibi was solid?"

"That's right," replied Rose. "He was the ex-boyfriend of Heather Brown. At the time, his alibi did check out. The victim's body was in the Cumberland River for a week or more. The time of death was estimated, leaving doubt about the exact date of her disappearance."

Jeff Stone was waving his hand frantically. The chief pointed at him and nodded.

"I'm Jeff Stone from the *Nashville Star Daily*. My question is for Detective McMahon. Based on what Detective Sergeant Goodwin said, if you had seen through the suspect's alibi sooner, four victims would still be alive—is that correct?"

Mike thought. *Stone is always trying to make Rose and me look bad, and he can't say anything positive—he's always looking to stir the pot!*

"What you're saying sounds simple, Jeff, but it isn't. Detective work is like trying to solve a jigsaw puzzle. Sometimes the pieces fit, and sometimes they don't. Things aren't always as cut and dried or black and white as we'd like. In our job, we turn over one stone at a time and move on. Sometimes we must go back and turn over a stone again because we may have missed some details. That's what happened in this case. We eventually figured it out, but sometimes it takes time. Unfortunately, other lives were lost. However, we saved the kidnap victim by figuring it out when we did, and God only knows how many more lives we might have saved by catching the suspect before he killed again."

As Mike finished, the room erupted into cheers and clapping. Red-faced, Jeff Stone took his seat, mumbling to himself.

The next reporter, Drake Davidson, asked, "Who was the kidnap victim, Detective McMahon?"

"Sorry, Drake, I prefer not to disclose that information. I'm sure you understand the victim is going through a stressful time, and identifying that individual in the media would cause more stress and anxiety."

The next reporter, Paul Parker from Fox news, asked, "Was the kidnap victim a member of NSGI?"

"Yes, the kidnap victim was a member of NSGI," Mike replied without further elaboration.

Jeff Stone interrupted and asked, "Detective Sergeant Goodwin, I understand that the suspect is wounded and in the hospital. Is that correct?"

"Yes, that's correct. To save the kidnapped victim's life, I shot the suspect in the shoulder before he could strangle the victim. It was a superficial wound, and he's resting comfortably at a Nashville hospital under police guard."

After Rose and Mike answered several more questions, the chief ended the news conference.

Just as the chief had finished speaking, all four MNPD cell phones began to vibrate. Viewing the text message on their screens, they couldn't believe what they read.

"Oh, my God," the chief said, the blood draining from his face.

Lieutenant Foster's jaw dropped, his face turned a bright shade of pink, and he looked like he was about to have a heart attack. His mouth stayed open, but nothing came out.

Rose and Mike both felt their stress level shooting back into the stratosphere as they read:

SUSPECT ESCAPED! WHEREABOUTS UNKNOWN!

The chief went over to the mayor and whispered into his ear. Mayor Hardy, shock registering on his handsome face, was speechless. Without another word, Chief Cummings waved at the others to follow, and they all made a hasty exit.

Seeing the police officials leaving in a hurry, Jeff Stone rushed to the mayor and asked, "Why did all the MNPD people leave, Mr. Mayor? I thought they would stay and mingle with the media."

"They would have, Jeff, but an emergency arose, and they got called away."

"What kind of an emergency?"

"I don't know," the mayor lied. "If you'll excuse me, I've got to go to the men's room." He turned and rushed off, his stomach in knots.

Stone stood frozen, looking bewildered, his reporter instincts on high alert, sensing something fishy was going on.

CHAPTER 34

C huck pretended to be asleep. When the nurse left the room, it took less than thirty seconds to pick the lock on the hand-cuff, using a paperclip he had found on the bedside table. Chuck ripped the IV attachment from his arm and jumped out of bed. Finding his clothes in the closet, he removed the sling from his right arm. Dressing slowly, Chuck tried to ignore the jabbing pain in his wounded shoulder. He put the sling back on, silently creeping toward the door. Holding a metal bedpan in his left hand, he struck the guard with a vicious blow on his head. The young officer slipped to the floor like a wet noodle—out cold. Chuck bent down, pulled out the officer's pistol, and made a mad dash toward the stairway exit sign. When he reached the ground floor, he sprinted through the front entrance. Spotting an idling taxi, he yanked open the driver's door, and with his good hand, he grabbed the unsuspecting cabbie and flung him to the pavement, kicking him hard in the stomach. Chuck slid behind the wheel, managed to put the car into gear, and took off like a bat out of hell, leaving black tire marks on the pavement and smoke rising into the air. As he drove, he noticed a cell phone lying on the passenger seat, like a gift under a Christmas tree. Without warning, a severe pain stabbed at his brain. He closed his eyes briefly, and when he reopened them, he became Charlie again.

* * *

After leaving the news conference, Rose and Mike returned to the squad room. They were trying to come to grips with the disturbing news. Charlie Cook/Chuck Connors sped away in a Music City Taxi taxicab. The taxi driver provided the plate number, and a BOLO went out to all MNPD and state trooper units with a description of the suspect.

"If you were him, where would you go?" Rose asked.

"That's a good question," replied Mike. "With his warped mind, who knows?"

"I'm sure he wouldn't be stupid enough to return to his apartment."

"He's probably ditched the taxi by now and hijacked another vehicle, or he may be lying low and hiding out somewhere," Mike said.

"Do you think he'd try to contact any of his friends?" Rose asked.

"He probably knows his friends as Charlie, and Chuck may not know or remember Charlie's friends. To be safe, I'll contact the three names Charlie gave us the day we interviewed him and ask them to let us know if he tries to contact them."

"That's a good idea."

After twenty minutes, Mike talked with all three of Charlie's friends and updated them on the situation. Each of Cook's friends agreed to call if he contacted them.

A minute later, Lieutenant Foster came rushing out of his office. He was red-faced and out of breath. "A patrol car just radioed in, and the two officers reported they found the taxicab abandoned in the Opry Mills parking lot near the Bass Pro Shop. He may still be in the area, so I've dispatched several units to help with the search. Detective McMahon, you'd better get your ass over there and help coordinate the search effort."

"I'm on it, sir," Mike said. He grabbed his coat and headed for the door.

With the siren shrieking, Mike pulled off the Briley Parkway onto the Opryland Mall entrance road twenty minutes later. He spotted several cruisers with their lights flashing near the Bass Pro Shop. Stopping next to a cruiser, he jumped out and hurried to the abandoned taxi. Flashing his badge at the two officers beside the car, Mike asked, "Are you the officers who found the vehicle?"

"Yes," the older of the two said. "We were on a routine patrol of the mall lot when we spotted the car sitting with no one in it. We checked the plate, and it matched the number on the BOLO, so we called it in."

"Did you happen to see anyone matching the suspect's description?" Mike asked.

"No. The suspect must have been long gone by the time we got here," the same officer said.

Mike said, "We'd better search the area, including the mall. The suspect could be on foot and still in the vicinity."

Mike was just about to gather the other officers to hand out assignments when a gray-haired woman in her late fifties came hurrying toward them. She was short, overweight, and out of breath and began speaking a mile a minute.

"I see you've been checking this taxi. Looking for the driver, are you?"

"Yes, we are. And your name is?" Mike asked.

"I'm Gloria Brookes, and I work at the Bass Pro Shop in the clothing section."

"Did you happen to see the driver?" Mike asked.

"About forty minutes ago, I came out to have a smoke, and I saw a small car pull up next to this taxi. A skinny young girl with short blonde hair tapped on the driver's window. The driver looked to be sleeping. He woke up, and seeing the young girl, he opened the door, got out, and hugged her. He was a large man, and his right arm was in a sling. Like a drunk, he staggered to her car and entered on the passenger side. Because of his size, he appeared to have difficulty adjusting to the cramped little car. The girl hopped in, and the car took off like a scared rabbit."

"Do you remember what color and type of car it was?" Mike asked.

"I sure do," she said. "It was a red and black Mini car—red body, black roof. It looked like the car used in the Paris chase scene of a Jason Bourne movie. I think it was *The Bourne Identity*—I'm a big Matt Damon fan."

"The car was probably a Mini Cooper. By any chance, did you get the plate number?"

"Yes and no, it happened so fast. I do remember part of it, though. It was one of those personal plates. I think the first word was SONG. Sorry, but I can't remember the rest. As I said, it all happened so fast."

Mike asked, "Do you remember if they were Tennessee plates?"

"Yeah, they were Tennessee plates."

All this time, Mike had been scribbling furiously in his notebook. Before letting the witness go, he asked for her contact information and jotted it down.

Handing her his card, Mike said, "If you think of anything that might help our investigation call me anytime on my cell number. Thank you, Gloria. I appreciate your help,"

Mike called dispatch, identified himself, and said, "This is an update on the escaped suspect in the 'Guitar String Strangler' case. He has abandoned the taxi. Repeat he has abandoned the taxi. Change the BOLO to look for a Mini Cooper with a red body and a black roof. The driver is a woman with short blonde hair; her passenger is the suspect we're looking for." Mike gave Charlie Cook's description, along with the partial plate information the witness had provided. Before signing off, he asked the dispatcher to have a police helicopter join the search.

When he finished the call to dispatch, Mike told all the officers to head out. He sent them in different directions to cover as much ground as possible. No one seemed to know which way the suspect car had gone. The logical conclusion—she had taken the Briley Parkway.

After all the cruisers had left, Mike sat behind the wheel thinking. *Chuck or Charlie has a female accomplice; we'll know her name if we get a hit on the license plate.*

CHAPTER 35

J ust as Mike was about to leave and join in on the search, a call came in from dispatch. The dispatcher said the personal plate read SONGGAL, and the registered owner was Rita Clair Thompson. The car was a red 2014 Mini Cooper with a black roof. The dispatcher gave an address in Hermitage, and McMahon jotted it down.

Holy shit, Mike thought, all excited. *Who would have guessed? I can't figure out the connection between Rita Thompson and Charlie Cook. There's something funny about this whole mess.*

With the siren screaming, Mike squealed out of the Opry Mills parking lot. When he reached the Briley Parkway, he radioed dispatch. He asked to have the other patrol cars rerouted to the address in Hermitage and to use flashing lights only—no sirens. They were to park on the street a block from the house to await further instructions.

Mike cut the siren when he was a few miles away. When he pulled onto the street, two cruisers had beaten him there. They were waiting, as instructed, on the road a block from the address. Mike waved for the police cars to follow. He parked a few houses away, opened the trunk, and put on his Kevlar vest. Drawing his Glock, he cautiously approached the house with several officers following, guns ready. The officer directly behind him carried a battering ram.

The tiny, well-maintained, gray-sided bungalow on Dockside Drive looked like a dollhouse. A bow window with black shutters overlooked the manicured front lawn and cement driveway that contained a newer blue Dodge Ram pickup truck. There was no sign of the Mini Cooper.

"They're not here. Maybe they spotted the line of police cars headed into Hermitage, figured we were on to them, and took a detour," Mike said.

"It looks that way," said the officer with the battering ram.

"Let's check it out anyway," Mike said.

He told the officers to wait in the driveway while approaching the front door. Standing on the small front porch, McMahon rang the bell and yelled, "MNPD. Open up!"

A few seconds later, he heard a man shout, "Just a minute; I'm coming."

Mike held his pistol with both hands pointed straight ahead. A deadbolt turned, and a chain rattled. The door opened, and a short, slender, gray-haired man in his late sixties stood there with a cane, a confused look on his wrinkled face. Since the man posed no threat, Mike holstered his pistol, introduced himself, and showed his badge.

"What's going on?" the man asked. His confusion turned to fear when he saw several police officers standing in his driveway.

"Are you Mr. Thompson?" Mike asked.

"No, I'm Bill Simpson.

"Is this where Rita Thompson lives?"

"Yes. Rita rents a room from me, but she's not here. Why do you want Rita? Is she in trouble?"

Mike ignored his questions. "When did you last see her?"

"She left a few hours ago. Rita received a phone call and took off. I haven't seen or heard from her since."

"Did she say who called and where she was going?" Mike asked.

"Of course not, and I didn't ask. It's none of my business. As I said, Rita rents a room and comes and goes as she pleases."

"Do you think the caller was a male or female?"

"I don't know, and I don't care. As I said, it's none of my business."

"Do you know where Rita works?" Mike asked.

"She spends most of her time at the NSGI office at the reception desk, and every second weekend Rita works as a hostess in the restaurant at the Embassy Suites Hotel."

"Mr. Simpson, do you mind if I come in and look at Rita's room?"

"Don't you need a search warrant or something to do that?"

"As the property owner, I don't, not if you give your permission. I won't be searching, and I only want to look at her room," Mike said.

"Okay, but don't disturb anything. I don't want to upset Rita, thinking I was snooping in her things."

When Mike entered Rita's bedroom, he glanced around. A framed picture on top of a white four-drawer dresser caught his eye. Rita's arm was around the waist of a large man that towered over her. The man in the photo was Charlie Cook.

Turning toward Bill Simpson, Mike pointed at the picture and asked, "Do you know the man in this picture?"

"Why yes. That's Rita's half-brother, Charlie Cook."

"Do you mind if I borrow the picture?" Mike asked.

"I don't know, Detective. I might get into trouble with Rita."

"Let me worry about Rita, and I'll make sure she gets it back soon," Mike assured him.

"Okay, I guess you can take it if you promise to return it."

"Thanks, Mr. Simpson. I appreciate your cooperation."

Mike picked up the picture, said goodbye, and left.

Bill Simpson stood staring out the living room window, watching the police officers leave. He scratched his head, confused, wondering what was going on.

Before he drove off, Mike checked in with dispatch, but they had nothing to report. It was as if the Mini Cooper had vanished into thin air.

CHAPTER 36

Rita was surprised when she received a call from Charlie. After he explained where he was and what had happened, he pleaded for her to come and get him. Driving as fast as she could without attracting attention, Rita pulled into the Opry Mills Mall parking lot a half-hour later. Charlie was in the taxi, fast asleep. She tapped on the window, and his head snapped to attention. When he saw Rita, Charlie smiled, opened the door, and got out. He gave her a relieved hug and then squeezed his massive frame into the passenger side of the small car. Charlie moved the seat back until it stopped, but he still felt cramped. Rita started the car, and the small vehicle sped off, headed for the Briley Parkway.

"Charlie, what mess have you gotten yourself into now?" Rita asked.

"The cops seem to think I'm the 'Guitar String Strangler.'"

"What? Are you?" Rita screamed, shock registering on her face.

"No way, sis, they must have me confused with someone else. You know me, I wouldn't hurt a fly."

"I'd like to believe you, Charlie, but there must be a reason they're after you. Are you still having those blackouts you told me about?"

"Yeah, I think so. The last thing I remember, an ambulance took me to the hospital with a gunshot wound. Next thing I know, I'm in a taxi where you picked me up."

"Maybe you should see a doctor and try to get some help. If you're not careful, those blackouts could get you killed."

"Where should we go?" Charlie asked.

"I don't think we should return to your place. I'm positive the cops will be watching it. My place is out because it's too small, and Mr. Simpson is there, and he may get suspicious."

"Let's find a motel where we can hide until we figure out what to do next," Charlie suggested.

"Okay. I know just the place, but we've got to make a quick stop'"

Rita pulled into a strip mall and ran into a costume shop. A few minutes later, she came out with a bag containing two wigs—a black one for herself and a blond wig for Charlie. Next, Rita went into a variety store and returned with shaving cream, a package of disposable razor blades, and scissors. While inside, she used the bank machine and withdrew four hundred dollars from her savings account.

"It might be best if we try to disguise ourselves. When we get to the motel, I'll put on my wig before registering. You stay in the car, and I'll sneak you into the room when the coast is clear. You'll have to shave off your goatee and get rid of your ponytail. If you're going to wear the blond wig, it won't look good if any of your black hair is showing."

"Okay," Charlie agreed.

Arriving at the motel, Rita parked outside the front office. She casually walked into the reception area and booked a room, paying up-front with cash for three nights. When the coast was clear, she hurried Charlie into room 112. Once he was safely inside, Rita moved the car to the back of the motel, hiding it on the far side of a large dumpster. Returning to the room, she heard Charlie singing happily in the bathroom.

* * *

Back in the squad room, Mike made copies of the picture. An email with the photo attached went out to every TV station within a two-hundred-mile radius. The message stated that the two suspects were wanted for questioning in the "Guitar String Strangler" case. It warned that the suspects were considered armed and dangerous and advised anyone spotting them not to approach them but to call the MNPD immediately at the local or toll-free number included in the email.

After all the newscasts, early and late editions had shown the picture and given information about the two suspects, nothing happened. No calls came in, not even a crank call.

CHAPTER 37

At 4:15 p.m., Mike picked up Suzanne and headed to Murfreesboro Road for their five o'clock appointment with two investigators from OPA. Upon their arrival, a cheerful receptionist ushered them into an interview room. They sat on uncomfortable folding metal chairs across the table from two middle-aged investigators. The men introduced themselves as Sergeant Tim Thomas and Lieutenant Steve Baron. They explained the procedure, and Suzanne and Mike signed a form giving their approval to record the interview. As the recording began, Brookes stated the date, time, location, and names of all parties present and the reason for the interview. During the questions and answers, Mike emphasized that Detective Sergeant Goodwin had no choice but to shoot the suspect to save Suzanne Taylor's life. When asked, Suzanne's story matched Mike's version of what had happened. The interview took just under one hour to complete.

As Mike and Suzanne left the room, they saw Rose walking toward them, looking pale and tense,

As she approached, Rose asked, "How did it go?"

"It went well," Mike said. "Don't worry. You'll be back on the job in no time, partner."

"You'll do fine, Rose," Suzanne said. "Good luck!"

* * *

Mike arrived in the squad room the following day feeling tired and stressed. He had tossed and turned all night, thinking about Cook's escape, and was sure he wouldn`t enjoy reading this morning's *Nashville Star Daily*. Mike knew Jeff Stone would be out to crucify him and Rose even though they weren't responsible for Cook's escape. Or were they? He couldn't help but think that if they had placed another guard in his room, Charlie would still be in custody.

Rose interrupted his thoughts when she approached his desk and said, "Good morning. I hope you slept a whole lot better than I did?"

"I don't think I got more than an hour or two. I kept playing everything over in my mind, wondering if we had done things differently, Cook wouldn't have escaped. I keep second-guessing the decision to place only one guard outside his room instead of placing another guard inside his room. If we had done that, I don't think he would've escaped."

"Blaming ourselves won't change things. That's water under the bridge. We've got to catch Cook before something bad happens. Maybe I should say you'd better catch him because I'm still on admin duty."

"Yeah, you're right—I'd better get my ass in gear and figure out where Cook could be hiding. Easier said than done," Mike said, his forehead wrinkling into a worried frown.

"Maybe I can help you brainstorm and come up with some possibilities. No one has to know."

"Good idea. I can use all the help I can get. By the way, how did your interview go?"

"I think it went well. It was hard to read those two cold faces. This admin duty drives me bonkers, and I can't wait to get back on the job and collar that maniac."

Just then, Lieutenant Foster appeared wearing a wide grin on his face. "I just received a call from Chief Cummings. He's been pushing OPA to get a ruling on the shooting. Usually, it takes two or three days, sometimes longer, to decide. I'm happy they've ruled in your favor and cleared you, Sergeant Goodwin. You're back on active duty. I've never seen a ruling come through so fast. The chief must have twisted a few arms on your behalf. He sends his congratulations."

Rose couldn't believe what she had just heard! She screamed, jumped up and down, hugged Lieutenant Foster, and said, "That's great news, Lieutenant!"

Foster hadn't expected such a jubilant reaction. His face turned pink, and when Rose released him, trying to sound gruff, he said, "Don't thank me, thank, Chief Cummings. Now get the hell out of here and go find that psycho." He turned, started to whistle, and headed for the sanctum of his office.

Mike gave Rose a hug and a peck on the cheek. "Congratulations! It's good to have you back."

"I can't believe it! Oh, what a beautiful morning," Rose said, beaming from ear to ear.

"Getting back to the case," Mike said, "we haven't heard anything from the surveillance we placed at Charlie's and Rita Thompson's addresses. I'm sure they figured we'd be watching their places."

"I'm guessing they're in a cheap motel in the Nashville area. We can rule out expensive hotels because I don't think they can afford them. I bet they've stayed off the interstates, knowing that the state police would also be searching for them," Rose said.

"That sounds logical. Let's talk with Lieutenant Foster and see if he can find a few units to start searching motel and small hotel parking lots for Rita's vehicle," Mike suggested.

After a brief meeting with Lieutenant Foster, he agreed with their plan. A few hours later, after assigning search grids, several patrol cars began searching for the suspects. Before leaving for their designated area, Mike opened the morning paper and wasn't surprised to see the headline. He groaned as he began to read:

"GUITAR STRING STRANGLER" SUSPECT ESCAPES!

By Jeff Stone, Investigative Reporter

I attended a news conference yesterday morning. The meeting in the city council chambers announced the capture of the suspect called the "Guitar String Strangler."

You could almost hear everyone breathe a collective sigh of relief. That relief, however, was short-lived. At the end of the news conference, the MNPD officials received a message that the killer had escaped. They rushed from the building without telling anyone what had happened. Why did they not inform the media of his escape?

My source informed me that the suspect sustained a non-life-threatening right shoulder bullet wound during his capture. An ambulance rushed him to Nashville General Hospital for treatment. The following day, while alone in his room, the suspect picked the lock on the handcuff that attached his wrist to the bed railing using a paper clip. He found his clothing, dressed, and used a metal bedpan to knock out the police officer stationed outside his room. Grabbing the officer's pistol, the suspect dashed down three flights of stairs and out the front entrance. The suspect spotted an idling taxicab in the parking lot and threw the unsuspecting driver onto the pavement. He jumped into the vehicle and sped off.

A short time later, the abandoned Music City Taxi taxicab was in the Opry Mills Mall parking lot near the Bass Pro Shop. An eyewitness, Ms. Gloria Brookes, said she saw the suspect take off in a Cooper Mini with a red body and black roof, driven by a young female. At press time, the police dragnet has failed to find the suspect and his accomplice.

Why did the MNPD assign only one officer to guard the suspect? Would he have escaped if they had posted a second guard inside the room?

We now have a suspected serial killer on the loose. There is no doubt in my mind he will kill again if not apprehended soon. Are you looking over your shoulder? You should be if you are part of the Nashville music scene!

"Read this, Rose. Jeff Stone is on our case again. That relentless bastard doesn't want to quit. He didn't say it, but I know he's blaming us for Charlie's escape. I'm still baffled how he gets his information so fast."

As Rose read the article, her blood pressure began to rise, and her face felt like it was on fire.

"You're right about Stone. He is relentless," Rose said, feeling the heat once more.

"I know our superiors and the mayor won't be pleased when they read the paper. Poor Lieutenant Foster, he may consider retirement before this case is over," Mike said with a half-hearted laugh.

Rose said. "We'd better get out of here before he reads Stone's article."

Slipping into their coats, they made a beeline for the door just as Lieutenant Foster picked up the *Nashville Star Daily*.

After Mike and Rose checked several smaller hotels in their assigned area without any luck, they decided to stop for a coffee.

They sat silently, each deep in thought, sipping their steaming coffee. Finally, Mike looked at Rose and said, "I could kick my ass for not putting another guard in Cook's room. If I had thought to do that, we wouldn't be out here spinning our wheels trying to find a needle in a fucking haystack."

"I should've thought of it too. There's no sense crying in our beer."

"Speaking of beer, I could use a drink right about now. Maybe a few beers might help ease this gut-wrenching feeling in my stomach," Mike said.

Rose laughed and said, "I feel the same way. My stomach has been churning all morning."

They finished their coffee and walked back to the car. Mike checked with dispatch, and none of the patrol cars had spotted the Cooper Mini.

Their next stop was the Drake Motel. The sign at the front entrance read: "Stay Where the Stars Stay." The parking lot contained several beat-up cars and a rusty black GMC pickup truck. It didn't look like any stars were there now, and there was no Cooper Mini.

"Where the hell are they?" Mike asked, clearly frustrated.

"Maybe they didn't go to a motel," Rose said. "What if they went to a friend's place instead? If they did, it might take a long time before we find them—especially if the friend has a garage where they can hide Rita's car."

"Any friend would be taking a huge risk hiding them, knowing they would be harboring fugitives. The only way that might happen would be if they forced their way in using the gun Cook stole from our police officer," Mike said.

"I guess that's possible, but I still think they're in a motel."

"We've got to keep looking and pray we catch a break," Mike said without much conviction.

* * *

Although small, the efficiency unit at the Break-Away Inn contained everything necessary to prepare meals–dishes, pots, pans, cutlery, microwave, bar refrigerator, and a stainless-steel sink. The room had two double beds, two threadbare brown upholstered wing-back chairs, and a white wooden table with two matching chairs. A large-screen TV hung on the wall across from the beds. The bathroom had a decent-sized shower and smelled of fresh paint, and it appeared to have undergone a recent renovation.

Their first night was uneventful. Charlie watched a few crime shows on TV while Rita read a Harlequin Romance novel. Before the eleven o'clock news came on, they were both sound asleep.

They slept in the following day until 10:00 a.m. After showering, Rita purchased coffee and four Egg McMuffins for breakfast at a nearby McDonald's. When the maid knocked on the door, Rita said she didn't need the room cleaned and sent her away.

At two o'clock, Charlie said he was starving. Rita left the room again. For lunch, she returned with submarine sandwiches and two chocolate milkshakes.

At five-forty-five, Rita walked to a nearby Domino's and picked up a large meat lover's pizza and two Cokes. While she was gone, Charlie sat watching TV. When the six o'clock news came on, he was shocked to see his and Rita's picture on the screen.

The female announcer said, "The Metropolitan Nashville Police Department has issued a state-wide alert for the couple shown in this picture. The man is a suspect in five recent murders here in Nashville. The police suspect he is the serial killer labeled the 'Guitar String Strangler.' His name is Charlie Cook, but he also calls himself Chuck Connors. His female accomplice is Ms. Rita Clair Thompson, a half-sister to the suspected killer. The female suspect was driving a red Cooper Mini with a black roof and a personal Tennessee license plate that reads SONGGAL. The suspects were last seen fleeing from the Opry Mills Mall parking lot and are still at large. They are armed and considered to be dangerous. If you should spot the suspects, do not attempt to confront them. I repeat, do not attempt to confront them. Please get in touch with the MNPD immediately ." The MNPD local phone number and the toll-free number flashed on the screen. "In other news...."

Charlie turned the TV off. He couldn't believe what was happening. He said to the TV and empty room, "I didn't kill anyone— this is all a big mistake. And I don't call myself Chuck Connors." Feeling exhausted, Charlie lay down on the bed, and a few minutes later, he was snoring like a freight train.

When Rita returned with the pizza and drinks, she found Charlie asleep. Not wanting the pizza to get cold, she gently shook him and said, "Charlie, wake up. It's time to eat."

Slowly he opened his eyes, looking disorientated and still half-asleep. In a few seconds, when his head cleared, he stared at Rita for

W . D .   F R O L I C K

a long moment. Without warning, he shouted, "Who the hell are you, and where am I?"

Stunned by his hostile reaction, she said soothingly, "It's me, Charlie, your half-sister, Rita."

"Charlie? Who the hell's Charlie? My name is Chuck," he yelled.

CHAPTER 38

J ust before six, Mike dialed Suzanne. When she answered, he said, "Hi, babe. I want to let you know that Rose and I will be working late. We're still searching motels, trying to find the escape car, and we still have several motels to go in our search grid. Don't worry about dinner. I'll grab a bite on the fly—and don't forget to keep the door locked and don't answer it for anyone. I'll be home as soon as I can."

"I'm scared, Mike. I won't feel safe until you're home."

"Don't worry. Everything will be fine. Love you!"

"Love you, too. Goodbye."

Rose called Paul and gave him the same news. She had just hung up as Mike stopped the car in front of the Break-Away Inn. They got out and walked into the front office reception area. An attractive young dark-haired woman of East Indian origin sat behind the counter.

Rose said, "Good evening. I'm Detective Sergeant Goodwin of the MNPD, and this is my partner Detective McMahon."

The two detectives presented their badges.

"We're looking for the two people in this photo. Would you happen to know if they're staying here?"

She glanced at the picture and said, "As far as I know, they're not staying here."

"Are you positive?" Rose asked.

"Yes, Detective, I'm sure."

"Okay," Rose said. "Thanks for your time."

W . D .   F R O L I C K

When they were outside, Mike said, "There's no Mini Cooper out front. Let's check behind the motel."

Walking around the corner to the side street, they had a complete view of the parking lot but did not see anything that resembled Rita's car.

Spotting the dumpster, Rose said, "Let's check behind that dumpster."

When they got there, the parking space was vacant.

"Shit," Mike grumbled. "I thought we might get lucky and find it."

"Yeah," Rose agreed, "that seemed like an ideal spot to hide a small car. Looks like another brick wall."

"What else is new?"

After leaving the Break-Away Inn, they checked the last few motels on their list without success and decided to call it a night.

At 9:20 p.m., when Suzanne heard Mike walk through the door, she jumped off the sofa and ran to greet him.

Wrapping his arms around her, Mike said, "How's my favorite girl?" He gave her a tender kiss, and she responded in kind.

"I'm great," she said. "The album's coming along fine, and we've tracked and recorded vocals for five songs already."

"That's good news. You seem pleased. Are you happy you chose Frozen North over Southern Heat?"

"I'm ecstatic, and I've never been happier. The Frozen North gang is great to work with, and the sound producer Mark Bush and engineer Jesse Potter are getting out of that state-of-the-art studio is blowing me away."

"I can't wait to hear it. When you become a big superstar, will you still have time for a beat-up homicide detective like me?"

"You bet your sweet ass I will. I might even take you on tour as my bodyguard."

Mike chuckled. "Yeah, I think I'd like that. You've got one hell of a body to guard."

Suzanne giggled, grabbed his hand, and led him into the bedroom. They had a refreshing shower together and spent the next hour massaging and pampering one another before making love.

Stress-free, they slept soundly, with Oliver curled up and purring at their feet.

* * *

When Rose arrived home, she felt tired and stressed out. Jill was already in bed, fast asleep. She went into her daughter's bedroom, pulled up Jill's covers, kissed her lovingly on the forehead, then went to look for Paul. She found him in his home office reading legal documents.

"Hi," she said. "Sorry, I'm so late and missed putting Jill to bed. How was your day?"

At first, Rose thought that Paul had not heard her. Finally, he looked up without smiling and said, "I'm getting tired of feeling like I'm the only parent in this house. I don't think our marriage is working. I've drawn up divorce papers, and here's a copy for you to read," he said handing them to Rose.

For a long moment, she stood there in silence. It felt like a knife had just penetrated her heart. *Wow,* she thought, I *didn't expect this!* As Rose took the papers, her eyes began to fill with tears. Turning abruptly, she ran down the hallway to the bathroom. After locking the door, she stood staring at herself in the mirror. Suddenly, the dam burst and tears flowed down her cheeks.

Rapping gently on the bathroom door, Paul said, "I've packed a bag and will stay in a hotel tonight. I'll come by in the morning around eight and spend the day with Jill. Even though tomorrow is Sunday, I presume you'll be trying to find your escaped killer. We can talk tomorrow evening and plan a schedule for looking after Jill. If you need me, call my cell."

Rose composed herself a little, and with a strained, shaky voice, she said, "Yes, I've got to work tomorrow. Thanks for looking after Jill. I appreciate it. Okay, let's talk tomorrow evening. "We can talk and work something out when I get home."

"Sorry, it has to be like this," Paul said. "I know my timing sucks. You'll find I'm more than fair when you read the papers. You might want a lawyer to read them as well. See you tomorrow evening."

W . D .   F R O L I C K

"Okay. Goodbye."

Paul's footsteps faded in the hallway. The front door opened and closed, and she heard his key locking the door behind him—then silence.

Rose unlocked the door and went straight to the liquor cabinet in the family room. She poured herself a stiff drink of Scotch and tossed it back in one gulp. After refiling her glass, She sat on the sofa, and tears began to flow again. Rose felt as if her world was coming apart at the seams.

CHAPTER 39

S unday morning, waiting for Rose to arrive, Mike kept busy with paperwork, and he took a few minutes to read the *Nashville Star Daily* sports section.

Rose was unusually late. When she walked into the squad room, it was almost nine-thirty. She plunked herself down at her desk and stared into space.

"Why the long face? You look like you've just lost your best friend," Mike said.

Rose didn't appear to have heard a single word he had said. She shook her head slightly and said, "What did you say?"

"I said why the long face?"

"Paul wants a divorce. He dropped the bombshell on me last night."

"Oh, no," Mike said, stunned. "I thought things were heading in the right direction. You were going to counseling, and it seemed to be working. What happened?"

"I don't have a clue. I thought things were improving. Then, Paul hits me between the eyes without warning. It shocked the hell out of me. I know I've been keeping long hours with the case, but I didn't think things were that bad."

Smelling liquor on her breath, Mike asked, "Are you okay? Maybe you should take some time off until you can get your head around it."

"No. It's better if I keep myself busy with work. Taking time off will give me more time to brood, and that's not good. Working will help to keep me sane."

"You smell like a brewery. How many have you had?"

"I've had a few—maybe a few too many. Do I look that bad?"

"I hate to say this, but you look like shit! Will you be able to function?"

"I'll be okay. Working will take my mind off things. I'd rather not talk about it."

"Let's get out of here. You could use a gallon of black coffee to sober you up."

"Where do you want to go?"

"We can plan our next move at Starbucks."

Just as they were about to leave, Mike received a call from the dispatcher. He said, "We just received a message from the Break-Away Inn reporting that a cleaning lady found a young woman named Rita Thompson tied up and gagged in her room. The male suspect is in the wind."

"Okay, thanks. We're on our way," Mike said.

He informed Rose of the situation. They grabbed their coats and sprinted for the door.

McMahon turned off the siren and stopped the car in front of the Break-Away Inn. As they walked into the reception area, Rita Thompson sat in a wingback chair, looking pale and frightened.

"Hi, Rita, are you okay? Do you remember me? I'm Detective Sergeant Goodwin."

Without acknowledging Rose, Rita began to speak rapidly. "When Charlie woke up, he wasn't Charlie anymore. He seemed to turn into another person and didn't even know me. He's been having blackouts. When I called him Charlie, he went berserk and said his name was Chuck. He must have knocked me out with something heavy like a lamp. When I woke up, I had a splitting headache, and he tied my hands and feet and gagged me with a ripped-up bedsheet. When the maid came to clean the room, she must have heard my muffled screams. She went to the office and got the manager. They came back and freed me."

"Wow," Mike said, "you're lucky he didn't kill you. Did he take your car?"

"I'm sure he did. I left my keys on the nightstand next to my bed, and when I checked, they were gone."

"Where was your car parked?" Rose asked.

"I parked it behind the motel on the other side of a large dumpster."

"That must have been the empty spot we saw," Mike said.

"I'll go to the car and radio dispatch to put another BOLO on the Mini Cooper. He could be anywhere by now," Rose said.

Mike said, "Rita Clair Thompson, I'm arresting you for accessory after the fact. After stating the Miranda rights, he asked, "Do you understand these rights?"

Rita nodded and said, "Yes, I think so."

"Please stand," Mike said.

Rita stood, and Mike handcuffed her hands behind her back and led her through the doorway to the car. He placed a hand on her head, guided her onto the back seat, closed the door, and said to Rose, "Before we put her in a holding cell, I think we'd better stop at a hospital. Rita might have a concussion."

"Okay. Sounds like a good idea," Rose agreed.

After doing a few tests, the emergency room doctor at Nashville General said that Rita had sustained a mild concussion but would be on the mend after a few days of rest. To help with her headache, the doctor provided some extra-strength headache tablets and said Rita was good to go.

Once Rita had been processed and jailed, Mike decided to check and find out if the BOLO had obtained any results. So far, the suspect was still in the wind.

An hour later, a guard brought Rita into the interview room where Rose and Mike were waiting. She still looked tired and disorientated.

"Rita, you have a choice to have an attorney present before questioning if you so desire," Mike said.

"I don't think I need a lawyer."

"Are you sure?" Rose asked.

"Yes."

"Since I've already read you your rights, if you don't object, we would like to record this interview, Mike said.

"Okay. I have no objections."

Mike started the recorder, stating the date and time. He named the parties in attendance and noted that the suspect, Rita Clair Thompson, had her rights read to her previously and agreed to the interview without the presence of an attorney.

"Rita," Rose said. "Do you know where you are?"

Rita paused, looked at Rose, then at Mike, and said, "Yes. I'm at the police station."

"Do you know why you're at the police station?" Mike asked.

"I think so. Is it because I helped my brother Charlie?" Rita asked.

"Yes, it is, Rita," Rose said. "Charlie is wanted for a crime, and you broke the law when you helped him escape. Consequently, by helping him, you harbored a fugitive. Under the Tennessee Criminal Code, you were an accessory after the fact. Do you understand what that charge means?"

"Oh," Rita said, sounding unsure. "I didn't know that I had done that. When he called, he said he needed me to pick him up. He told me the cops were after him but said he was innocent and needed time to think. I had to help him because Charlie's my half-brother?"

"Nevertheless," Mike said, "what you did is a Class E felony, for which you could face a jail sentence of up to six years and a fine."

Rita looked bewildered. "Gosh, that sounds serious. Maybe I should have a lawyer."

"Do you want a lawyer?" Mike asked.

"It might be a good idea," Rita said.

"Who would you like to call?" Rose asked.

"Gee, I don't know. I can't afford a lawyer. I don't have much money."

"If you can't afford an attorney, one will defend you without charge. Would you like us to arrange that?" Mike asked.

"Yes, please," Rita said.

CHAPTER 40

C ook was still on the loose Monday morning, and Rita was in a holding cell. She had a 10:00 a.m. appointment to meet with her attorney, Ms. Donna Dean, a public defender specializing in criminal law.

Jeff Stone wrote another scathing article regarding the performance of the MNPD. He said the detectives in charge dropped the ball, allowing the suspect to escape. Stone hadn't mentioned their names, but his accusation pissed off Mike and Rose. They were sure Lieutenant Foster would call them in for another ass-kicking if they didn't catch the killer before he struck again. If that happened, Mayor Hardy would be on the phone daily, screaming at Chief Cummings. Chief Cummings would be hollering at Lieutenant Foster, Lieutenant Foster would yell at Mike and Rose, and Jeff Stone would write another article criticizing the MNPD for their incompetence.

Mike's cell phone rang, and he answered without thinking to check the screen.

"Detective McMahon," he said.

"Hi, Detective, it's your buddy, Chuck."

It was his normal voice—no distortion.

"Chuck, where are you? Are you calling to turn yourself in?"

He laughed and said, "Not likely. I'm calling to tell you I'll be back in action soon."

"Don't do anything stupid, Chuck. You need help. Turn yourself in, and I promise we'll treat you fairly. You need a professional to help you with your condition."

"What condition? I don't need any help. All I need is someone to listen to my songs, someone who will appreciate my great writing. That's the trouble with the Nashville music industry; no one wants to listen. There are just too many songwriters. Maybe if I kill off a few more, there will be less competition, and I'll have a chance. I was thinking of starting my own publishing company. I've got two names, ' Killer Songs' and 'Treble Clef Music.' What do you think? Great names, huh? Which one do you like the best, Detective?" He laughed again.

Mike ignored his question about the publishing names and said, "I have a few connections with publishers and record companies. Maybe I can help. I'd like to hear your new song, 'Suzanne', and I'm sure I could get a publisher to listen to it. What do you say? Can I help you?"

"What you're saying sounds good, Detective, but you're trying to trick me. And why would I let someone else share the royalties when I can publish it myself?"

"I'm not trying to trick you," Mike lied. "I know I can help if you give me a chance."

"I'll think about it. Talk to you soon." The line went dead.

Rose had been listening to the conversation. When Mike hung up, trying to lighten the mood, she laughed and said, "It sounds like Chuck likes you, Mike. He keeps calling you, and I get the feeling he's lonely. He may even have a crush on you."

"I'd like him to have a crush from a hammer as I hit him on his fucking psycho head."

Rose laughed again and said, "Temper, temper, I know it's not funny, but between what's going on at home and this crazy case, I've got to do something to relieve the tension—a little warped cop humor can't hurt."

"It's time to get serious and back to business. Somehow, we'd better come up with Chuck's location and catch him fast before he kills someone else. If that happens, we're fucked with a capital 'F.' We can kiss our careers goodbye, and Jeff Stone will have a hay day writing about it," Mike said.

Just then, it hit him. "I didn't look at my screen when he called, and it's probably the same "Unknown Caller." As Mike checked his phone, he couldn't believe his eyes. "Holy shit," he bellowed. "It shows, Jason Briggs."

"What? You've got to be kidding me."

"Seriously, that's what it says."

"What's their connection? I didn't think they even knew each other," Rose said.

Mike rushed into Lieutenant Foster's office and filled him in on the call from Chuck.

"I'll assemble a SWAT team and have them join you at Briggs' address. Let's hope he's still there."

* * *

Chuck knew the cops would be looking for the vehicle he had taken from the motel belonging to that girl who said her name was Rita. They would also search for a large man with black hair and a goatee. Chuck noticed his goatee was gone, and he was wearing a blond wig. He wasn't sure who the girl named Rita was. She had said that she was his half-sister, and she had called him Charlie. Who was Charlie? A voice in his head told him not to kill her. For some reason, he had listened. Maybe he was getting soft—anyway, he was fresh out of guitar strings. Perhaps he should stop at a music store and buy a few packs. That thought made him smile. He laughed.

Once he had decided where to go, Chuck stayed away from the main arteries taking every side street toward his destination. When he was a few blocks away, he pulled the car into a large shopping mall and parked among the hundreds of vehicles. He looked around and didn't see anyone in the immediate vicinity. Chuck left the car and casually began walking toward a residential area. Ten minutes later, he knocked on the door of Apartment C.

"Who is it?" a male voice called out.

"It's me—your friend Chuck."

"Just a minute."

The door opened, and Jerry Briggs grabbed Chuck and pulled him inside, looking to see if anyone had followed him.

"Chuck, what the hell are you doin' here?" Jerry asked, giving him a bear hug.

"I need a place to crash for a while. Hope you don't mind, Jerry?"

Jason Briggs walked out of the kitchen and into the living room.

"Charlie, what's goin' on, man?" Jason asked.

"Who's Charlie? My name is Chuck. And who are you?"

Jerry gazed at Jason with a startled look on his face.

"Chuck," Jerry asked, "do you have a twin brother?"

"No, Jerry, are you crazy? I don't have a twin brother—but it looks like you do."

After moving in with Jason, Jerry grew a beard, shaved his head, and had a gold stud inserted into each earlobe. He looked exactly like Jason; an untrained eye couldn't tell them apart. Jerry looked at Jason and said, "I met Chuck at Tootsies, and when my truck wouldn't start, he gave me a lift home."

"Oh," Jason said, "for a minute, I thought he was Charlie Cook, a guy I met at NSGI."

"Well," Jerry said, "everyone has a double. I guess Chuck is Charlie Cook's double."

"Nice meetin' you, Chuck," Jason said, still bewildered. He shook Chuck's left hand since his right hand was in a sling.

"We were gonna smoke a little weed, Chuck. Would you like to join us?" Jerry asked.

"Nah, but I'll have a beer if you've got one."

"They're in the fridge in the kitchen," Jason said.

"Thanks," Chuck said. "Do you mind if I use your phone to make a quick call? I forgot to bring mine."

"No problem," Jason said. "It's on the wall near the stove."

Five minutes later, Chuck returned, sipping a beer, and asked, "What's with all the weapons on the kitchen table? He laughed and said, "If I didn't know better, I'd swear you're terrorists looking to start a war."

"Shit." Jerry frowned, glancing at Jason. "I thought you put them back in the bedroom closet."

"Sorry, I never got around to it," Jason said.

"I read about your escape in the paper, Chuck. You use guitar strings to kill people; we're gonna use guns," Jerry said.

"Who the hell are you going to kill?" Chuck asked.

Without warning, he felt a sharp pain inside his head. Chuck's eyes glazed over, and he staggered slightly. He appeared to black out for a split second. Before Jerry could jump up and steady him, he regained his balance. After opening his eyes and shaking his head, Chuck became Charlie.

Jerry continued. "We were online and liked what GLF is all about. It's a new organization, and it stands for Global Liberation Front. We decided to become radicalized," Jerry said with a laugh. The brothers sat on the couch, giggling, puffing away, and getting high.

"Yeah, we want to stir up a little shit," Jason said. "We're plannin' on gettin' even with NSGI for revokin' my membership. We'll head over to publisher night tomorrow and shoot up the place. I think those Canucks from Frozen North Music will be there, and we'll make them pay for not likin' our songs. Do you wanna join us, Chuck?"

Charlie thought. *I must be in Jason Briggs' apartment. Are my eyes playing tricks on me? I'm seeing' double—Jason Briggs times two!*

"Jason, did you say you were gonna shoot up NSGI tomorrow night?"

"Yeah, Chuck, why don't you come along? It'll be a real blast. Get it—a real blast! Pow, you're dead," Jason said, using his finger as a gun.

Chuck? Who the hell's Chuck?

"My half-sister Rita Thompson will be there. Are you gonna kill her too?"

"We're gonna kill every shithead in the place, even your half-sister. What the fuck's a half-sister anyway? Hey, Jerry, are you my half-brother?" Jason laughed, slapping Jerry on the back.

"No, Jason, I'm your whole brother." They both doubled over and laughed hysterically.

Inside, Charlie was beginning to boil. *These fuckers are pissin' me off, and nobody's gonna kill Rita.*

Realizing he was wearing a wig, Charlie yanked it off and tossed it, hitting Jason in the face. That's when he felt the hidden pistol under his shirt. Charlie reached behind his back, pulled the gun out, and yelled, "Bang, bang, you're dead." He fired two quick shots, and the Briggs brothers died instantly with their eyes wide open.

Rose had her ear on the door when the two gunshots rang out. A SWAT team member with a battering ram was poised and ready. Rose stepped aside and gave the signal—it took a fraction of a second—the door exploded inward, and everyone charged into the living room.

Without hesitating, Cook placed the gun to his temple and squeezed the trigger, spraying blood and brain matter from the hole in his head.

Jason Briggs and Jerry Briggs appeared to be unconscious on the couch. A closer look revealed both brothers were dead! Each man had a bullet hole in his chest. The air was heavy with gunpowder and the sweet smell of marijuana smoke.

"Shit," Mike yelled. "What a fucking mess!"

Three SWAT members went to check out the other rooms.

"Clear!"

"Clear!"

"Clear!"

"You won't believe what's on the kitchen table," one of the SWAT team members said when he returned.

Mike and Rose followed him back into the kitchen. Lying on the table were two Glock 17 semi-automatic pistols, two UZI Sub Machine guns, and several ammunition boxes.

"What the hell is this all about?" Rose asked, looking confused.

"I'd say whatever it is, they were up to no good," Mike replied.

"It looks to me like they were getting ready to start a war," Rose said.

"I don't get the connection between Charlie and the Briggs brothers. I know that Charlie knew Jason from NSGI; whether he knew Jerry is debatable. Maybe Charlie learned that Jason had been screwing his girlfriend, Heather Brown, and came over for revenge," Mike surmised.

"Could be," Rose replied, "but now we'll never know for sure."

"I wish I knew what the Briggs brothers had planned. Were they involved in some terrorist group or conspiracy? We may never know, but they were nutty enough to do something crazy just for kicks."

"That question will drive us crazy for a while. I hate loose ends, and those weapons are certainly loose ends," Rose said.

Mike glanced at the coffee table and said, "I wonder whether that laptop computer will have any answers. Why don't we take it back and have a computer specialist check it out?"

"Good idea. You never know what we might find," Rose said.

Three hours later, the ME and techs had finished processing the scene, and the bodies were on their way to the morgue. Rose picked up the computer, and they headed back to headquarters.

As Mike drove, Rose asked, "What's your opinion? Did Charlie suffer from DID, or do you think he was faking it?"

"God, that's a tough question. Now that he's dead, I doubt we'll ever find out. Even if they could study his brain to see if it showed any abnormalities, there's nothing left to check. I guess we'll never know. I'm leaning in the direction that he did have a split personality."

When they arrived at the precinct, Rose found Joey Sawyer, a young computer tech specialist. She told Sawyer what to look for, handed him the computer then joined Mike in Lieutenant Foster's office.

Mike told the story with all the gruesome details. Foster sat back in his chair and sighed. "The chief will be happy to hear the news and get the press and mayor off his back. Great job, you two! You both deserve much credit for all the hard work and long hours you put into this investigation. Maybe I`ll get a good sleep tonight. I hope my wife will like me again now that I won't be so grumpy." He laughed as he reached for his ulcer tablets and swallowed two down with a sip from a water bottle. For once, the vein on his forehead looked normal.

That night, Mike and Rose went home with the world's weight lifted from their shoulders. Mike went home to a warm embrace and a tender, loving kiss from Suzanne, while Rose went home to an empty shell of a house. Jill had been staying with Rose's sister, Marilyn, for the last few days because of her long work hours. She hoped that would all change for the better now that the serial killer case was over. Nothing had changed—Paul still wanted a divorce. Rose poured herself a double Scotch on the rocks, sat at the kitchen table, and cried.

CHAPTER 41

T he following morning, when Mike picked up the *Nashville Star Daily*, as he expected, there was another article by Jeff Stone.

GUITAR STRING MURDER SUSPECT KILLS TWO, THEN COMMITS SUICIDE

By Jeff Stone, Investigative Reporter

Yesterday, a raid by the MNPD SWAT team and homicide detectives Sergeant Rose Goodwin and Detective Mike McMahon found three male bodies in an apartment in a high-crime district of the city.

The victims, Mr. Jason Briggs and Mr. Gerald Briggs, identical twin brothers, both 25, were found dead in their apartment, along with the body of the suspected "Guitar String Strangler," Charlie Cook, 25, also known as Chuck Connors. It appears Mr. Cook murdered the brothers with the handgun he took from a police officer guarding him during his escape from the Nashville General Hospital a few days earlier. After killing the Briggs brothers, Cook turned the gun on himself and took his own life.

The police found several assault weapons on the premises but could not explain why they were there. Were Jason and Gerald Briggs part of a terrorist group or some radical organization?

Who knows? Answers will probably not be forth-coming since all parties are deceased.

In past articles, I have been highly critical of the MNPD—especially Detective Sergeant Rose Goodwin and Detective Mike McMahon. I want to take this opportunity to thank the MNPD—and extend a special thank you to the two lead detectives mentioned above. Good job, Detectives—we feel safe once more! Sleep well, Nashville!

After reading the article, Rose turned to Mike and said, "Maybe Jeff Stone isn't such a rotten egg after all."

Mike laughed and said, "I wouldn't hold my breath. The next time we screw up or take too long to solve a case, he'll be all over us like a cheap suit."

"Yeah, I guess we should enjoy it while we can," Rose said with a bright smile.

Mike thought. *God, it's good to see her smile again!*

Joey Sawyer entered the squad room, approached Mike and Rose, and said, "I checked the laptop and found the user had been on several terrorist websites, including ISIS. I printed this email message from a dude named Muhammad X welcoming Jerry and Jason Briggs to GLF." He handed Rose the computer and the printout to Mike.

"Thanks, Joey," Rose said as Sawyer turned to leave.

Mike began to read. *Welcome, my brothers, to GLF. We are proud that you have decided to join us in our fight for justice in a world of imperialist tyranny. Your first target, NSGI, is approved. We wish you good luck. May Allah be with you. Yours in liberty, Muhammad X.*

"Who the hell is GLF? And who is Muhammad X?" Rose asked.

"They're a new terrorist group formed here in the United States," Mike said. "I presume Muhammad X is the leader's name, but I doubt that's his real name."

"Shit, not another terrorist organization—as if there aren't enough of them in this crazy world already," Rose said, looking disgusted.

"Well," Mike said, "it's obvious the brothers became radicalized. Thank God Charlie blew them away before they could carry out their plan to kill innocent people at NSGI."

"Yeah," Rose smiled, "good old Charlie. It was Chuck who was the psycho."

Mike laughed and said, "We'll never know for sure, will we?"

Mike's desk phone rang. It was the DA's office. They informed him that Public Defense attorney Donna Dean had negotiated a plea bargain with the DA on Rita Thompson's felony charge for accessory after the fact. She pleaded guilty and was given three years of probation with no jail time. Instead of a fine, the judge imposed three hundred hours of community service. In making his decision, the judge considered that Rita Thompson had no prior criminal record.

Two weeks later, Suzanne's album hit the stores and the Internet. Her first single was released to all country radio stations worldwide. The song, "Don't Throw Our Love Away," sung as a duet with Marven Jones, quickly became a top ten billboard hit, and Marven and Suzanne began a nationwide tour of country radio stations to promote the single.

After taking a few days off, Mike and Rose were back on the job.

Several days after the "Guitar String Strangler" case was closed, Rose and Paul were officially divorced, and they agreed to share joint custody of their daughter, Jill.

Mike's dad had met an attractive widow on the golf course. They started dating, and his father seemed happy and enjoying retirement in sunny Florida.

Mike's sister, Joanne, a real estate lawyer, still lived in Dearborn and was happily married. She and her husband, Tom, were expecting their first child in a few months. Mike was excited and looking forward to becoming an uncle for the first time.

Frozen North offered Mike a job as Suzanne's bodyguard. Although tempting, he still enjoyed catching killers and bringing them to justice. He gave the offer serious consideration, but in the end, he politely declined, deciding to stay with the MNPD.

W. D. FROLICK

While Suzanne was on the road, Mike attended anger management sessions and began exercising at the gym again. He and Suzanne talked on the phone daily, and although they missed each other a lot, they both agreed that all the travel was necessary for her career. Good thing Mike had Oliver for company. He had purchased a gadget that looked like a flashlight that shone a small red dot that Oliver chased. Mike would laugh as Oliver ran like a dog chasing his tail in circles. It passed the time for Mike and tired Oliver out. Afterward, the cat would curl up with Mike on the couch while he watched TV. Within an hour, they would both be sound asleep.

Mike went to Bruno's Clothing Shoppe and purchased a sleek new navy-blue suit using the gift certificate Suzanne had given him for Valentine's Day. He thought, *Now I won't look like Columbo!*

Unknown to Suzanne, Mike had become a closet songwriter. He'd pull his Fender acoustic guitar from under the bed and write songs for hours. His latest two songs, written about Suzanne, were "While You're Away" and "Missing You."

The night before Suzanne was due to arrive home for a few days, his home phone rang as Mike was working on a new song. The screen showed Rose Goodwin.

"Hey, Rose. What's up?"

"Hi, Mike. We just got called to another crime scene."

"Shit! What happened?"

"A record company executive was leaving his office after working late tonight, and someone surprised him in the parking lot behind his building before he could get into his car. You'd better sit down because you won't believe this—another victim strangled with a guitar string."

"Holy shit, here we go again!" Mike said, exasperated. "Did we get the wrong guy, or do we have a copycat?"

Rose let out an amused laugh. "Gotcha—just kidding—sleep tight!"

He was about to reply, but Rose had already hung up.

Mike laughed. *That little devil—I'm glad she hasn't lost her sense of humor.*

He was still smiling and thinking about Rose when his cell phone vibrated on the coffee table.

The screen showed dispatch.

Shit! What now?